Readers Love Scotty Cade

I0659699

An Unconventional Courtship

"This is a very nice story with interesting characters… Sure, some of the romance may have been over the top at times but it was still fun to read."
—On Top Down Under Book Reviews

"The author does a fabulous job of building the story and the sexual tension between Tristan and Webber. It may have taken them two years to come together but when the do it's absolutely beautiful and their chemistry together is combustible."
—Guilty Indulgence

"*An Unconventional Courtship* is another entertaining release by Scotty Cade… These two are perfect for each other and sometimes, you just need a story that makes you happy to read.
—Literary Nymphs

An Unconventional Union

"Cade's novels are for the 'grown and sexy' set… *An Unconventional Courtship* was the first Scotty Cade book that I read, but it certainly was not to be my last. I truly enjoy this writer's work."
—Mrs. Condit & Friends Read Books

"Beautifully written with characters that live and breathe off of the written page, *An Unconventional Union* is one of my favorite books I've read this year. Mr. Cade has once again gave this reader several hours of pure reading enjoyment, and I can't wait to see what he has in store for us!"
—Top 2 Bottom Reviews

The Mystery of Ruby Lode

"This novel was just a cornucopia of wonderful elements that it is hard to know where to begin… Parts of this book will have you in tears so have the tissues handy as you will need them."
—Scattered Thoughts and Rogue Words

"There are some difficult and painful things happening throughout the book, and I felt for all of the men in this story. I enjoyed spending time with them and am very glad I went along on their adventure."
—Gay List Book Reviews

By SCOTTY CADE

Published by DREAMSPINNER PRESS
http://www.dreamspinnerpress.com

SUNRISE
OVER
SAVANNAH

SCOTTY CADE

Dreamspinner Press

Published by
Dreamspinner Press
5032 Capital Circle SW
Suite 2, PMB# 279
Tallahassee, FL 32305-7886
USA
http://www.dreamspinnerpress.com/

This is a work of fiction. Names, characters, places, and incidents either are the product of author imagination or are used fictitiously, and any resemblance to actual persons, living or dead, business establishments, events, or locales is entirely coincidental.

Sunrise Over Savannah
© 2014 Scotty Cade.

Cover Art
© 2014 Anne Cain.
annecain.art@gmail.com
Cover content is for illustrative purposes only and any person depicted on the cover is a model.

All rights reserved. This book is licensed to the original purchaser only. Duplication or distribution via any means is illegal and a violation of international copyright law, subject to criminal prosecution and upon conviction, fines, and/or imprisonment. Any eBook format cannot be legally loaned or given to others. No part of this book may be reproduced or transmitted in any form or by any means, electronic or mechanical, including photocopying, recording, or by any information storage and retrieval system, without the written permission of the Publisher, except where permitted by law. To request permission and all other inquiries, contact Dreamspinner Press, 5032 Capital Circle SW, Suite 2, PMB# 279, Tallahassee, FL 32305-7886, USA, or http://www.dreamspinnerpress.com/.

ISBN: 978-1-62798-652-6
Digital ISBN: 978-1-62798-653-3

Printed in the United States of America
First Edition
February 2014

As always this book is dedicated to my husband, Kell. Your continued support means more than any words can acknowledge. I love you! And to our great friends and fellow boaters John and Pat Gercon and Norton Gerard and Stephen Locke, with whom we were traveling when the inspiration for this novel smacked me on the head. We love you all!

CHAPTER ONE

THOMPSON GRAY stood at the end of the dock, both hands clutched tightly around his steaming cup of coffee in a feeble attempt to fend off the early morning November chill. The sun was just starting to peek above the barrier islands separating the Atlantic Ocean from the fast-moving tide of Savannah's Intracoastal Waterway. Georgia's glowing morning sky was filled with hues of red and orange, and the slightest hints of fuchsias and pinks seemingly arranged to announce the arrival of another beautiful fall day. But not for Thompson. "Four years," he said to himself as he fought the tears stinging the backs of his eyes.

He gazed at the brilliant display and thought only of her. This peaceful ritual of coffee and sunrise was one he'd shared with his wife Caroline every morning after they'd bought the Thundercloud Marina just over six years ago. But this morning he stood alone, as he'd done daily for the last four years, to the day, since Caroline's sudden death at the age of twenty-eight. He shivered against the chill and took another sip of his coffee, hoping the hot liquid might eventually warm his core, but knowing better. On this day, every year since her death, he couldn't escape the icy chills and the impending sense of doom, the loneliness and anxiety, that filled his being.

He thought back to that dreadful day, as he'd done most mornings since her death. The brain aneurism that had taken Caroline from him had come out of the blue. She'd been perfectly healthy—or so they had thought—with no prior warning except a slight headache when she'd awakened that morning. As was always her way, she'd popped a couple of aspirin and never complained. She'd taken him by the hand and led him down the dock with the excitement of a child. It was her favorite time of day, but neither of them had realized this day was to be their last sunrise together. In a flash, life as he'd known it had changed forever.

They'd been assisting a captain as he docked his boat for the evening. She'd bent down to secure a line when Thompson heard a loud gasp. He'd looked up to see her grabbing her head with both hands and collapsing in the very spot where he was now standing. In his mind's eye, he saw her unconscious body lying on the dock. He clearly remembered the fear and panic that had been in his voice as he desperately called her name. He saw himself scooping her limp body into his arms and felt the vibration of the dock under his feet as he ran, frantically yelling for someone to call 911.

By the time they'd arrived at the hospital, she was already dead. She'd never even regained consciousness.

Thompson tightened the grip on his coffee cup, fighting the memories of that wretched day. If the stabbing pain in his heart was any indication, he should be as dead as Caroline, but unfortunately, he'd been left alone to exist in his own nonexistence. He lost the fight against the impending tears and wondered briefly if he was crying for Caroline or for himself. With no clear answer, he allowed the tears to slide down his cheeks freely. He closed his eyes, and his legs started to tremble so badly he could no longer support his own weight. In an act of desperation, he dropped to his knees and slammed the coffee cup against the dock, causing it to shatter like the pieces of his broken heart.

THOMPSON AND Caroline had grown up just two doors apart, played together with the other kids around them, and, starting from the age of thirteen, had spent their summer vacations sitting on the dock watching the boats come and go at the Thundercloud Marina. They'd make up stories about where they were coming from, where they were headed to, and who owned them. Sometimes when it was really busy, they would help the owner by collecting trash from the boats or delivering newspapers in the morning. As soon as they were old enough,

Thompson and Caroline had worked as dockhands, and that's when their love for the marina life really began.

As their friendship progressed, they'd become inseparable, and the two of them would get to work just before daybreak, have coffee together while the sun peeked over the horizon, and start their day by casting off travelers—snowbirds, as they were commonly called—making their way south for the winter and then eventually north again for the summer.

They'd gone to Savannah State University together, married right after graduation, and purchased the marina with the help of Thompson's grandfather.

Until Caroline's untimely death, it seemed like they had the perfect life and were living their dreams. Then in one instant, everything changed. The morning after her death, he walked out to the dock and watched the sunrise alone for the first time and vowed to continue their morning ritual as long as he lived. It was where he felt closest to his wife. It was all he had left of her.

AFTER THE moments of grief and anger had temporarily passed, Thompson got to his feet. He wiped away the tears with his fingertips, looked around, and prayed no one had seen his breakdown. He was grateful when he remembered that his only dockhand had quit two days ago and most of the many snowbirds that filled the marina had not yet awakened. He walked to the office to get a broom and dustpan and headed back down to clean up his mess. As he swept the remains of his coffee mug, the mundane chore helped to calm him and he began to regain his composure. His mind again drifted back to that time. During her funeral, so many people had given him words of encouragement. "Time will heal your open wounds," they'd all said. But the last four years hadn't healed anything. His guilt about being the one still alive had done an excellent job of keeping him frozen in time. Today, he still felt as devastated as the day he'd lost her. Tears threatened to fall again as the emotions and harsh memories all came flooding back.

During the first year after she'd died, he'd turned his back on everyone. Friends tried to stay connected, but he didn't want their sympathy. He just wanted to be left alone. Everyone had meant well, but he just couldn't bear the "everything will be okay" speech day after day. It would never be okay. Time would not heal him. Nothing could heal him. Eventually, everyone had given up on him. He didn't blame them. He was sure he'd have done the same thing if the situation had been reversed.

The one person who hadn't given up on him had been his longtime best friend, Prince. His real name was Henry Charming. His family called him Hank, but ever since high school, because of his striking good looks and his last name, most of their friends had called him Prince Charming. They'd been best friends from childhood. More than best friends, actually. But things began to change when Thompson suddenly brought Caroline into the mix. Prince had slowly pulled away from him, but after Caroline died, he'd come back into Thompson's life and tried to rescue him. He'd had spent the better part of two years trying to bring Thompson back from the darkness that had encompassed him. But a person can only do so much, and it had all come to a head early one morning.

Thompson remembered the day as if it were yesterday. Prince had been trying to convince him that this morning ritual was not helping him and that he needed to give it up. In his usual way, Thompson had ignored him and proceeded down the dock with Prince on his heels. By the time they'd reached the end of the dock, it had been obvious to Thompson that Prince's patience had finally run out. At the top of his lungs, arms flailing, he'd again tried to convince Thompson he needed to let go of the past and try to start living his life. Prince had finally broken down in sobs when he'd told Thompson that although Caroline was dead, he was still alive and he was doing her memory an injustice by not living his life to the fullest.

Prince's words weren't anything Thompson hadn't already known, but it was a harsh brush with reality to hear them out loud. He'd flinched internally but had kept his expression blank and had given no response. Eventually, Prince had dropped his head, turned, and walked away for what Thompson had instinctively known was the last time. On one level, he'd known Prince was his only lifeline, but on the other, he was grateful Prince had finally given up on him too. After all, he'd given up on himself.

THOMPSON'S MIND drifted back to reality. *Was Prince right? By holding on to this stupid ritual, am I holding on to the past and making everything worse?*

"No," he mumbled to himself. "I can't. Caroline was my life and we were happy until…. This is my last connection to her. To not do this would be like erasing the one thing I have left of her. I can't pretend this moment we shared every morning never existed. Like *we* never existed."

But deep down he also knew that Prince had been right. After her death, he was still solidly stuck in place, sinking little by little with no visible way out. He realized for the first time that he wanted to get out. He wanted a life, but he had no idea how to go about it. Everyone still treated him like a ticking time bomb. He'd been so unreachable in the weeks, months, and even years that had followed her death that his friends no longer tried to approach him.

He poured the remnants of his coffee mug into the trashcan and started walking back up to the office. *Caroline, I know I'm broken, but I have no idea how to fix myself.*

CHAPTER TWO

DOCTOR GARNER Holt stepped through the companionway of his fifty-five foot sailboat, *AquaTherapy*, carrying a hot cup of coffee and a plate containing a stale cinnamon bagel and what little cream cheese he could scrape out of the container. "Guess it's time for a grocery stop," he said to himself as he examined his breakfast. He balanced the plate and cup, trying not to spill either as he made his way onto the bow and took a seat. There was a gentle breeze blowing out of the east and the sun was now peeking just above the horizon. He looked up out of habit to check his rigging and was amazed how the impending sun was causing the lingering dew to glisten like little diamonds. He caught movement to his left and saw a very regal blue heron perched on an old log along the bank with its long beak hovering just above the water, waiting for breakfast to swim by.

His gaze was interrupted when he heard a splash and turned to see a pelican floating right off the starboard bow with its head tipped up and a lump wiggling as it went down its throat. "Damn, even the bird's breakfast is fresher than mine," Garner chuckled, taking a bite out of his bagel and chewing and chewing and chewing. After he swallowed, he inhaled the fresh air and sighed. Despite his breakfast, there was beauty in every direction, and he savored the simple moment. "I could never have seen this stuff from my office window at the hospital," he mused.

For the last nine years before his early retirement, he'd been the head of psychiatrics for the Mount Sinai Medical Center. Back then he'd been a very career-driven man, working twelve to fourteen hours a day. In the beginning, the grueling schedule had been exhilarating, but over the years it had proven to be very detrimental to any sense of a personal life. His job had always come first, which didn't leave much time for a healthy relationship, though in the beginning he'd tried to juggle both. One failed attempt after another had convinced him that he just wasn't cut out for relationships, and eventually he stopped trying. Ultimately, the burnout he'd heard about started to descend on him, and the last two years had been a real struggle. One morning he looked in the mirror and realized he no longer recognized his own reflection. He had deep circles under his eyes. He was pale in color and looked much older than his thirty-six years. That morning, he'd decided enough was enough. In the weeks that followed, he'd resigned his position, sold his apartment and all of his belongings, and started to simplify his life. Growing up, he and his dad had been avid sailors. He'd always enjoyed the isolation and quiet pleasure it brought and had dreamed of sailing off into the sunset one day. The day he bought his shiny new Beneteau Oceanis was his "one day!" That had been almost six months ago, and as he made his way to points south, he'd not once regretted his decision to trade his hectic job for a life of exploration on the water.

GARNER LOOKED around again and mentally complimented himself. He'd made a great choice yesterday afternoon when he'd chosen to anchor in this very secluded cove just north of Savannah. He'd been on the water for a few months and recalled his journey, which had started in Manhattan. On his first day out, he'd followed the East River to Sandy Hook, New Jersey, spent a few days on the beaches of the Jersey shore, and then sailed the Atlantic Ocean to Cape May, where he entered Delaware Bay. From there, he'd made his way down to the Delaware River and through the manmade waterway connecting the Delaware River with the Chesapeake Bay called the C&D canal. He'd taken his time and enjoyed the many great anchorages along the Chesapeake, eventually ending up in Norfolk, Virginia, where he entered the Intracoastal Waterway, or the "Ditch," as boat captains call it.

His plan would take him along this well-traveled waterway as far south as Biscayne Bay, where he would again venture out into the Atlantic Ocean and head for the Florida Keys. When he was tired of the Keys, he would head east to the Bahamas and eventually the Caribbean and the Virgin Islands.

Garner finished breakfast and rubbed his aching jaw. "I've got to get some groceries before my jaw gives out."

He went down below, stowed his gear, secured the cabin, and headed topside again to raise the anchor and get his day started. He pressed and held the engine heater button for ten seconds, then pressed the starter. The Westerbeke diesel turned over several times, but it didn't start. *What the hell? She always starts immediately.*

He gave it a few seconds and then tried again. Still nothing. "Damn," he hissed. "This day is going downhill pretty fast."

Garner glanced at the fuel gauge and mumbled to himself, "Half full." He checked the other gauges. Engine temperature. "Good." Oil pressure. "Good." After verifying everything topside, he went down below and opened the engine compartment. He checked the oil and coolant, and both were well within the normal operating ranges on the dipsticks. Next he checked the fuel filter. It appeared to be clear. Lastly he inspected the water intake strainer to make sure it wasn't clogged, and it was clear as well. He went topside again and gave it one more try. Nothing. The engine easily turned over so he knew it wasn't the battery.

He put his hands on his hips and stared at the starter buttons, willing the damn things to work. *It just doesn't seem like the engine is getting any fuel.*

"Fuck it," he said as he went down below again and searched his boat files for his membership card. "That's why I pay a yearly fee for a towing service."

He unclipped his cell from his belt and dialed the number, requesting a tow to the nearest marina. He gave the guy his name, his boat's name, and his GPS coordinates, then ended the call.

While he waited for the towboat, he checked his waterway guide and found the nearest marina was the Thundercloud Marina, about three miles north of his present location. He once again retrieved his cell phone and dialed the number from the waterway guide and waited. After several rings, someone answered.

"Thundercloud Marina, this is Thompson."

"Good morning, Thompson, my name is Garner Holt. I'm anchored off the Intracoastal a few miles south of you, and I'm having some engine problems."

"Sorry to hear that, Captain. How can I help?"

"I just requested a tow from BoatUS," Garner shared. "The guy said he would be here in about an hour, and we're approximately three miles south of you. Do you have a mechanic on site who can take a look?"

"Yes, sir, we do," Thompson said. "What type engine?"

"A seventy-five horsepower Westerbeke diesel."

"Got it," Thompson said. "I'll have someone standing by when you get here."

"Thanks, man, I'll see you in a couple of hours."

"We'll be waiting."

Garner ended the call. *Nice telephone voice.*

IN A little under an hour, Garner spotted the towboat entering the anchorage. He acknowledged the boat's arrival with a wave and went about his business setting lines and fenders, preparing his boat for towing. Garner watched as the towboat approached from the stern and pulled up along his port side.

When he got a look at the boat captain, his jaw dropped. He was gorgeous. His short jet-black hair reflected the sunlight and his piercing blue eyes held Garner's gaze. He was shorter than Garner's own five foot eleven inches, but built like a man who came by his physique naturally. Broad shoulders and a huge chest led down to a flat stomach and small waist.

"I hear someone needs rescuing," the towboat captain joked.

Garner smiled and started to speak. Then his smile quickly turned into a frown when he saw the guy nonchalantly glance at the rainbow flag sticker on the stern of his boat. *Just my luck. I'm in the backwoods of fucking Georgia when someone finally notices that damn sticker. I knew that thing would get me in trouble one day.*

Garner took a few seconds to curse his "out and proud" best friend for adhering the sticker to his stern without his knowledge the morning he'd shoved off from New York. When he'd found it later that day, Garner had known exactly who'd put it there and had called his friend to give him a shitload of grief. The only response he'd received was "If you're going to cruise around God knows where, at least people need to know you're gay. How else are you gonna get laid?"

Garner was startled out of his thoughts by a strong voice. "If you need rescuing, I'm the only Prince Charming in sight," the captain teased, looking around. He eventually stuck out his hand. "I'm Prince Henry Douglas Charming."

You can rescue me any day was the first response that popped into Garner's mind, but he thought better of it. "You're it, huh?" Garner teased, accepting the outreached hand with a smile and returning the firm grip. "Garner Holt," he said, offering the captain the bowline and then the stern.

"Ouch!" the man said with a wink. "I know I'm no Tom Cruise, but am I that bad on the eyes?"

Garner looked at the guy with apprehension. *I do believe he's flirting with me.* "Uh, sorry; that really didn't come out the way I'd planned." Garner crossed his arms over his chest and gave the guy the onceover. "Prince Charming, huh?"

The towboat captain blushed a little, and Garner thought it was adorable.

"Okay, okay. You got me; I'm not really a prince. But... the Charming is real," the captain stammered. "My friends call me Hank. Well, that's not true either. Most of the guys I grew up with call me Prince. Get it—Prince Charming? But I prefer Hank."

"I get it, and I'll remember that, Hank," Garner said as he attached two spring lines, one forward and one aft, and then looked back up at the captain.

"Ready to go?" Captain Charming asked.

Garner looked around and nodded. "I think so, yeah."

"You wanna hop over and ride with me?"

"Hell yeah!" Garner wanted to say, but he went with, "Sure, why not. I've been alone on this boat for quite a while. The company sounds nice."

Hank flashed a huge smile in his direction and offered his hand.

Minutes later, side by side at the helm, they were carefully leaving the safety of the anchorage and slowly beginning their journey down the Intracoastal Waterway toward Savannah.

OUT THE corner of his eye, Garner watched as Hank skillfully captained the two boats down the waterway. Garner's fifty-five-foot sailboat was much larger than the twenty-five-foot towboat, but Hank did it with a confidence and skill that made it look easy.

Every now and then Hank would glance back and forth between him and the waterway and smile sheepishly. They had said little since their humorous exchange of words earlier, and Garner was feeling a little uncomfortable. In the silence, his mind had time to ramble. *Maybe he wasn't flirting with me at all. Maybe he's just a nice guy, and I've been alone too long and was just reading more into it.*

"So," Hank said, interrupting Garner's thoughts. "*AquaTherapy*, huh? Do you get it or give it?"

Garner chuckled. "A little of both, I guess. I'm sure you know how it is being on the water. Everyone has a story."

"Yep," Hank answered with a knowing tone. "See and hear it every day."

Hank looked like he was about to elaborate, then stopped and picked up his VHF radio. "One sec."

He held the radio to his mouth and began making a security call. Garner looked up and saw a tug pushing a barge in their direction. He kept quiet and listened as Hank received passing instructions from the tug captain.

"Nice job," Garner said after they had successfully maneuvered their boats past the tug and barge.

"Thanks."

They went along in a comfortable silence for another few minutes before Garner spoke again. "So, Charming, huh?" was the first thing that came to his mind. *So much for smooth talk.*

Hank laughed. "Yeah. I use it a lot when I rescue people; it's sort of a tense time for the boaters and it often breaks the ice. But I promise you I came by it naturally. It's my given name."

So he uses it on everyone to break the ice. Garner suddenly felt very foolish. He nodded and turned away to hide the embarrassment he was sure was clearly evident on his face. "I can see how that might put people at ease."

Before Garner could actually put both feet in his mouth again, Hank broke the silence. "How long have you been on the water?"

Garner exhaled, a bit more comfortable with where the conversation was now going. He explained that he left New York harbor about twelve weeks ago. He recounted his travels and was surprised that Hank seemed genuinely interested and asked a lot of questions. He did his best to answer accurately, trying to remember one stop from another and the different anchorages.

"Do you have a final destination in mind?"

"Not a concrete one. I mean, I thought I'd head down to Key West and spend some time there. If I get bored, I'll cross the Gulf Stream to the Bahamas and maybe end up in the Caribbean for the season. Since I retired, my time is my own."

Hank whistled. "Sounds like a dream come true to me."

"It kind of does, doesn't it?" Garner agreed. "So what about you?"

Hank tossed him a coquettish glance. "Li'l ole me? What about me?"

"How did you end up captaining a towboat?"

"My story isn't nearly as exciting as yours, but I'll share it just the same."

Garner leaned against the communication arc, crossed his arms over his chest, and waited.

"In my senior year in college, I worked for the guy who owned the local BoatUS, or Towboat US, as it was called then, and I found that I really enjoyed being on the water. About a year later, I opened a little boat store, nothing too big, just some small center console jobs, and I really enjoyed that too, but then I started missing being on the water. So when the BoatUS franchise became available, I bought it. That way I get the best of both worlds. I have a general manager who runs the boat store, which gives me the freedom to take off when I need to rescue damsels in distress or, in your case, stranded boaters."

Garner smiled. "Sounds like a marriage made in heaven."

"Whoa! Who said anything about marriage?" Hank said with a straight face. "We just met less than an hour ago."

Garner felt the blood drain out of his face, but before he could say anything, Hank started laughing. "I'm sorry, I couldn't pass the opportunity by. I'm only teasing."

Garner released a breath and punched Hank on the arm. "I meant the two companies."

"Ouch!" Hank said, rubbing his arm. "I knew what you meant. Look, I saw the rainbow flag on your boat. Does it mean what I think it means?"

Garner suddenly felt flushed. He'd never been in the closet, but unlike his best friend, he wasn't the "in your face" or "out and proud" type. He took a deep breath and released it. "I guess the cat's out of the bag. Yep, I'm a big ole homo."

Hank's smile was beaming. "Well thank God, I thought my gaydar was malfunctioning."

Garner nudged Hank with an elbow. "You too?"

Hank smiled and nodded. "Guilty as charged."

"Well, go figure," Garner mumbled. "Who would've thunk it?"

Hank tilted his head to one side in a questioning gesture. "What do you mean? There are a lot of 'mos in the marshes of south Georgia."

Garner laughed. "You know, I've heard of sightings, but I never thought I actually see a South Georgia 'mo up close."

"So now that you have, what do you think?"

"Not bad. Not exactly what I expected, but not bad at all."

Hank slapped Garner on the back and squeezed his shoulder. "Yankees! How'd they ever get in?" he drawled in a thick Southern accent.

Before Garner could come back with a witty reply, they rounded a turn and Garner saw the Thundercloud Marina. A man waved from the shore and started walking down the dock toward them. Garner watched and then gasped when he got a good look at the man. This stranger was one of the most handsome men Garner had ever seen. Even the gorgeous Hank looked like chopped liver, and Hank was clearly filet mignon.

"Hey, Thompson!" Hank shouted out as he inched the boats toward the dock. "Appreciate the personal service."

The man smiled genuinely and Garner thought it must be the Fourth of July by the way his face lit up. "My pleasure, Prince."

Garner raised a forefinger up to his jaw and slapped it closed as he stared on. *Holy Jesus, what a good-looking man.*

CHAPTER THREE

GARNER VAGUELY heard someone calling his name. "Uh, Garner? Garner!"

Garner shook his head. "Yeah! What? Sorry!"

"If you don't mind, would you hop to your boat and stand by to throw Thompson the bow line as soon as you're within reach?"

"Will do," Garner stammered as he climbed onto his boat.

While he waited for Hank to inch his boat alongside the dock, he was unable to turn away from the man awaiting their arrival. He looked to be about six feet two or three inches tall and about thirty years old. His dark-blond, shoulder-length hair was naturally sun-streaked and beautiful, but what got him were the man's eyes. Even from a distance, Garner could see they were the color of sparkling emeralds. In the bright sunshine, they glimmered brilliantly when the man flashed his deeply dimpled smile. Because of his career choice, Garner had always been able to read people pretty well, and he thought he picked up on a great deal of sadness embedded behind those beautiful eyes despite the bright smile.

The man's facial features, including those spectacular dimples, were fine and chiseled but not the least bit feminine. He was wearing a light-blue Thundercloud Marina T-shirt stretching tightly across his broad chest, and his low-rider jeans rode well on his hips, exposing just the waistband of his plaid boxers. And from what Garner could see through his clothing, the man appeared to be very well built.

Hank must have noticed Garner's interest and gave him a knowing smile. "Down, boy. Thompson's a real looker, isn't he? But don't get too excited; he's unavailable."

Garner nodded and silently cursed himself for being so transparent and allowing his libido to overrule his brain.

When he was in reach, he threw the man the bowline. After it was secure, the man walked down the dock and Garner tossed him the stern line as well. When the line was securely around the cleat, the man stood up and Garner's eyes locked on his. They held each other's gaze, and Garner felt like he was under some sort of spell as he stared deeply into the most gorgeous green eyes he'd ever seen. The close proximity allowed him to see specks of citrine sparkling from deep within, mesmerizing him and making it impossible to look away. But Garner didn't appear to be alone in the intensity of his gaze; the stranger didn't break the stare either.

Finally, the man shook his head and smiled. He stuck his hand out. "I'm Thompson Gray. You must be Garner."

The two men again stared at each other silently. *That requires an answer, you fool!* Garner tried to recover. "Uh yeah, Garner. Garner Holt, that's me." *Way to go, you idiot.*

Thompson frowned. "Sorry you're having engine problems. Hopefully we can get you fixed up and back on your way in no time."

Garner thought about his verbal comeback. He really wanted to say, "No way, I'd rather stay right here and look into those eyes for the rest of my life," but "Hope so" was all that came out.

Thompson looked up to a building on the shore, then back at Garner. "My diesel guy should be right down to take a look."

"Thanks, I really appreciate that."

The VHF radio attached to Thompson's hip went off. "Excuse me," he said as he unclipped it and brought it to his mouth. He walked to the other end of the dock as he answered the hail.

FROM HIS boat, Garner's gaze followed Thompson until he couldn't see him anymore. He picked up movement out of the corner of his eye and turned to see Hank hopping on board. Then Hank slapped him lightly on the back. "Thanks for your help docking, I appreciate it."

"No problem, glad I could do something."

Garner instinctively glanced back in Thompson's direction, and it obviously didn't go unnoticed by Hank.

"He's really striking, isn't he?" Hank said, watching Thompson as well.

Garner blushed a little and nodded.

Hank chuckled. "It's okay, I had such a crush on him when we were teenagers. And hell… everyone has that same reaction when they meet him for the first time."

By the way Hank was following Thompson's every move, Garner wasn't so sure that he'd ever gotten over said crush, but he kept that tidbit to himself.

Garner attempted to relax a little. "Does he own the place?"

"Yeah, it's his. He and his wife used to own it together, but she died. What is it? Three, no four years back now."

"She must have been so young. What did she die from?"

"A brain aneurism." Hank pointed to the corner of the dock right off the bow of Garner's boat. "Right over there."

Garner didn't know Thompson, but felt an unusually strong wave of sadness for the guy. The therapist in him was kicking in. "Oh man. That sucks. And right here on the dock. How can he come to work and not relive that every day?"

Hank shook his head. "To be honest, I'm not sure he doesn't relive it every day. He's never really gotten over it. And such a great guy too, would give you the shirt off his back if you needed it."

Suddenly Garner was picturing Thompson with no shirt on and again silently cursed himself. *For the love of Pete, stop it, Garner. He's straight and a widower. Leave the poor guy alone.*

Before Garner could say anything, an elderly guy with a cigarette hanging out of his mouth walked down the dock carrying a tool bag. "I hear someone's having engine problems."

Garner raised a hand. "That'd be me."

The man took the cigarette out of his mouth, stubbed out the end on one of the pilings, and stuck it in his top pocket. "I'm Titus, but folks around here call me Bubba. What seems to be the problem?"

Garner threw both hands in the air. "Hell if I know. She turns over, has fuel, I checked the filters and the intake, but she just won't start. The damn boat is brand new."

The mechanic toed out of his boat shoes. "Permission to come aboard, Captain."

Garner gave him a mock salute. "Permission granted. I'm Garner, by the way."

The two men shook hands and Bubba headed down to the engine compartment. "Give me a couple of minutes to take a look, then give her a crank for me," Bubba instructed over his shoulder.

"Just say the word, I'll be standing by."

When Garner was once again topside, he caught Hank staring at him with a huge smile on his face. "What?" Garner asked.

Hank took a few steps closer and whispered. "You're every bit as handsome as Thompson."

Garner felt the flush come on as the blood crept into his face. He chuckled nervously. "Seriously, man, when was the last time you had your eyes examined?"

Hank shook his head, but said nothing.

"Give it a crank," Bubba yelled from down below.

Garner again pressed and held the engine heater button for ten seconds, then pressed the starter. The engine turned over as it had earlier, but it just wouldn't start.

"Okay, that's enough," Bubba yelled. "When did she come uncranked?"

"She ran fine yesterday and then just wouldn't start this morning."

A few minutes later he popped out of the engine room. "From what I can tell, everything looks okay. I'm gonna get my gear and do a compression check."

"A compression check, what does that mean?" Garner questioned.

"Nothing good," Bubba explained. "I know you don't want to hear this, but this is my third compression problem on this model of Westerbeke diesels. Supposedly the manufacturer has fixed it now, but they identified the same problem on hulls one through eighty-seven. Do you happen to know the hull number on your boat?"

"Eighty-three. I just bought her," Garner said with a great deal of regret. "If this is the problem, how long will it take?"

Bubba shook his head. "It's hard to say. The last replacement took six weeks. The biggest problem is getting the new engine here."

Garner felt his eyes go wide. "Replacement? New engine? Six weeks!"

Bubba frowned. "I'm afraid so. But luckily for you, you're still under warranty. Because of that, you might just have a little more pull with the manufacturer. Maybe the company you bought the boat from might even be able to help apply some pressure."

Garner sat down and rested his arms and head on the steering wheel. "New engine," he whispered.

He felt Hank's hand land on his shoulder and give a quick squeeze. "Sorry, man."

Bubba dug the half-smoked cigarette out of his top pocket, brought it to his lips, and fished a lighter out of his pants pocket. "Let's not panic yet, boys," he mumbled while the cigarette bounced up and down. "Let me get my gear and run the test; then we'll know what we're dealing with."

Garner lifted his head. *He's right. Maybe it's not a compression problem at all. Maybe it's something totally different.* He allowed himself to hope, just a little.

Garner felt Hank squeeze his shoulder again and then remove his hand. "Look, man, I hate to leave you in your time of need, damsels in distress and all of that bull, but I've got to get back to the store. How about allowing me to take you to dinner tonight?"

Garner considered the invitation and then looked up at Hank. "Sure. I'll be here at least one night or six weeks, who knows. But either way, your invitation sounds very nice."

"Great, I'll call you after lunch to see what Bubba comes up with and we can make plans then."

"You need my cell?" Garner asked.

"Nope, it's still in my phone from your call this morning."

"Duh! Sorry, man, my head's all over the place right now."

Hank laughed as he hopped into his boat. "I'll take her back to her slip before I leave for the store."

Garner waved and tossed the lines as Hank backed the towboat away. When Hank was finally out of sight, Garner focused on his engine and the worry crept back into his mind. He sighed, ran his fingers through his hair, and turned, only to stop dead in his tracks when he saw Thompson coming toward him. His heart started racing, and he felt all sorts of butterflies milling about in his stomach. *What is it with you and this guy? This is not like you, Garner.*

"What's the verdict?" Thompson asked as he approached the boat, his green eyes sparkling.

"Not sure yet," Garner replied with a shaky tone. "Bubba went back to the shop to get his compression testing equipment."

"That doesn't sound good."

Garner let out a nervous chuckle. "From your mouth to God's ears."

He noticed that Thompson seemed to be just as ill at ease as he was, and for some reason it relaxed him a little.

"Just know you're welcome here as long as you need to be," Thompson said with a tentative smile.

"Thanks. I'll let you know as soon as Bubba gives me the news. He said it could be as long as six weeks."

Thompson whistled. "That long, huh?"

"What in the hell am I going do around here for six weeks?"

Thompson smiled again. "My deckhand just quit; maybe I'll put you to work."

"And maybe I'll just take you up on that offer."

"The offer stands," Thompson said as the radio on his hip started squawking again. "Duty calls. Let me get this. I'll check back in with you in a bit."

"Thanks, man, I really appreciate it."

GARNER PACED topside as Bubba ran the diagnostics on his engine. He'd been down there for at least an hour when he finally poked his head up through the companionway door.

When Garner saw Bubba's expression, he froze and felt the blood drain out of his face.

"I'm afraid I was right," Bubba said with a bit of apprehension. "It flat-out failed the compression test."

Garner stopped pacing and threw both hands up in the air. "How can this be? It's a brand-new boat."

"Hey, don't shoot the messenger," Bubba reminded him. "From what I've been told, this engine is a new model and the manufacturer gauged the exhaust incorrectly. They should have used a three-inch exhaust system, but instead used a two-inch system. The smaller system didn't allow the exhaust to exit quickly enough, which created too much pressure per square inch, a backpressure in excess of ten psi. The psi should never be over two or three in the worst of conditions. And there you have it."

Try to stay calm! Garner said to himself as his head began to throb and his heartbeat increased with every breath. He paced a few times. *Stay calm, hell!* He stopped and looked at Bubba. "What the fuck!" he barked. "They sold me a new fucking boat knowing it had this issue. You would think someone would have had the decency to mention it."

Bubba had a very concerned look on his face. He put his hands up, palms out. "Okay, man, you might want to calm down a little. I promise we'll get it all sorted out."

Garner looked down and started pacing again. He inhaled and released a few times, and when he looked up, Bubba was still staring at him with the same look.

Garner smiled sheepishly. "Sorry for the meltdown, Bubba. I thought I put these episodes behind me when I left New York. Okay, where do I start to fix this?"

Bubba dropped his hands. "Well, as far as I'm concerned the pin is out of the grenade. All we can do now is see who's willing to pay for the damage from the explosion. If it were me, though, I'd start by getting on the horn with whoever you bought this boat from and inform them of the problem."

Trying to get his meltdown under control, Garner put his hands on his hips. "Okay. Okay and you're right," he reassured Bubba. "It'll all work out. It's not like I have somewhere to be by a certain time. So what if I have to spend six weeks in Savannah. It could be a hell of a lot worse."

Bubba seemed to relax a little. "Who did you buy this boat from, man?"

"SunMarine out of Norwalk, Connecticut, why?"

Bubba took off his ball cap and scratched his head. "SunMarine, that's a good thing," he said. "The last boat we had with this problem was purchased from SunMarine as well, so I'm on a first-name basis with the service manager."

Encouraged, Garner fished his cell out of pocket. "Thanks, Bubba, will you stay around while I make the call in case they want to talk to you?"

Bubba nodded and dug through his pocket for another cigarette. "Sure thing."

Garner waited for Bubba to light up and when he didn't, Garner must have given him a strange look.

"Trying to quit," Bubba said without being prompted. "I was at two packs a day when I took the plunge. My plan was to smoke one less cigarette each day, and as of today I'm proud to say I'm down to two. I get one tomorrow and then I'm a free man. The hardest thing I've ever done."

Garner smiled. "Gotta love a disciplined man. I've never smoked, but I know it's a bitch to kick."

"Yes, sir," Bubba replied, puffing out his chest just a little. "I space myself a few puffs at a time throughout the day to make the cigarettes last longer, and so far so good. But in between smokes, keeping the damn thing in my mouth sometimes helps to cut the cravings. I know it sounds silly, but it works."

"Hey, if it works, who cares how silly it sounds."

Bubba nodded, but seemed pleased with Garner's response.

Garner found his sales rep's name in his contacts and placed the call. After a lengthy and sometimes heated conversation between him and his rep, Bubba took over for the mechanical end of the conversation. When Bubba was through with them, he handed the phone back to Garner. After everything was all said and done, SunMarine agreed to cover the replacement of the engine, the labor to do the job, and even to expedite shipping the new engine to Savannah. In addition, they also agreed to pay for his dockage for as long as he had to be there.

The only problem Garner could see was the Westerbeke plant gave his rep an ETA of four to five weeks for delivery because the plant was behind in production. To address that issue, SunMarine offered him a new Yanmar engine instead. They promised they could get it there at least two weeks earlier, but Bubba advised against it because of the different configuration, so Garner stuck with the Westerbeke.

Garner pressed the end button on his phone and sighed with relief. He looked at Bubba. "Thanks for all that. I'm not sure I could have handled that alone."

Bubba smiled. "Sure you could have, son. Just might have taken you a little longer is all."

Garner looked around the marina reluctantly. "I guess I should find Thompson and tell him he has a new tenant."

Bubba must have seen the distressed look on his face and smiled weakly. "Don't worry, son, the time will fly by, you'll see. And who knows, you might actually like it here."

Garner fell silent, seemingly lost in thought. When he didn't respond, Bubba grabbed his tool bag and lifted it up to the dock. "Next week I'll start removing the old engine in preparation for the new installation. Should only take me a few days, though. In the meantime, if you need me, you know where to find me."

Garner held out his hand. "Thanks, Bubba, you've been a lifesaver."

The two men shook hands. "Welcome to the neighborhood, son."

They walked up the dock together, Bubba heading to his shop and Garner in search of Thompson. Bubba had suggested he start with the marina office, and Garner found Thompson sitting behind his cluttered, paper-covered desk talking on the telephone. When Thompson heard the door open, he looked up and flashed Garner that radiant smile. He waved him over and motioned for him to take one of the chairs in front of his desk. *God, I hope he can't see what that smile does to me.*

Thompson finished his call and plopped the phone back in its carriage with a thud. He looked at Garner with a sympathetic look. "Any news?"

Garner sighed and cracked his knuckles, a move he knew he did when he was nervous. *Why in the hell am I so nervous?* He met Thompson's eyes and finally spoke. "Yeah, and none of it good, unfortunately."

"I'm so sorry, man," Thompson said. "What can I do?"

"For starters, you can put me and my boat up for the next month and a half," Garner said with a chuckle.

Thompson smiled. "Not a problem. Six weeks, huh? That's not good."

"Nope, not good at all," Garner said, shaking his head.

He explained the situation in detail and could clearly see the sympathy building in Thompson's gaze. "So it looks like you're stuck with me for a while."

Thompson flattened both hands on the top of his desk and stood. "Not stuck at all. I'm glad to have you." He offered Garner his hand and Garner accepted it. The grip was firm and strong and he knew he held on a little longer than he should have, but he was grateful for the touch. "Thanks, I really appreciate how great you and Bubba have been."

"Bubba's the best," Thompson said in a reassuring tone. "He'll get you all fixed up and, while he does it, he'll take damn good care of you."

"I have no doubt. He seems to be a really nice guy."

Thompson sat back down, scratched his head, and looked at Garner from under his eyelashes. "If you were serious about keeping busy while you're here, I can still use the help."

"I never really gave it much thought, but I don't see why not."

Thompson's expression changed to one of concern. "I can't pay much, but I promise I'll keep it interesting."

"Don't take this the wrong way," Garner said, a little uneasy with the turn in the conversation. "I mean I'm not bragging or anything, but I really don't need the money. I just know me and feel certain I would go crazy with nothing to do for six weeks."

"I can understand that," Thompson teased. "And hey, I'm not a proud man, I'll take you any way I can get you."

Garner started imagining all sorts of inappropriate things, reluctantly shifting in his chair to relieve the ache that was quickly building in his groin. The uncontrollable blush invaded his cheeks and feelings of embarrassment overtook him.

Their eyes met briefly and Garner felt sure Thompson knew what had been going through his mind, which only made his blush more intense.

Thompson looked a little unnerved and cleared his throat. "Uh sorry, I didn't mean that the way it sounded," he admitted with a nervous chuckle. "Sometimes things I mean to say come out all wrong. It's like the filter between my brain and my lips occasionally has a meltdown."

Garner smiled and did the only thing he could do. He stood very carefully, keeping his hands in front of his groin. "Happens to the best of us. Uh… about the job, can I take today to get settled in and start tomorrow morning?"

"Sure thing," Thompson said, looking relieved to be over the awkward moment. "We get started at seven. Is that too early for you?"

"No, not at all, I've always been an early riser."

"Okay then, it's settled."

They shook hands again, Garner still trying to cover his groin with his other hand, and then he left the office, making a beeline for his boat. He mentally kicked his own ass all the way down the dock. *What in the hell is wrong with you? Now I'll bet he thinks you're some kind of pervert. Stupid, stupid, stupid! Why can't you control your stupid libido? Every time you've been around him you act like a babbling teenager.*

As he continued to chastise himself, his cell phone rang. He fished it out of his pocket and didn't bother to look at the caller ID. "Hello!" he barked.

"Oh, that doesn't sound like a happy 'hello,'" the caller said.

"Excuse me!" Garner replied with an indignant tone.

"Whoa, big guy, it's Hank Charming. If this is not a good time, I'll call back later?"

Garner felt himself blush again. *Damn it, Garner! Get it together.* "No! No, sorry, man, just having a bad day."

"I gathered as much. Not good news about the engine, huh?"

Garner climbed onto his boat and paced on the bow. "Not at all, looks like I'll be around for six weeks or so while they change it out."

Hank's tone lightened. "Man, I sure am sorry for you, but I am very happy for me."

Garner couldn't help but chuckle. "Thanks, I think."

"For what? I'm just being honest," Hank said with a mischievous tone.

"Making me laugh, I guess. I haven't felt much like laughing in the last few hours."

"Wanna talk about it?" Hank asked.

"Sure, why not."

As he paced, Garner filled Hank in on all the details regarding the engine and his job offer from Thompson.

"I'm really sorry about the engine, but Thompson's a good guy and he'll be great to work with. In fact, I think I might be a little jealous."

"Of him or me?" Garner asked.

Hank paused for a second, apparently contemplating his answer. "Both, I guess," he finally said. "He can be very charming, no pun intended, and he's quite the looker too. I told you I had the biggest crush on him when we were in high school. In fact, I wouldn't mind spending all day looking at both of you. What a fantasy that would be."

Garner howled. "That's very funny. And… flattering, but I hardly think we're gonna get naked so you can watch us do God knows what for your enjoyment," he teased.

"Fine then," Hank snickered. "Be like that." No longer able to keep it together, he burst into laughter. "I'm just yanking your chain, Garner. And just so you'll know, I'm not a pervert or stalker or anything."

The word "stalker" got Garner's attention, but he quickly pushed it out of his mind and tried to come back with something witty. "Now I'm really disappointed," he said with a sigh. "I haven't been stalked in quite some time."

"Okay, big guy, if we keep up this line of conversation, I think it might get me in some serious trouble. Sooooo, we still on for dinner?"

"Sure, why not."

"Perfect. If it's all right, I'll come by around seven."

"Absolutely. We can have a glass of wine on board, then head out."

"Sounds like a plan. See you at seven."

"See you then. Bye, Hank."

Garner disconnected the call and had to admit he did feel a bit better. *Maybe it won't be so bad hanging around for six weeks. Hank seems like a nice guy, and he's awfully easy on the eyes.*

The term "easy on the eyes" suddenly reminded him of Thompson. In his conscious brain, he knew Thompson was off limits, straight *and* a widower, but there was just something about him. And… he was damn hot.

Still pacing on the bow of his boat, Garner was deep in thought. He realized his attraction wasn't just because Thompson was hot. He thought he'd picked up on something between them, not of a sexual nature, but he'd felt some sort of connection, like Thompson needed help or something. His brows furrowed when he thought about Thompson losing his wife. *How horrible that must have been for him.* Then he remembered the moment they'd met. Thompson's welcoming smile had been so brilliant, and Garner had been struck by the rich color of his eyes. They were gorgeous and intense, but he also remembered a deep sadness to them. He felt like Thompson was still carrying around a great deal of pain.

He scratched his head. *Hank said Thompson's wife had died several years ago?* It was obvious to him the wound was still very raw. He felt certain of that. Working together for the coming weeks might shed some light, but until then, he'd damned well better keep his libido in check. *The last thing Thompson needs is a swooning gay man on his heels!*

THROUGH THE heavily tinted glass of the window overlooking the marina, Thompson watched his new tenant and soon-to-be temporary employee pacing back and forth. Even at this distance and with a cellphone blocking half of Garner's face, he could see how stressed out and uncomfortable he looked. *I guess it's justified after the day that poor guy's had.*

Staring intently, Thompson had to admit he felt a little voyeuristic, but something about the stranger intrigued him. Garner's shaggy wavy brown hair, streaked with blond highlights, framed a slender, handsome face with striking features and a strong jawline. His wide shoulders led to a small waist and naturally muscular legs. If he was being honest, he'd have to admit the guy was a knockout. "Hell, I'll have to beat Hank off him with a stick," he mumbled to himself.

When Thompson thought about all the people that passed through his marina, he wondered what it was about this guy that held his attention. He met interesting people all the time. A lot of really nice people and some real assholes. It was just the nature of the business— but for some reason he'd taken an instant liking to this vagabond.

There were two things Caroline had repeatedly teased him about. The first was he put a great deal of stock in first impressions. And the second, he was way too sensitive. Of course, over the years, he'd repeatedly proved her right on both counts. And today was no different.

He'd surprisingly offered Garner a job after knowing him for less than an hour. That must say something about "first impressions." And… he remembered there was something about the way Garner had looked at him when they'd first met, something that had touched him in some way. There was the "way too sensitive" part.

Through the large window Thompson noticed that Garner had just ended his call. He'd taken a seat in the cockpit and was now gazing out over the waterway. The tension in his face seemed to ease a little, and he looked much more relaxed now. For some reason, that made Thompson feel better. But out of the blue, Garner looked to the office and stared at the large window overlooking the marina as if he could see Thompson watching him. Thompson knew that was impossible through the tinting of the one-way glass, but he still had to fight the urge to turn away. Garner's stare was penetrating, and he felt it all the way down to his toes. Then he had a flashback to their initial meeting. It had felt much the same way. It wasn't just the way Garner had looked at him; it was as if he'd been looking into him.

Thompson was totally mesmerized by what was happening. He'd always thought that someone's eyes said a lot about the person, and there was definitely something about Garner's rich brown eyes that made you feel connected to him. He didn't have to wonder about the last time he had a connection with someone like that. The images all came flooding back vividly. Even as kids, it had been Caroline's amethyst eyes that had hit him like a ton of bricks. He'd never seen eyes that color before, the blue so deep it bordered on purple.

The memory of Caroline's eyes hit him hard, and the huge gaping hole in his heart started to ache again. Now in his memory he saw the same beautiful eyes lifeless, the bright amethyst fading to a dull gray as she'd died in his arms. He jerked his head from side to side in an attempt to force that vision from his mind, but the image was etched in his brain forever. *Fuck, Thompson! You can't keep living like this. You've got to find a way to move on.*

His attention was drawn back to Garner when he stood and disappeared through the companionway. Thompson was oddly disappointed, but he didn't know why. He looked down at the mounds of paperwork on his desk and sighed. *Enough stalking, you idiot, time to get to work.*

AFTER A couple of hours of shuffling papers, he'd barely put a dent in the stack and finished nothing. He was ill at ease but didn't know why. For the umpteenth time today, he turned his attention to Garner. He needed to put employment paperwork together for him to sign in the morning and had no idea where to find the crap. He opened and closed one desk drawer after another, his frustration level growing by the second as he feverishly searched for the necessary forms. He looked up at the ceiling and sighed. "God, Caroline, why in the hell can't I be as organized as you were?" The word "were" forced a lump into his throat, and he had to struggle hard to swallow it down. *Stop it!*

Finally, as if guided by an invisible hand, he opened the first drawer again and immediately put his hands on the file labeled "New Employee Forms." He searched the files, found the right forms, stapled everything together, and laid them aside and sighed quietly.

It was times like this when, although he knew Caroline was never coming back to him, he'd hope beyond hope that it was her subtly guiding him and reminding him that she was still with him in some small way.

Mentally exhausted, he folded his arms on his desk and lowered his head, laying it gently on his forearm. When he was like this and his brain could no longer process a simple thought, it always managed to drift back to Caroline. He pictured her like he'd done so many times since her death, happy and healthy. As his mind wandered back to happier times, he longed for the companionship and comfort he felt when he was with her. She'd been his best friend, and while their life together had not been a passionate one, it had been full and satisfying, and his dedication and their deep connection had always seemed to be enough.

His mind drifted back to their childhood. When they weren't in school, he, Caroline, Prince, and a few others had spent their days together playing, fishing, and hanging out on the water. He and Prince played baseball on the school team together, and Prince had been his best friend. Wherever you saw one of them, you saw the other. Then everything came to a crashing halt when Caroline—

Thompson was startled out of his thoughts by a tapping on the door. He raised his head and looked up. Hank was standing in the doorway. Thompson ran his fingers through his hair. "Hey, Prince, what's up?"

Longing for some glimpse of the relationship he and Hank had once had, Thompson was hoping that Hank would throw a fit and protest the "Prince" nickname like in the old days, but like most of his friends, they treated him with kid gloves.

"You okay, Tommy boy?" was all he said.

Thompson sighed. "Yeah, man, just a little tired is all."

Hank looked at his watch and then gave Thompson a compassionate look. "It's six forty-five, man, why don't you call it a day already?"

"Soon," Thompson promised. "I've got to close out the day, and I still have this mound of paperwork to tackle."

Sighing, Hank said, "You know it will all be here tomorrow, right?"

Thompson chuckled. "Yeah, that's what I told myself every day for the last two months, and you know what, I was right. It's still here."

Hank smiled. "Just don't kill yourself, okay? Tomorrow's another day."

"Don't remind me," Thompson whispered, not missing the concern in his voice.

"What?"

"Oh nothing. What brings you back here at this hour? Got a call?"

"Nope," Hank said sheepishly. "A date."

"A date?" Thompson said with a tone in his voice that surprised even him. "With whom?"

"None other than your handsome new tenant."

"Garner?"

Hank brought the fingers of his right hand up to his mouth, blew on his nails, and rubbed them against the T-shirt stretched tightly across his chest. "Yes, sir."

"Garner's gay?" Thompson asked.

"As a goose," Hank teased.

Thompson couldn't hold back his smile. No matter how many times he'd heard Hank use that term, he never got the "gay as a goose" reference.

"Well imagine that," Thompson said.

"Who would've thunk it?" Hank responded. "A guy like that going to dinner with a guy like me."

"Hey, man, don't sell yourself short, okay?" Hoping to get a rise out of him, Thompson added, "From what I remember, you're a great kisser."

Hank's face quickly turned pink, and for a second he looked like he was going to come back with some kind of snappy retort, but as usual he hesitated.

In one last attempt, Thompson added, "And you'd make a great wife."

That sort of did it.

"Hey!" Hank whined. "Why do I always have to be the wife? Oh hell, why am I asking you that question? It's not like I'll ever be Mrs. Thompson Gray."

Thompson instinctively flinched at the reference to his wife, and the two men stared at each other for a second.

"I'm sorry, man, I didn't mean it like that," Hank said, obviously regretting the words the second they left his mouth.

"I know you didn't, Hank. It's okay. Forget about it."

Hank nervously glanced at the clock over Thompson's desk. "I need to get going. I'll never get the opportunity to be Mrs. Anyone if I can't show up for a date on time."

The mood lightened again, and Thompson chuckled, waving his hand in the air. "Get out of here and have a good time."

Hank gave the thumbs-up. "Just don't stay too late, okay?" he added right before he closed the door.

Thompson missed his best friend and the way they used to be. But he didn't think he deserved to have Prince in his life again. He'd thrown that chance away a couple of years ago. Besides, even if he wanted to try to recapture what they once had, he wouldn't even begin to know where to start. Sadness and regret again overtook him. Just when he thought it couldn't get any worse, he felt a strong twinge of jealousy creeping up his spine. He rolled it over in his mind, trying to determine its origin. What was it suddenly eating away at him? Was it all the memories of how close he and Prince used to be? Or was it something more? He continued to sort through the feelings as best as he could, but made little headway. He eventually closed his eyes and tried to let it all go. Suddenly his eyes sprang open in a panic, and he felt the blood drain out of his face. *Oh fuck no, Thompson! You are not jealous because Hank and Garner are going on a date!*

CHAPTER FOUR

GARNER RAN a brush through his long wavy hair as he stared at his reflection in the mirror. *I do believe it's time for a haircut,* he mused. *I think I'm starting to look like Popeye the Sailor.* He fisted his hands, arched his arms, and worked them from side to side. "Well, blow me down!" he recited in a gruff voice and then snorted repeatedly, remembering the way the sailorman had laughed on reruns of the cartoon he'd watched as a kid. He stopped and shook his head, amused with himself. "You've been alone way too long, my friend." *Blow me down?* He had to laugh again when he realized the implication of that statement. Especially since he was going on his first date in over six months.

Allowing his gaze to drift lower in the mirror, he turned his attention to what he was wearing. *I hope I'm not underdressed.* He looked at the yellow polo shirt and admired how it highlighted the tan he'd acquired from long hours on the water. His eyes falling even lower, he turned his body to the side and eyed the canvas belt embroidered with brightly colored nautical flags adorning the blue jeans that rode low on his hips. The simple fact that he cared about what he looked like just might be a hint that he was feeling a little excited about his date. It hit him like a ton of bricks when he'd realized he'd actually missed human contact. He smiled weakly. He'd been alone for long stretches at a time during his journey; why, he hadn't considered how being in solitary for so long might affect him. Bearing in mind the events of the day, the fact that he was smiling at all was a miracle. He ran the brush through his unruly hair one last time, smirked, and reluctantly put it down. *This is as good as it gets, Popeye.*

He looked out of the porthole to complete darkness. *What the hell time is it?* He glanced at his watch. *Wow! Six forty-five already. If I hurry, I might have time for a beer before Prince Charming comes a-calling.* On the way out of his cabin, he sprayed a little cologne on his shirt and hit the light switch. He stopped at the control panel and turned on the outdoor lights and then bounced into the galley. He was reaching in the fridge for a Corona when he heard a knock on the hull and a familiar voice. "Permission to come aboard, Captain?"

Garner chuckled. He rolled his eyes and grabbed an extra beer. "Permission granted, Prince," he yelled as he climbed the companionway stairs.

"Oh no!" Hank bellowed. "Don't you dare start calling me that!"

When Garner was topside, he found Hank toeing off his boat shoes, about to step aboard. Garner froze and his heart fluttered when he got a look at his date. Hank's jet-black hair, cropped short on the sides but longer on the top, was still a little damp and glistened in the bright moonlight. He was wearing nicely fitted jeans and a royal-blue T-shirt that made his eyes look even bluer than they had in the bright sunlight earlier that day. His white jacket was thrown over his shoulder as if he had stepped right out of a Nautica fashion magazine ad.

"Is something wrong?" Hank said, apparently noticing his stare. "Am I dressed okay?"

Garner snapped his mouth shut. "Um, yeah. As a matter of fact, you look incredible."

Not knowing what else to say, Garner nervously shoved the beer in Hank's outreached hand. "I hope you like Corona? No lime, though, sorry."

Hank took the offered beer. "As a matter of fact, I do." Hank switched the cold beverage to his other hand and reached out for a shake. "Good to see you again, Garner."

Garner accepted Hank's large, warm hand. "Sorry, I'm a little nervous. This is my first date in a very long time."

With their hands still locked in place, Hank pulled Garner a little closer and sniffed the air. "For someone who hasn't had a date in six months, you certainly remembered to smell fantastic and look just as good."

Garner smiled. "Thanks. But I had nothing to do with the very questionable 'looking good' part, that would all be my parents. And… I guess you should be thanking Dolce & Gabbana for the smelling-good part."

Hank raised his beer. "To your parents, then. Oh… and Dolce & Gabbana too."

"Hear, hear." Garner said as he touched the neck of his beer bottle against Hank's.

With that, Garner led Hank down below and they settled across from each other in the salon.

Hank looked around and nodded. "Nice digs," he said, throwing one arm over the back of the couch, stretching his legs out in front of him, and crossing his feet at the ankles. "So, how was the rest of your day?"

God, even his feet are gorgeous, Garner thought, looking down. *Long, slender, and tanned, beautifully shaped toes, and nicely manicured nails. No gnarly sailor toes for him.*

Garner looked up and met Hank's eyes. "Uh, pretty good. I met with Thompson for a little while. I start working tomorrow."

Hank threw Garner a questioning look. "That soon, huh?"

Garner shrugged. "Might as well. It's not like I have anything else to do. Besides, it might be fun."

"Well, if you get bored," Hank offered, "you can always come out with me on BoatUS calls."

Garner tilted his head to the side, thought for a second, and then nodded. "That might actually be fun too."

"You're welcome to tag along anytime."

"Thanks, I appreciate that."

There was an awkward moment of silence, and Garner started nervously tapping his fingers on the back of the couch.

"I… I hope you're hungry," Hank asked, downing the last of his beer.

"Starved," Garner admitted quickly. "All I had today was a stale cinnamon bagel for breakfast and an apple for lunch."

Hank stood. "Then we need to get you fed."

Garner stood as well and reached for Hank's empty beer bottle. "So, where are we going?"

"I'm taking you to a Savannah favorite. It's called The Olde Pink House. Certain times of the year it can be a little bit touristy, but the food is great and the architecture of the historic building is magnificent."

Garner tipped back his Corona bottle and swallowed the last of its contents. "I'm sort of an amateur architectural buff, so tourists or no tourists, it sounds perfect."

Garner locked the boat and the two men walked up the dock. "I'm parked over here," Hank said, pointing to a pristine, pearly-white four-door Ford F150.

"New ride?"

Hank hurried in front of him and opened the passenger door. "Yeah. The businesses are going to be a little too profitable this year, so my CPA told me to spend some money. She said it was either spend the money on the business or give it to the government in the form of taxes." Hank raised a finger. "Don't get me wrong. I'm not anti-government or anything, and believe me, I pay my fair share of taxes. But if it comes down to taxes or a new truck, hell, I'm going for a new truck any day."

"I'm with you on that!" Garner said right before Hank closed his door. *When was the last time anyone opened a door for me? I guess chivalry is still alive and well in the South!*

He watched Hank cross in front of the truck to the driver's side. The door opened and Hank hopped in before sliding the key in the ignition and turning it until the trucked purred like a kitten. "Off we go."

AFTER COVERING a plethora of topics from Garner's new sailboat and his journey so far to Hank's boat store and towboat business, Hank pulled into a parking lot across the street from the restaurant. "Here we are."

"I see where it gets its name," Garner chuckled, looking at the pink, stately mansion.

"Kind of obvious, huh?"

"Ya think?"

"She was built in the 1780s for one of Savannah's founding families, who made their money in cotton."

Garner scrutinized the building and its architecture. "Georgian style, right?"

Hank slapped a hand down on the seat between them. "I love a man who knows his architecture."

Garner laid his hand on top of Hank's and was about to come back with a witty response about mentioning "love" on their first date, when he stopped midthought. He caught a glimpse of the transom light above the main entrance of the restaurant and was mesmerized by the wavy glass and the way it caught the light. "That transom light over the front door is magnificent."

"The oldest known in Georgia," Hank said rather proudly. "They call it a fanlight, though, because of the circular way it fans over the door."

"Magnificent," Garner repeated.

"This building was one of the only to survive the great fire of 1796 and is said to be haunted by the original owner, James Habersham Jr. He supposedly hanged himself in the basement in 1799."

Garner opened his door. "Come on, I can't wait to check this place out."

Hank laughed. "Has that effect on most everyone."

They crossed the street, and Hank suddenly stopped. "Oops, I forgot my phone. Sorry, I'm on call tonight. I'll be right back."

"No problem." Garner looked up and again gave the building a once-over. "I'll be here," he replied.

Garner was so mesmerized by the sight in front of him he hardly noticed when Hank disappeared from his side. For some reason, the Greek portico with its grand columns held his interest for the longest time. Until, of course, he forced his eyes to move up to the large palladium window above the portico. "What a great example of

Colonial architecture," Garner mumbled, lost in the understated elegance.

Hank returned and stood next to him. "I'm sorry, what did you say?"

"Oh, just talking to myself. This place is stunning."

Side by side, they walked up the front steps and into the foyer. "I'll be right back," Hank said as he made his way to the hostess stand.

Garner stood frozen in place, taking it all in. He looked from left to right. There were rooms on each side of the foyer and a simple but very elegant Georgian stairway leading to the second floor. Before Garner could peek into any of the other rooms, Hank returned with the hostess, who led them up the main stairs. They reached the second floor and entered a large foyer with rooms in every direction. The hostess led them down a wide hallway toward the front of the house and into what Garner could only describe as a grand ballroom.

The room ran the entire width of the house and on each end of the longest wall were two massive recessed fireplaces. In the center was a large, round table boasting a gigantic floral arrangement; a large number of other tables were strategically placed with ample room for maneuvering. As they were led through the dining room, Garner glanced around and saw that every table was occupied with customers seemingly enjoying their dinners. The hostess stopped and placed menus and a wine list on a table for two in a private corner next to one of the fireplaces. "Yo'orrr serva will be right with you," the middle-aged hostess said with a thick Southern drawl, then disappeared.

Garner thought he must have looked possessed as his head spun in every direction. "So… charming," he mumbled.

"I'm glad you like it," Hank agreed. "It's one of my favorite places."

Garner turned around in his chair and looked out over the room. "I swear, if I squint my eyes, I can see people in formal period clothing sipping cocktails and dancing at what must have been grand parties thrown here."

Hank's broad smile was contagious, and before he knew it, Garner was smiling as well. Hank placed his phone on the table and reached across to cover Garner's hand with his own.

Garner had a quick flash of butterflies in his stomach at the simple gesture. He had to admit he liked what he knew of Hank Charming. Garner squeezed Hank's hand. "So what did you do before you set out on the water?"

Garner started to answer when out of the corner of his eye he saw a waiter approaching the table. He watched Hank's expression change to one of surprise and then disappointment when he obviously recognized the attractive blond-haired man.

The waiter stepped up to the table, crossed his arms over his chest, and looked Hank up and down. "Long time, no see, Hank," he said, turning to Garner and giving him a once-over as well. The waiter quickly dismissed him and turned his attention back to Hank.

"I felt certain that thing was broken," the waiter said, referring to Hank's cell phone lying on the table.

Hank didn't look up from the wine list and seemed to ignore the comment. "How are you, Sam?"

"Doing just fine, man, thanks for asking," the waiter said sarcastically. "Who's your friend?"

"Oh sorry, that was very rude of me. Sam Lester, meet Garner Holt."

Sam reached out and shook Garner's hand. "How do you do?"

"Just fine, thank you," Garner said.

"Can I get you gentlemen something to drink while you study the menu?" Sam asked.

Hank looked up. "Chardonnay okay?"

"Absolutely."

He then met Sam's glaring eyes. "We'll take a bottle of the Baileyana Chardonnay, please."

"Very well. I'll be back to tell you about the specials in a moment."

The waiter turned on his heel and made a beeline for wherever he was headed.

"History?" Garner asked with a slight smile.

Hank frowned. "Yeah. We went out a few times. I'm sure you'll learn soon enough that Savannah is a very small town and the dating pool is *very* limited. And just for the record, Tuesdays used to be one of his nights off, so I thought we were safe."

Garner laughed. "Hey look, you don't owe me an explanation. Would you feel more comfortable if we went somewhere else?"

Hank's expression lightened. "Would you mind?"

Garner saw Sam walking across the dining room carrying the bottle of wine. "Of course not."

When he reached the table, Garner took the lead. "Uh, Sam, I'm very sorry, but I'm suddenly not feeling well. I think we're gonna have to leave."

"Oh?" Sam said, not looking at all surprised. "I'm sorry to hear that."

Garner gave Hank a sympathetic look and winked. "I hate to ruin our evening, but can you please take me home?"

"Of course."

Thankful for the rescue, Hank folded his napkin, placed it on the table, and stood. He walked around and pulled out Garner's chair. "Let's get you home and into bed."

Sam snickered rather loudly.

Garner nodded and stood. "Thank you, Hank." He grabbed Hank by the arm, and unable to pass up the opportunity to give Sam a taste of his own medicine, he quickly added, "As long as you'll join me."

This time Sam didn't just snicker; he put the wine bottle on the table and placed his hands on his hips. "Well, aren't you confident? Trust me, it won't be long before he gets tired of you and moves on to someone else."

"Not if I get tired of him first."

Sam huffed as he grabbed the bottle of wine and stormed off, cursing under his breath.

Hank guffawed. "You're so bad!"

Garner winked at Hank again. "I'm sorry, he was being mean to you and I couldn't allow that to happen."

Hank bowed his head. "Thanks for defending my honor."

"Listen, Hank, you might be a prince, but I can be a queen when I need to be, and queens protect their princes."

On their way out, still chuckling over their silliness, Hank showed Garner all the other dining and sitting rooms as well as the cellar bar. Even as they crossed the street and climbed into the truck, they were still laughing.

"So what, did you just not call the guy back or something?" Garner asked.

"What? No!" Hank said. "I would never do that."

Now extremely curious, Garner asked, "So… are you gonna tell me what happened or am I gonna have to beg?"

"I've got to admit, the thought of seeing you beg is pretty enticing, but I'll tell you and save the begging for something else. I just think you're going to be disappointed."

Garner crossed his arms and smiled. "I'll be the judge of that."

"It was nothing more than a few dates," Hank explained. "That's why I'm in shock that he's still so bitter."

Garner felt a slight grin overtake his lips. "Do you want to know what I think?" he asked with a teasing tone.

Hank cocked his head to one side, returning the smile. "Sure. Why not?"

"Well… I think there's a lot more to the story than you're letting on," Garner confessed. "But if you don't feel comfortable sharing, I totally understand. It's really none of my business."

"No. It's not that," Hank protested, apparently still trying to decide if he wanted to share. "Oh, what the hell," he conceded. "Okay, I still think you're going to be disappointed, but here goes. One night at a bar, Sam bought me a beer. He was with a few friends and they were ready to go shortly after I arrived, but on his way out, he asked if I would have dinner with him. He's handsome and I was flattered and he looked like a nice enough guy, so I said yes. A week later we had a very nice dinner.

"A couple of nights after that, I invited him over to my house for dinner and he showed up pretty looped."

"You mean drunk?"

"Yep, and halfway through dinner, he was all over me like a cheap suit. I mean, I couldn't keep the guy's hands off me."

"I'll remember that," Garner teased.

Hank swatted him on the arm. "Stop it. Do you want to hear the rest of the story or not?"

"Sorry."

"So, it took forever to get him out of my house that night, but I finally managed it. The next day when he sobered up, he called and apologized profusely, blaming it on a really bad lunch shift at the restaurant, and begged for an opportunity to make it up to me. He really did seem sincere, so I gave him another chance."

"Let me guess," Garner said. "Bad idea?"

"How'd you know?"

"Okay, go on."

"Well, this time he invited me to his house for dinner, which should have been my first clue. When I got there, I was certain he was well on his way to being drunk again, but not wanting to be rude, I gave him the benefit of the doubt. About twenty minutes after we finished dinner, he excused himself, I assumed to go to the bathroom. Much to my surprise, when he returned, he was buck-ass naked."

Garner smacked Hank on the arm this time. "No way."

"Oooooh yes."

"What did you do?"

"I got up and left. When he called the next day, I thanked him for dinner but told him I didn't think it was going to work out."

"And let me guess—he didn't get the hint."

Hank started the engine, then put both hands on the steering wheel and looked at Garner. "Bingo. He called a couple times a day for a week until I guess he finally gave up."

"Poor guy," Garner said.

"Thanks. It was really uncomfortable and still is, as you can see."

"I was talking about Sam."

"What?"

"Come on, Hank, you broke his heart. But thanks for telling me the story. I made some great mental notes."

Hank pulled out of the parking lot. "You've got to be kidding me. Right?"

"About you breaking his heart? Sure. But not about taking mental notes," Garner assured him.

"What mental notes?"

"First two on my list, no drinking and no getting naked," Garner teased.

"Hey, that's not fair," Hank whined. "I want to get drunk and naked with you."

"Do you now?" Garner asked.

"Hell yeah."

AFTER BURGERS and a couple of beers at the local sports bar, Garner and Hank were still laughing when they got back to the marina. The relaxing effect of the beers had only intensified the humor of the night and made them laugh harder while talking about the look on Sam's face when they'd left the restaurant.

Halfway down the dock, Hank grabbed Garner by the arm and stopped him. When their eyes met, they held each other's gaze. Hank slowly cupped Garner's face in his hands and placed a gentle kiss on his lips.

When Hank pulled back, Garner whispered, "Thanks, that was nice."

A split second later he felt Hank's lips covering his again, but not so gently this time. Hank launched a full-on assault and Garner was prepared for the attack. His mouth opened for Hank and within seconds, he was lost in the onslaught. Suddenly struggling to breath, Garner remembered where they were and pulled away. "Not here."

He took Hank by the hand and led him down to the boat.

Garner fumbled with his keys, unlocked the companionway door, and turned on the cabin lights. Before he could go any farther, he was spun around and pressed against the light switch, turning the lights off again. But light or no light, Garner could see Hank's fierce blue eyes blazing into his. Frozen in Hank's regard, Garner didn't move when Hank raised both hands and placed them on the wall on either side of Garner's head. He again felt Hank's lips pressed against his, seemingly not wanting to break the intense connection. Garner ran the fingers of one hand through Hank's thick black hair, cupping the back of his head and pulling him in closer while he hooked a finger of his free hand in one of Hank's belt loops and allowed his hand to hang freely.

Hank felt so damn good Garner didn't want to stop. It'd been so long since he'd felt any intimate human contact, he was flying high in the moment. Then a little voice went off in Garner's head. *This is your first date, Garner. And besides, you're only here for six weeks; do you really want to get involved with someone? You suck at relationships, and Hank clearly wants more than a one-night stand.*

Garner brought both hands up between them and rested them on Hank's chest. He gave a gentle nudge, and Hank broke the kiss, giving him a concerned look. "What's wrong? Are you okay?"

Garner smiled. "I'm way better than okay, but we need to think about what we're doing here."

"I know exactly what I'm doing," Hank said.

Garner sighed.

Hank wrinkled his face. "Have I done something wrong?"

Garner ran his hand down the side of Hank's face. "Of course not. You've done everything right, that's why it's important to me to be honest with you."

Hank took a couple steps back and leaned against the galley counter. "I'm listening."

Garner's head was still reeling from the kiss, but he did his best to get his thoughts together. He took a step toward Hank and stood in front of him while resting his hands on Hank's shoulders. "Look. I have no idea where your head is, but I'm only going to be here for six weeks. Even if I were going to be here longer, I suck at any relationship that has the word 'lasting.'"

Hank tilted his head, giving Garner a confused look. Garner ran a hand through his own shabby hair. "Okay, let me rephrase that. If I didn't think you were a great guy, I would jump your bones right here."

"So you don't sleep with great guys? Is that it?" Hank asked.

"No. I mean yes. Oh hell. None of this is coming out right."

Hank crossed his arms over his chest, seemingly enjoying Garner's squirming.

"Let me start over," Garner said. "I do think you're a great guy and the question is: do either one of us want to get involved in something for just six weeks?"

Hank dropped his head and sighed. "I get it. But you could be here for longer if you wanted to, right?"

Garner thought about the question. "Technically yes. But I made myself a promise that I was going to see the world a little at a time, and well, to be honest, I don't know if I'm willing to break that promise. And besides, this is just our first date, and as I said, historically I suck at relationships. You may end up wishing I'd get out of here a hell of a lot sooner."

"I hardly think—"

Garner pressed a finger to Hank's lips, stopping him midsentence. "We're going to see a lot of each other around here, so let's just take it a day at a time and see where it goes, okay?"

Hank groaned in obvious frustration but gently kissed Garner's finger. "Okay, you win. But only because I know I can win you over and I believe you're worth the wait."

Garner dropped his head. "Thank you. And for the record, I really do think you're a great guy."

Hank smiled.

"How about a nightcap? I have some cognac I received as a gift and I've been saving it for a special occasion."

"I like being a special occasion. Sure, I'd love to try it."

Garner dug through his liquor cabinet and pulled out an ornate bottle with a rich caramel-colored liquid inside.

"From the looks of the bottle, I'll bet that's some pretty expensive stuff," Hank said.

Garner held the bottle up and turned it in his hands before stopping to read the label. "It's called Courvoisier L'Esprit, and I think you're right. I tried looking it up online once and couldn't even find this particular vintage anywhere."

He pulled two brandy glasses out of the cabinet and poured them each about a third of a glass. "It's a beautiful night; do you want to go topside?"

"Great idea."

STARTLED AND confused, Thompson bolted upright when he heard loud noises. He rubbed his eyes and looked around the dark room trying to figure out where he was. When his eyes began to adjust, familiar things started to come into focus and he remembered. *My office. I must have dozed off on the couch in my office.*

He wasn't surprised. He'd pulled the same routine many times when he worked late and didn't feel like going home to an empty house. Rubbing his eyes, he tilted his head to the side when he heard the noises again. Listening intently, he realized the sounds were muffled voices mixed in with hearty laughter. He swung his legs around and stood, wincing a little when his bare feet came in contact with the icy concrete floor. He walked over to the large window overlooking the marina and stared into the dark Savannah night. He saw two men walking down the dock and blinked a few times to try and bring the faces into focus.

When the men walked under one of the overhead dock lights, he recognized them. *That's Garner and Hank.* Watching from the shadowy confines of his dark office, Thompson for the second time in one day felt like a voyeur, but he didn't turn away. He looked on as they strolled leisurely down the dock, stopping only when Hank grabbed Garner by the arm, then cupped his face with his hands and kissed him. When the kiss ended, it appeared as though they exchanged a few words, and Hank's lips again covered Garner's, this time more passionately. He looked away, not wanting to invade their privacy, but his curiosity got the best of him and he turned back to the window. Garner was now leading Hank down to his boat at breakneck speed. After they boarded, Garner appeared to be fumbling with his keys, and then they disappeared below. A second later the cabin lights came on and Thompson saw their silhouette in the eerie glow of the tinted porthole, bodies pressed tightly together. A second later the cabin went dark.

Thompson felt another strong pang of jealousy. The only difference between this time and the last was the bulge in his jeans telling him he didn't have to wonder of what or, actually, of whom he was really jealous. *Fuck no, Thompson! You're not jealous.*

GARNER CRAWLED into his bed and set the alarm on his iPhone for 6:00 a.m. As he stretched out in his comfortable berth, he couldn't help but think of Hank. He'd have to be careful with this one. His new friend had been absolutely charming and had quite a sense of humor. After their discussion, they'd laid up on the deck sipping their cognac and staring up at the bright stars glowing against the satiny midnight blue of the dark Georgia sky. They'd giggled and made out like teenagers, against his better judgment, until the sexual tension had become too much for either of them to handle. Garner had said his goodnights and sent Hank home before he did something he didn't want to. Not true, he knew. He wanted to do it all right, but he also knew he shouldn't.

CHAPTER
FIVE

GARNER WAS breathless as he looked down into Hank's sapphire-blue eyes glistening in the dimly lit stateroom. He was holding Hank's bare feet just below the ankles, and he took comfort in Hank's hands resting on the backs of his thighs, guiding him forward with each thrust. Hank's tight opening felt warm and welcoming as it surrounded and consumed him with each slow and deliberate move. His heart was beating so fast it seemed his veins might not be able to handle the massive flow of blood coursing through them, and he closed his eyes to try and calm his libido.

Garner's head rolled back as his release quickly raced through his body with desperate need. He did his best to hold his orgasm at bay, wanting to enjoy every last thrust, but now he was pumping frantically. Garner opened his eyes and froze. He was shocked to no longer have Hank's blue eyes looking up at him; instead, he was now gazing into the sparkling citrine of Thompson's lust-filled emerald eyes, and hell if they weren't peering right into his soul. Caught up in something he couldn't understand or control, he was unable to break away and instinct had him moving again. As his length slid in and out of Thompson with reckless abandon, he felt more than saw Thompson's lube-covered hand rhythmically moving up and down his long, fully erect shaft. At the sight of Thompson beneath him, he could no longer control his impending release and came to the sounds of strumming guitars.

Guitars? Strumming guitars? What the fuck?

Garner opened his eyes and realized his iPhone alarm was vibrating and filling the empty cabin with the annoying sound of strumming guitars. "Why in the hell did I think strumming guitars were a good way to start each day?" he asked himself in frustration.

He quickly silenced the alarm and buried his head beneath his pillow. His mind wandered back to his dream and he sighed, remembering it so vividly. He'd started out having sex with Hank and then ended it with Thompson beneath him. *What the fuck was that all about?* Still lying on his stomach, he moved ever so slightly to relieve the pressure on what he thought was his normal morning wood when realized he was lying in a cool, wet, sticky mess. He rolled his eyes and moaned in frustration. *This did not just happen. How the fuck old are you, Garner? A wet dream? Really? And about Thompson Gray, no less?*

Garner lifted his soiled body out of the bed, stripped the sheets, tossed them to the corner of his stateroom, and headed for the shower.

STEPPING OUT of the hot, steamy glass enclosure, the physical evidence of his teenage pubescent nightmare long since washed down the shower drain, Garner reached for the bath towel he'd laid on the toilet seat earlier. The corner of his mouth inched up into a very small smile when he inhaled the aroma of fresh brewing coffee. He had to admit he was just a little pleased, considering the sexual overload his brain was experiencing lately, that he'd remembered to set up the coffee maker and hit the auto-brew button before he'd gone to bed.

He dried off quickly and wrapped the towel around himself, tucking the end in at his waist. Using a hand towel, he wiped a circle in the heavy fog covering his mirror until he could clearly see his reflection. He placed both hands on the counter and leaned in. "A wet dream, Holt?" he mumbled in a disgusted tone. "At your age?"

As the steam slowly started to reclaim the circle he'd just cleared, he leaned in closer. "Look, I don't know what's going on with you right now, but you've got to get your shit under control."

Eventually his face turned into nothing more than a blur, and three beeps ended his mental chastising. The coffee maker told him the brewing process was complete and a fresh hot cup of java was waiting for him in the galley.

When he stepped out of the steamy warmth of the master head and into the cool air of the hallway, he shivered against the iciness of the chilly November morning. The teak and holly floor was cold against his bare feet, and goose bumps began to quickly form on his damp skin. To hell with the cold. He needed caffeine and the galley was the quickest place to get it. Quickly moving through the dark cabin, he turned on lights as he went, stopping at the thermostat and pressing the up temperature button a few times until he heard the heat kick on. It would take a few minutes for the boat to warm up, and he contemplated turning and bolting straight for the warmth of his bed, but he remembered the soft linens in a pile of wet, gooey mess in the corner of his stateroom and cursed under his breath, pushing that thought out of his mind.

When the first sip of hot coffee touched his lips, he imagined the surge of caffeine as it traveled through his veins, waking up his limbs one by one. He went back to his stateroom, dressed in jeans, a T-shirt, and a sweatshirt, and carried his boat shoes to the companionway stairs. He looked out of the galley porthole and saw the glow of the impending sunrise. He grabbed a jacket, stepped into his shoes, and carried his second cup of coffee topside. He settled in the cockpit and watched as the swirly hues of orange, pink, red, and amber crested above the barrier islands like a child's first-grade watercolor.

Motion caught Garner's eye, and he turned to see Thompson standing with coffee cup in hand on the end of the dock, no more than thirty feet away, glowering at the view in front of him. Every now and then he would bow his head, but just as quickly he would look up again, seemingly unable to turn away from the approaching sunrise.

When the sun was fully visible above the horizon and all the vivid colors had blurred into a steady orange-yellow glow, Thompson wiped his cheek with the back of one hand and turned. He froze when his eyes locked on to Garner's, but he didn't break the connection. Even from thirty feet away, Garner could see the red blush coloring Thompson's face. His look reeked of embarrassment and defeat, and Garner's heart began to ache for him. Not ache in a "sexual" or "longing for him" way, but in a "need to take care of or protect him" way. The way you feel when someone you care for has been badly hurt and you want to wrap your arms around that person and hold on tight so they don't get hurt again. And his first inclination was to do just that. Jump off his boat, wrap his arms around Thompson, and hold him until he was able to absorb some of the pain that was so evident in Thompson's face. Then a light bulb went off in his head. *This must have something to do with his late wife. Hank said she died down here on the dock.*

Before Garner could say anything, Thompson's face went void of any feelings. He straightened his shoulders and cleared his throat. "Good morning! I didn't realize anyone else was up at this hour."

Garner smiled, trying not to look as concerned as he felt. "Morning," he replied with a sense of cheer he didn't feel. "I've always been an early riser. You know, career goals and all that 'early bird gets the worm' crap."

Thompson seemed to relax a little and smiled, the stress softening around his eyes.

Garner held out his cup. "I've got a full pot. Can I get you a refill?"

Thompson looked down at his cup hesitantly. "Sure, why not. We have a few minutes before this place gets cranking."

"Good," Garner said, motioning with his free hand for Thompson to come on board.

Thompson kicked off his Sperry loafers, climbed aboard, and took a seat next to Garner.

Garner stood and reached for Thompson's half-full cup of cold coffee. "How do you take it?"

"Black's fine," Thompson replied.

Garner stepped into the companionway. "You got it, I'll be right back."

While Garner filled both cups with steaming hot coffee, he was still baffled by Thompson's earlier behavior. No. Baffled wasn't the word. Concerned was more like it. He just couldn't shake the overwhelming sadness on Thompson's face when he turned, saw Garner, and their eyes locked. And he couldn't understand the strong feelings brewing within him to help and protect this man. But protect him from what? He topped off the cups, deciding there was nothing more he could do short of asking Thompson outright, and he certainly didn't want to add insult to injury and embarrass the man further. He would do the only thing he could do. Ask Hank about it when they next talked.

Again heading topside, he got to the stairway leading up the companionway and stopped. Thompson's feet were eyelevel and fidgeting nervously. His navy-blue socks with the gold toes were bouncing back and forth almost like he was running in place. He cleared his throat to let Thompson know he was coming up the stairs and the fidgeting suddenly stopped. He climbed up and handed Thompson the hot coffee, hesitating while he decided where to sit. If he took his previous seat, he would be sitting right next to Thompson, which would seem odd because the cockpit was very spacious and had ample seating. On the other hand, Thompson had sat down right next to him earlier, so he threw caution to the wind and plopped down in his original seat. Their legs brushed ever so lightly, but Thompson didn't shift or move over. Out the corner of his eye, Garner watched Thompson stare down at the dark brew as if the answers to every question in the world were held in the rich black liquid in his cup. He seemed to be lost in thought for a bit, but eventually blew on the hot liquid and took his first sip. "This is good," he mumbled, almost to himself.

"Thanks."

There was an uncomfortable silence, so Garner made a quick attempt at filling the void. "So. What's on the agenda for my first day, boss?"

Thompson looked up with a crooked smile on his face, obviously relieved that he was off the hook and didn't need to explain what Garner had just witnessed.

"Well, let me see," Thompson said, tilting his head back and looking up to the quickly developing blue morning sky, then back down. He met Garner's eyes. "On last count, which was last night, I think we have seven departures and twelve arrivals."

Garner nodded. "That many, huh? What time is checkout?"

"Checkout is eleven, but most departures are on their way between first light and eight o'clock."

"And check-in?" Garner asked.

"Noon. But again, most arrivals start coming midafternoon, about three o'clock or so, and continue steadily until dark."

"What do you anticipate my hours being?"

"Listen," Thompson said with a slight smile. "Beggars can't be choosers, so however much time you want to give, I'll take."

Garner chuckled. "It's not like I have anything else to do and I do want to help, so whenever you need me, I'm here."

Thompson flashed him that striking smile, dimples prominently displayed, and those stupid unidentifiable feelings about caring for and protecting this man were front and center again. *You really need to sort through these feelings, Garner, before you get yourself into trouble.*

"And what will you *need* me to do?"

Thompson didn't hesitate this time. "In the mornings, you'll help check out and cast off the departures. Midday it's fueling up and pumping out the holding tanks of transient boats and the afternoon is filled with check-ins. And then whatever needs doing in between," he added with a hesitant look.

"Okay. I'm in," Garner said with a nod. "How much does this gig pay anyway?"

Thompson's smile quickly faded, and Garner immediately regretted the question. He realized right then and there he'd work for free if it kept a smile on that man's face.

"That's the thing," Thompson said, tilting his head to one side. "All I can afford is fifteen an hour. Maybe sixteen if I skip lunch every day."

"Sold," Garner said without hesitation. "Fifteen it is. I can't have you missing meals and wasting away to nothing."

Thompson's smile covered his face again and Garner's heart filled with joy.

STANDING AT the end of the dock after casting off the last departure, Thompson was about to head up to the office for what seemed like the hundredth time when he stopped and looked at his watch. *Twelve thirty.*

His stomach had begun to quietly protest over the lack of food an hour ago, but now it was making itself know to everyone in a five-foot vicinity. The morning had gone by in a flash. Garner had been an eager student and his boating knowledge was already proving to be a great asset. He'd picked up all the marina systems and operations very quickly and had even taken over the VHF radio. He was handling the phone and answering what questions he could and taking messages for what he couldn't. Thompson felt lucky and grateful to have him on board, for however long he hung around.

He glanced down and saw a plastic grocery bag floating near the dock. *With my luck, someone's engine intake will suck that up and they'll blame me for not having a clean marina.* He knelt down, leaned over the edge of the dock, and scooped it up. When he stood and turned, he saw Garner's boat and had a flashback of this morning when his new employee had caught him teary eyed and exposed. He quickly remembered the embarrassment he'd felt and shook his head, trying to push the feelings out of his mind. A boat got his attention as it rounded the bend in the waterway, and he stared at it blankly as he struggled to get a hold of the rollercoaster of emotions he'd been experiencing lately.

Up until the anniversary of Caroline's death, most of his tears and emotions had long since dried up, leaving just the unbearable pain and emptiness to which he'd become accustomed. But then out of the blue, everything had returned with a vengeance. Between him slamming his coffee cup yesterday morning and his teary show of weakness this morning, he felt like he was finally starting to come unraveled. But as he relived the scene in his head, he didn't remember feeling like Garner was shocked at his behavior. In fact, he'd thought he'd seen some level of understanding or compassion in Garner's eyes, which confused the hell out of him. *He couldn't have any idea about Caroline. How could he?* Then it hit him. *Hank! Maybe Hank mentioned something to him? That would explain his reaction.* "Shit!" he mumbled. "Damn it, Prince."

Feeling disgusted with himself yet again, Thompson walked over to the trashcan, removed the lid, held it in the air, and disposed of the plastic bag. *Look at the bright side.* At least Garner had been kind enough not to push for an explanation. That would have really been awkward.

He positioned the lid back on the trashcan and turned. He froze again midstride and smiled, remembering how kind Garner had been and how much he'd enjoyed having coffee with him. He'd been very comfortable around the man, and that in itself was quite shocking. Normally after an episode like that, he would simply curl up into a ball and ride it out until he could function again. *Why this abrupt shift, and what is it with Garner Holt?*

Suddenly, the VHF radio hanging on his belt came to life. "Motor vessel *Seafari* hailing Thundercloud Marina, Thundercloud Marina, come back."

He put his hand on the radio to return the hail, but before he could unclip it from his belt, he heard Garner's voice. "*Seafari*, this is Thundercloud Marina. Captain, please acknowledge and switch to channel sixty-eight. That's channel six-eight."

Thompson smiled at the confident voice on the other end of the radio. Then his radio went dead as the two switched to another frequency. Thompson was again left in silence to contemplate the mess his life had become.

GARNER WAS enjoying his first day on his new job. It was hectic and fun, something different and exciting to experience since his journey from New York. Thompson had been a good, thorough, and patient teacher. It'd been a while since Garner had been around anything but his boat, and he felt like he was a little rusty. It had taken him a couple of hours to get back into work mode, but once he did, everything came back to him and he felt pretty comfortable.

"*Seafari*, welcome to Thundercloud Marina. Your slip for the evening will be Dock L as in Lima, slip three. Do you need fuel before we get you docked?"

Garner heard the office door open and close, and he looked over his shoulder to see Thompson entering. He gave him a wink and went back to work.

"That's a negative," the captain replied. "Can you give me instructions to Dock L?"

"Sure thing," Garner said, referring to a large map of the marina on the wall. He used his finger to trace the route. "Once you enter the marina, turn to starboard at the first opportunity and Dock L will be the third dock on your port side. Slip three is the last slip on your starboard side. If you go in stern first, it will be a port-side tie-up."

"Roger that," the captain replied.

"Once you make the turn to port," Garner instructed, "you'll see me on the dock waiting to assist you."

"Much appreciated, Thundercloud Marina, see you at the dock. *Seafari* switching back to channel one-six."

"Thundercloud Marina standing by on channels sixteen and six-eight."

Thompson crossed his arms over his broad chest and eyed up his new employee. "Nice job. Pretty soon you won't need me hanging around at all."

"I hardly think your job's in jeopardy," Garner said with a smile as he headed for the door. "I'd love to stay and chat, but I have a boat to dock."

Thompson flashed that brilliant smile Garner thought he would never get tired of, and his knees went a little weak.

"Good answer," Thompson said. "Come on, I'll give you a hand."

"I'd appreciate that, this is a seventy footer. I might need the extra hands."

THIRTY MINUTES later Thompson had his arm slung over Garner's shoulder, and he was laughing hysterically as they walked back up to the marina office. "Oh come on, at least you didn't fall in. I saved you, remember?" Thompson said, apparently trying to dial back his hysterics. "You have to admit it was pretty funny, though."

"Hilarious," Garner said, pretending he was upset. He stopped and threw Thompson's arm off his shoulder. "You keep that up and you're gonna have to get a new employee. And then I'll sue you for making fun of me." Garner quickly realized how ridiculous that sounded, and he burst into laughter himself, remembering the sequence of events.

Docking Seafari *had turned out to be quite an ordeal. Halfway through the process, the wind had starting kicking up and it had quickly become obvious the captain was somewhat inexperienced, which made matters worse. Garner had just secured the stern line and looked up to see Thompson fumbling with the two mid-ship lines. A gust of wind took the bow and started to push it away from the dock. Garner made a mad dash to get to the bow and catch the bowline from the first mate before* Seafari *collided with the boat next to them. Apparently Thompson had the same idea and the two collided pretty hard. The force of the impact had Garner going headfirst toward the water with bowline in hand when Thompson grabbed him by back of his shorts. Thompson pulled back on Garner so hard they both fell backwards, Thompson landing on his ass and Garner sitting on top of him.*

Thompson was still laughing so hard he was starting to tear up.

"That was so close, my friend," Thompson choked out. "Am I gonna have to put one of those child leashes on you to keep you from falling in?"

"You're getting funnier by the minute, but maybe," Garner teased.

Thompson wiped at the tears dotting his cheeks, apparently trying to get himself under control. "You know I'm only teasing you, right?" He rubbed his ass with his free hand. "And besides, I'm the one who landed on the bottom. That's going to leave a mark, you know."

Garner chuckled as he studied the man's face. "Yeah. I know you're teasing, and ah, I'm sorry about your ass."

Thompson seemed genuinely amused, and Garner realized he would end up in the drink every day if it put a smile on Thompson's face. He shook his head and smirked. "Oh and just for the record, I won't leave you in a jam. You got me at least until my boat is fixed."

Thompson bumped his shoulder against Garner's and started walking again. "I knew that. Like you have a choice anyway."

They walked in silence for a few seconds, and then Thompson stopped again. "You know, I haven't laughed like that in years. It felt really good. Thanks."

Thompson held out his fisted hand and the two men bumped knuckles.

"Glad I can provide some much-needed entertainment for you," Garner said. "Do you know your entire face lights up when you smile?"

In a split second, Thompson's expression changed and his head dropped. Garner immediately regretted the words, albeit not knowing why.

Silence loomed between them for a few seconds. Then Thompson looked up. "Yeah, my wife used to tell me that all the time. And the fact is, I would love to laugh more. But in the last four years, I haven't had much to laugh about."

This time Garner chose his words very carefully. "Yeah, man, I... I was sorry to hear about your wife."

Thompson just stared at him with no detectable expression. Garner held his breath and waited for the "mind your own business, asshole" response, but it didn't come.

Thompson started walking again. "Thanks, it's been difficult" was all he said.

When they reached the office, the phone was ringing.

Garner walked around the front of the desk and beat Thompson to the receiver. "Thundercloud Marina, Garner speaking."

"Well, look who's on the ball already, answering the phone and everything."

Garner laughed, recognizing Hank's voice. "Yeah, that's some feat, isn't it?"

"I tried your cell about an hour ago, but got your voice mail, so I thought I give you a try here."

"Oh sorry, I left it down on the boat. You know, first day of work and all."

Distracted and worried about Thompson, Garner watched him slide in behind his desk and start to shuffle some papers, seemingly miles away and deep in thought.

"So... how's your first day going?"

"It's going great, Hank, thanks for asking. How's your day?"

At the mention of Hank's name, Garner saw Thompson look up briefly but then continue to busy himself with paperwork.

"Pretty well," Hank said. "No rescue missions so far, and I actually sold a boat today."

"Congratulations," Garner said.

"Thanks. Will you help me celebrate tonight?"

"Maybe. I don't know what time I'll be out of here, but what did you have in mind?"

"I thought I'd cook dinner for you at my place."

Garner chuckled. "Should I plan on getting naked and jumping your bones?"

At that comment, Thompson stopped his busy work and was now looking up at him with a strange expression.

Garner covered the bottom of the phone with his hand and whispered, "Long story. But I'll explain later."

Thompson raised both hands, palms out, as if to say "None of my business," and went back to his paperwork.

"Very funny," Hank responded. "And before you jump to any conclusions, it's no pressure, okay? Just dinner. And for the record, you'll need to learn not to threaten me with a good time."

Garner crinkled his nose. "You're not the first person to tell me that."

"So, will you join me?" Hank asked again.

"Sure, but it will have to be later. Our last arrival is not expected to get here until around six or so this evening."

Thompson looked up again, waving one hand. "I can handle the last few arrivals," he whispered. "Go and have fun!"

Garner simply shook his head.

He heard Hank speak again. "How about if I pick you up at eight? Will that give you enough time?"

"I think that'll work," Garner replied. "See you at eight."

"I'm looking forward to it."

"Me too. Bye, Hank."

Garner hung up the phone and sat on the corner of Thompson's desk, but Thompson didn't look up. "Thanks for the offer to cover for me, but I pull my weight around here or I don't take a paycheck. Okay?"

Thompson still didn't look up, but he stopped shuffling papers and placed both hands flat on his desk. "Look, I've been doing this a long time and I can handle a few late arrivals by myself, so don't feel like you have to hang around until closing every night."

"Really?" Garner said, crossing his arms over his chest. "You wanna tell me where this is coming from, Thompson? One minute we're getting along and laughing and the next you're snapping at me about me wanting to pull my weight."

Thompson finally looked up. "I said… I can take care of the late arrivals."

"Of course you can, big man," Garner said with a bit of sarcasm. "This is your business and I'm sure you can do it all. But if you must know, I enjoy your company and I like working with you. There."

The stress lines in Thompson's face seemed to fade away, and his look turned to one of sadness. "I'm sorry, man," he said. "I get like this when something triggers memories of Caroline."

"Don't want to assume anything, but was Caroline your wife?"

"Yeah. I guess Hank filled you in, huh?"

"Not really, just that she died unexpectedly on the property," Garner confessed, the therapist in him again staring to kick in. "If you want to talk about it, man, just know I'm here. In my experience, it's sometimes easier to talk to a stranger than it is to talk to someone you've known a long time."

Thompson hesitated as if he was actually thinking about opening up to Garner, but when he spoke it was not what Garner was hoping for. "Won't do any good and won't bring her back." He sighed. "What's done is done."

"Well, just know it's an open invitation," Garner offered.

"Thanks, and I'm sorry I'm such a dick sometimes. And… by the way, I enjoy working with you too."

Garner smiled and put his hand on Thompson's shoulder. "Do you like me enough to let me borrow a vehicle sometime to go to the grocery store? I'm really getting tired of eating tuna fish and stale bagels."

Thompson laughed out loud, and his face lit up yet again. He opened the right top drawer to his desk and dangled a set of keys in front of Garner. "My black Avalanche is parked right outside. Why don't you go now while it's quiet."

"You sure?"

"Yeah, I'm sure."

"Thanks, man. Can I get you anything?"

"I'm good," Thompson said, handing him the keys.

"Oh yeah, can you give me directions to the nearest grocery store?"

Thompson jotted down some notes and went over them with him. "It's a few miles to Publix, almost a straight shot, though. You'll find everything you'll need there."

Garner rattled the keys and stood. "Thanks again and I'll make it quick. I promise."

"Take your time," Thompson said. "I have things under control here."

THE DOOR closed with a thud as Garner left the office. Thompson exhaled. "Way to go, asshole," he mumbled. "You're an emotional fucking mess lately, and he didn't deserve that shit from you."

He folded his arms, rested them on his desk, and laid his head down, closing his eyes. He needed to figure out what was going on and what had affected his emotions so quickly. The one thing he did know was that he liked Garner. A lot. And he felt comfortable around the man, which was odd because he hadn't connected with anyone on any level since Caroline.

In fact, he hadn't laughed like that since Caroline died, and it had felt so good to just let go. But what had changed his mood so suddenly? One minute he was laughing hysterically at his and Garner's episode and the next he was pissed off and snapping at the poor guy.

Was it Garner's reference to his smile and the fact that Caroline used to say the same thing that had set him off? Most likely; any mention or thought of Caroline usually sent him down an emotional path, but it was usually a melancholy one, not an angry one. But if not that, what else? He recalled eavesdropping on the conversation between Garner and Hank. He suddenly raised his head. *Oh hell no! I don't care what Garner and Hank do.* But just thinking about the conversation was making him tense up all over again. He kept hearing Garner say "Should I plan on getting naked and jumping your bones?" over and over again in his head. *God. I'm so fucked up!*

THOMPSON WAS down at the fuel dock pumping diesel fuel into a commercial fishing boat when he saw his truck pull into the parking lot. He felt a sudden wave of nerves course through him, and he cursed under his breath. He watched as Garner loaded a shitload of groceries into a marina cart, rolled it down the dock, and then unloaded the contents onto his boat. With little else to do but listen to the clicking of the fuel pump as the gallons and dollar amount rolled over and continued to climb, he kept an eye on Garner's boat. Ten minutes later, Garner reappeared with a bag of trash in hand and pushed the empty cart back up the dock. *Must have cleaned out his fridge.*

He watched as Garner parked the empty cart alongside the others and disappeared through the office door. His gaze shifted to the large window, imagining him standing on the other side scanning the marina, probably trying to locate him. With the pump still clicking, he allowed himself to think about the man for a minute. He didn't know what about Garner had touched him, but obviously something had. Sure, he had an easy, gentle way and seemed to make people feel comfortable around him from the get-go, including Thompson, but that wasn't all it was.

The pump abruptly stopped, interrupting his thoughts and signaling a full tank. He removed the nozzle and placed it back in the pump.

The captain walked up, digging his wallet out of his pocket. Thompson looked at the pump. "That'll be two thousand fifty-six dollars and fifteen cents."

The captain gave him a credit card, and Thompson was in the hut running the card when he heard the VHF radio go off at his hip. "*Excalibur* to BoatUS, over?"

He heard Hank's voice come over the radio. "*Excalibur*, this is BoatUS. Please acknowledge and switch to channel six-eight, please."

The other radio in the hut, monitoring channel sixty-eight, came to life. "This is *Excalibur*."

"What can I do for you today, Captain?" Hank's voice said clearly.

"I just dropped the hook a little north of mile marker five eighty with a fouled prop. Can you give me a tow back to my dock in Thunderbolt?"

"That's affirmative," Hank said. "I can be to you in fifteen or twenty minutes."

"We'll be here," the voice said.

Hank spoke again. "Can you give me a cell number in case I can't reach you by radio? Over."

"Sure thing," the voice said and then recited a phone number.

Thompson left the hut and was untying the stern of the boat he'd just fueled up when he turned and saw Garner getting the bowline. "You're back," he said. "Did you have any trouble finding the store?"

Garner shook his head as he tossed the line onto the bow of the boat. "Nope, your directions were spot on. Thanks again for the use of your truck."

"Anytime," Thompson said, doing the same with the stern. He waved to the captain and yelled, "All clear, Captain."

He then walked over and put his hand on Garner's shoulder. "I'm really sorry about snapping earlier."

"It's already forgotten," Garner assured him. "Don't waste another minute thinking about it. But speaking about earlier, I wanted to clarify something."

Thompson tilted his head to one side. "What's that?"

"I just wanted you to know that I was teasing Hank with that comment about getting naked and jumping his bones."

Thompson raised both hands again and smiled. "None of my business, man. You don't owe me any explanation. And I'm the last one to judge anyone, considering how together I am and all."

"No, really," Garner said. "I want to explain."

Thompson was now intrigued, so he didn't try to discourage Garner's explanation.

"So," Garner started. "When Hank and I had dinner last night, our waiter was a guy Hank had dated a few times, and the guy didn't seem too happy about seeing Hank out with someone else, so we left. Of course I asked what had gone wrong. I mean, the guy was good-looking as hell, and so Hank gave me the lowdown."

Garner recounted the story about Sam and Hank's dates, really focusing on the last date where Sam got naked.

Thompson tried not to act uncomfortable in any way, but hearing about Hank getting naked with someone was making him just that. In an attempt to mask his discomfort, he scratched his chin and said, "And getting naked is bad how?"

Garner laughed. "It was their second date, you asshole."

"Ohhh," Thompson said, forcing a smile.

Garner nodded and then his face took on a serious expression.

Thompson braced himself for something significant, probably questions about Caroline.

Garner shuffled from foot to foot nervously, but when he finally spoke, it wasn't about Thompson or Caroline. "Look, Thompson, I assumed you figured out about me being gay when I went out with Hank." A look of panic suddenly consumed Garner's face. "Oh God, please tell me you already knew about Hank?"

Thompson felt so relieved this wasn't about him that he just couldn't resist the opportunity to make Garner squirm. "I had no idea Hank was gay until you told that story. And furthermore, I think all gay people...." But the joke was on him because before he could even get the next line out about how appalled he was with homosexuals, he couldn't keep a straight face and lost it.

When Garner realized Thompson was fucking with him, he hauled back and let him have it right in the arm. Hard.

"Okay, okay! Sorry!" he said, rubbing his aching arm. "And before you hit me again, the answer is yes on both counts. And... the fact that I saw the rainbow sticker on your boat."

"Oh good Lord," Garner cursed. "I'll bet that damn sticker has been outing me all the way down the eastern seaboard. Shit! That's how Hank found out as well."

"Did I hear my name?"

Garner turned to see Hank walking down the dock. "And speak of the devil."

Hank waved them off. "Can't stop and chat, ladies, Captain Charming has someone else to rescue. I'll rescue *you* later," he added, looking at Garner.

Garner blushed and smiled nervously. Thompson had to admit he was enjoying seeing the seemingly together Garner a little off-kilter.

Once Hank was past them and preparing his boat, the conversation continued.

"So why did you put the sticker on your boat if you didn't want anyone to know you're gay?" Thompson asked.

"That's just the thing. I didn't," Garner explained. "A friend did it without my knowledge, and when I tried to pull it off, the damn thing started to tear and left a mark on the hull, so I said the hell with it and left it there. And for the record, I'm not trying to hide anything, I just don't go shouting it from every rooftop."

Thompson could feel the broad smile on his face as it grew wider and wider. He was surprised to realize that he was actually enjoying this. "I see" was all he could say.

"Now you're laughing at me," Garner said as he drew back to let Thompson have it again. But this time Thompson was ready and he rushed him, wrapping his arms around Garner and pinning Garner's arms to his side. "Now what are you gonna do?" he whispered in Garner's ear.

⛵

GARNER FELT a rush of something. He didn't know what, but the combination of Thompson's body pressed against his, his soft breath against Garner's ear, and Thompson's arms wrapped tightly around him was enough to send the blood rushing right to his groin. Horrified that Thompson might feel his growing erection, he decided he had to do something and do it quick. In a move that utilized gravity, he let his full weight help him down to a stooping position, slipping out of Thompson's grip, hopped backward like a ninja, and then returned to his full height, arms spread wide and fingers wiggling in a "bring it on" gesture.

"Damn," Thompson cursed. "That was a smooth move."

Garner's mouth turned up on one side and his expression changed to one of pride. "Damn straight, straight man. You got any other moves you want to try on me?"

Thompson threw his head back and howled with laughter for the second time in one day, so much so that he couldn't get a word out. He stepped closer to Garner, threw one arm around his neck, and dragged him back to the office, shaking his head and laughing the entire way.

CHAPTER
SIX

HANK WAS standing over the stove with a wooden spoon in each hand as the sound of Norah Jones wafted through the house. He was swaying and humming along to Norah's sultry version of the "Tennessee Waltz" while stirring a pot of yellow cheese grits with one spoon and a sauté pan of jumbo shrimp and Andouille sausage with the other. A thought suddenly hit him, and he turned his head to one side, deciding what to do about it.

He lowered the flame on both burners, picked up his cell phone, and opened his contacts, choosing the contact he'd programmed earlier that day for Garner. While the call connected and started to ring, Hank found himself swaying again to Norah's soulful sounds.

He stopped when he heard Garner's voice. "Hey, Hank." Garner had obviously checked the caller ID before he answered.

"Hey, man, how's it going?"

"Pretty good. Thompson and I just finished checking in the last arrival, and I'm about to head down to the boat to unwind for a second and then shower."

Hank felt a wave of panic and looked down at his watch. Six forty-nine. He went over his mental checklist. He still had to finish dinner, set the table, shower, and pick up Garner, and he had just over an hour in which to do it all.

"Hank?"

"Yeah, I'm here. Boy, do I need to get a move on, though. I just wanted to make sure you weren't allergic to shellfish or see if there was anything else I should know about your diet."

"Nope. No food allergies that I'm aware of."

"Okay, good. Gotta go! See you at eight."

"Okay," Garner said with a chuckle.

Hank ended the call and went back to the stove. He dipped his spoon into the simmering grits and brought the cheesy mixture to his mouth. "Ummmm, perfect. One down."

He turned off the burner, covered the pot, and turned his attention to the shrimp and sausage mixture.

As he pushed the shrimp and sausage around in the pan, listening to Norah sing "I Think It's Going to Rain Today," he thought about Thompson for some reason. Garner mentioning his name on the phone triggered a couple of memories that had stuck with him all day and he wasn't sure why. For starters, he'd stopped by the marina midmorning with some bagels for Garner and Thompson. When he'd found the office empty, he'd approached the large window and found them coming up the dock, Thompson's arm slung over Garner's shoulder and both of them laughing hysterically. The scene had struck him as odd because ever since Caroline's death, Thompson had been very reserved and mostly closed off. In fact, Hank hadn't seen him crack more than a smile for as long as he could remember. But then they'd stopped laughing suddenly, and it looked as though the mood or conversation had taken on a more serious tone. They had continued up the dock looking like each of them had more to say, and, not wanting to get in the middle of anything, Hank had slipped out unnoticed.

Then when he'd come back to the marina on that call, it looked like they were into something heavy again, so not wanting to interrupt this time either, he'd said hello, but chose not to stop and headed right for his boat. But as he was on the water leaving the marina, he saw Thompson throw his arms around Garner, saw Garner make some move to get free, then Thompson's arm was around Garner's neck, and they were walking up the dock laughing again. *I wonder what is going on with those two?* Then it hit him like a ton of bricks. *Holy shit! Am I jealous?*

Hank realized that he really liked spending time with Garner. He didn't know where it was headed, but he liked him enough to go along for the ride. He hadn't felt any type of connection to anyone in such a long time, and he was damned excited about it. Garner was smart, good-looking, sexy as hell, and had a wicked sense of humor. All the traits he liked in a man. Some of the excitement waned a bit with his next thought. *Six weeks, Hank! He's only here for six weeks. Be careful and don't go getting your heart broken.*

The sizzling sound of the food brought him back to reality, and he decided to push the thoughts to the back of his mind for now. Besides, he could ask Garner what was going on between him and Thompson tonight.

Hank tasted one of the shrimp. "Just about done," he said under his breath. "I think I'll let them marinate for a while and finish them off right before I serve them."

He turned off the gas burner, moved about the kitchen getting dishes, silverware, and placemats together, and headed for the dining room. "That Yankee isn't going to think twice about Thompson Gray when he gets a taste of my famous Southern Shrimp & Grits. A way to a man's heart through his stomach and all that."

When the table was set, he stood back and admired his work. He glanced at his watch again. *Forty minutes to go. Not bad, Hank. Not bad at all.*

GARNER WAS standing outside the marina entrance when he saw the white F150 round the corner. He waved as the truck pulled up and stopped. The power window came down and the driver leaned out. "Hellooo, sailor! Looking for a ride?"

"If you're going my way," Garner retorted.

Hank grinned and winked. "Oh yeah, I go your way."

Hank put the truck in park, hopped out, and stole a quick kiss on Garner's cheek.

"Thanks," Garner said. "You look great, by the way."

Hank was wearing a nicely pressed blue chambray shirt over a bright-orange T-shirt, khakis, and brown driving shoes.

"Thanks. You too."

Garner felt underdressed in his amber-colored V-neck T-shirt, blue jeans, and blue-and-gold Nikes. He ran his hands down the front of his shirt. "This old thing?"

Hank laughed and opened the door. "Yes, that old thing. I like the way it brings out the blond in your hair. Now get in there, silly."

Garner watched Hank run back around, jump in, and buckle his seatbelt. He moved with a confident grace and Garner liked it.

As the truck sped up, Hank leaned over and patted Garner's thigh. "How was the rest of your day? When I came back from my call, Thompson said you were out."

"Yeah, he asked me to run a marina guest up to West Marine to pick up a replacement bilge pump."

"God, I love that store," Hank said. "If I ever sold my business, I would really like to work there. The only problem I can foresee is I'd buy so much shit, I'd owe them money at the end of every pay period."

Garner nodded in agreement. "Me too. I'm afraid I'd be right there with you."

The short ride back to Hank's place was filled with the usual back-and-forth banter they'd become accustomed to in the short time they'd known one another.

In less than ten minutes, Hank pulled into the driveway of a beige bungalow-style home boasting a white wraparound porch with a swing, white wicker furniture, and green-and-white striped upholstery. Dark-green shutters and a pale-yellow door finished off the exterior. Garner thought it looked like something out of a magazine. The landscaping was perfectly manicured and the outdoor lighting was spot on. There was soft lamplight coming from all the windows, and the entire place looked warm and inviting.

"This is absolutely charming," Garner said, taking it all in.

Hank put the truck in park, rested both hands on the steering wheel, and stared at his house as if he was seeing it for the first time himself. "Thanks, I've owned it for about a year and just finished renovating the entire thing."

Garner opened his door. "Come on, I can't wait to see the inside."

Hank hopped out of the truck, apparently as eager to show off his place as Garner was to see it. They walked into a spacious foyer with at least twelve-foot ceilings. There was a round leather-inlaid drum table in the center with a bouquet of fresh flowers and a secretary with a Chippendale chair against the back wall. A powder room was recessed in the back right corner. Garner turned to the left and saw a formal dining room, complete with romantic table set for two. He stepped into the room, admiring one thing to the next. He stopped when he saw a large antique cupboard in the far corner loaded with some type of porcelain. "Everything is lovely, but this piece is spectacular."

"Thanks. It was my grandmommy Ellen's, right down to the very last piece of porcelain inside of it. It's one of my two prized possessions."

"And the other?" Garner asked.

Hank's very being seemed to be filling with pride as he took Garner by the hand and led him across the foyer to the formal living room.

"And this is the formal living room," he said with the wave of his hand.

Garner followed in awe, certain his mouth was hanging open from the sheer beauty surrounding him. There was a royal-blue tone-on-tone striped camelback couch sitting in the center of the room with two tapestry-upholstered Martha Washington chairs flanking a large fireplace. End tables and other accent pieces effortlessly placed here and there donned the room and created a comfortable but elegant feel. There was a hall at the far right, which Garner assumed led to the bedrooms, and closed double french doors across the back wall. But before he could ask where they led, he spotted a triple mahogany chest of drawers with shiny brass pulls against the back wall. "That's got to be the other piece."

"Bingo," Hank said. "You have a great eye."

He ran his fingers across the top of the long chest, admiring it. "I don't know about that, but it's hard to miss this example of fine craftsmans—"

Before he could finish his sentence, Hank's lips were covering his. It was a long, deep, and slow kiss. Hank's tongue explored every crevice of his mouth, and when it ended, it left Garner breathless and wanting more.

Hank brushed the side of Garner's face with the back of his hand. "I've been wanting to do that since I saw you early this morning."

Garner smiled at the compliment. Then something didn't sit right with that statement. He thought for a second. *This morning? I didn't see him until this afternoon.* "You mean this afternoon?" Garner corrected.

"Nope. This morning," Hank restated with a nonchalant tone.

Suddenly, memories of an earlier time back in New York when he'd had an overzealous admirer that had turned into amateur stalking flooded Garner's memory. *Stop it, Garner. He doesn't appear to be the stalker type. And besides, if he were really stalking you, would he tell you about it?* He pushed those ridiculous thoughts out of his mind, but he must have still had a concerned look on his face that didn't go unnoticed.

"Don't worry, I'll explain over dinner," Hank volunteered.

Garner opened his mouth to protest, but Hank held up a finger. "It's really nothing. I promise."

He felt Hank's hand again slip into his. He led Garner to the double doors across the back wall. He stopped in front of the doors and separated them, each disappearing into the walls. "Gotta love pocket doors," Hank said.

Garner nodded and stepped into the next room. Although much more casual, the den and kitchen area were really one big room separated by a large granite-topped island. The den side had a large overstuffed couch and two club chairs surrounding a massive coffee table all positioned in front of built-in bookcases and a sizable flat-panel television. To the left, the kitchen was gourmet all the way. Cherry wood cabinets with black granite countertops surrounded the area housing every stainless steel high-end appliance you could imagine.

Garner rested his hands on his hips and studied the rooms. "Functional, warm, and still beautiful. Well done, I really like it." He raised his nose to the air and inhaled deeply, recognizing wonderful aromas of simmering seafood and spices. "It smells really good in here too."

"Thanks, and that reminds me, I need to finish the shrimp." Hank headed across the room and stepped up to an eight-burner gas range, turning on one of the burners under a sauté pan. He looked over his shoulder. "You want to pick out some wine, or would you prefer beer?"

"Either is fine with me," Garner said.

"Okay if we have wine tonight?" Hank asked. "I'm in a vino mood. How about some white?"

Garner opened the door to the wine fridge and looked over the collection. "Fine by me," he said, choosing a Jean Dumont Sancerre from one of the shelves.

Garner looked around for an opener, but before he could ask, Hank pointed to a drawer. "In there."

Garner rummaged through and pulled out a corkscrew.

"What did you choose?" Hank asked. Garner held up the bottle label out. "Ah, great choice. One of my favorites."

Garner poured two glasses and handed one to Hank as he stood at the stove.

"Can I see the rest of the house?" Garner asked.

"Sure, this will be fine for a few minutes," Hank said, turning the flame down to a simmer. "Let's go."

With the shrimp simmering away again, Hank led him through the living room and down the hallway. Two large guest bedrooms with en suite baths were just as spectacular as the rest of the house, each distinct in its own way, but very inviting.

Hank's master suite was unbelievable. The room was very spacious, with a king-size bed positioned in front of a wall of floor-to-ceiling windows overlooking nothing but marshlands.

"That's cast, isn't it?" Garner asked, pointing to the windows. "I could get used to waking up to that view every morning. You must get a gorgeous sunrise."

"The best," Hank said. "Maybe you should try it one morning."

Garner chuckled. "Very subtle, Prince," he said wryly.

When they got back to the kitchen, Garner took a seat at the island, and Hank went right to the fridge and came back with an armful of vegetables and greens, dropping everything on the counter opposite Garner. He retrieved a knife and a chopping board and started sorting.

Garner stared down at his glass as he swirled the wine in a circular motion.

When he looked up, Hank was looking at him with a concerned look. "Okay, I've only known you for two days, but you get this look when you're thinking about something. I noticed it right after Bubba told you that it was gonna take six weeks to get your engine repaired and I'm seeing the same look now. Do you want to share?"

Garner felt silly but he had to know. "Look. I really am curious," he said, still staring at the wine glass and swirling. "And I know you said you'd tell me over dinner, but…."

"Ohhhh," Hank said as he stopped chopping, wiped his hands on a towel, and walked around the counter and sat next to Garner.

Garner watched him intently as Hank swirled his wine glass a few times, just as he had done, and eventually took a sip. He savored the wine in his mouth, sloshing it from side to side, then swallowed slowly. "Um, this is really good." The corners of Hank's mouth formed a slight smile.

Garner realized Hank was dragging this out on purpose and, much to his surprise, it was starting to annoy him. "You're enjoying this, aren't you?" he said with an expression that must have conveyed *and you're starting to piss me off.*

"Okay. Okay, I'm sorry," Hank said. "Yes, I was starting to enjoy seeing the almighty and powerful wizard of the big city get a little unnerved."

Garner had to smile at that. "Asshole," he mumbled under his breath.

Hank's mouth dropped open. "I heard that."

"If I didn't want you to hear it, I wouldn't have said it."

"Touché." Hank held his glass up and touched Garner's.

"So…?" Garner said with a steady gaze.

"It was nothing really," Hank explained. "I stopped by to bring you and Thompson some breakfast and you weren't in the office. I saw the two of you out on the dock. One minute you appeared to be laughing hysterically, and I had this sudden urge to kiss you. Then, by the apparent change of expressions on your faces, it must have turned into something more serious. I didn't want to get in the middle of whatever was going down, so I left before either of you saw me."

Garner felt relief flood his entire body. *Paranoid sissy.*

"Feel better now?" Hank asked.

Garner nodded. "Yeah, I do. Thanks."

Hank stood and once again took his position opposite Garner and began working on his salad. "So is everything all right between you two?"

"Yeah," Garner admitted. "At least I think so."

Hank gave him a questioning look and Garner took the opportunity to explain what had happened on the dock.

"Yeah, I'm not surprised," Hank said, chopping and looking up every now and then. "He's not been the same since she died."

"That bad, huh?" Garner asked.

"You have no idea. He took Caroline's death very hard," Hank explained.

"How long have you known him?"

"Since we were kids," Hank explained. "Thompson and I were best friends growing up, always together, but I knew Caroline as well. We all hung out together with a few other friends when we were younger. Funny thing, though: by age thirteen or fourteen something happened, and Thompson and Caroline became inseparable and it became the three of us."

"How old were they when they got married?"

Hank looked up and appeared to be mentally counting. "Twenty-one or twenty-two, I think. Not long after we graduated from SSU."

Garner nodded and took another sip of his wine.

"And here's the kicker," Hank continued. "During our junior year in high school, I fell in love with ole Tommy boy. I think I was in love with him as far back as I can remember, but didn't figure it all out until high school."

Garner almost spit out a mouthful of wine. "Ohhh, Hank!"

"'Oh Hank' is right. I mean, look at him," Hank continued. "He was always gorgeous, but he was kind and gentle and equally as sensitive and very touchy-feely for a guy. Had no problem walking down the street with his arm over my shoulder. I loved it and eventually mistook that for loving him."

Garner was still in shock. "How do you mean?"

"By this time, I knew I liked boys, but I kept it pretty much to myself. Thompson was always the sensitive one and Caroline was always the tomboy, so I figured in my teenage wisdom that he must be gay and she must be a lesbian. I'd worked this theory from every angle and kept coming up with the same conclusion. They were each other's beards."

Garner laughed out loud. "Way to go, Einstein!"

"Not so fast," Hank chuckled.

"Sounds like there's more to this story?"

"Now who's the Einstein?" Hank asked.

"Okay, moving along," Garner teased.

"I haven't talked about this in years," Hank said. "But remember. You asked."

Garner wiggled in his seat, rested his elbows on the counter, and looked up at Hank, who was looking straight down at his vegetables.

"Thompson and I were alone in the locker room after gym class, one of the few places he wasn't plastered to Caroline's side. It was our senior year and the last day of school, so we were in a really good mood."

"Yum. Locker rooms and everything," Garner interrupted. "This sounds like a gay romance novel in the making, and it's getting better by the minute."

"Very funny," Hank said in a facetious tone. "Do you want me to continue or not?"

Garner shifted in his seat again. "By all means."

"So where was I? Oh yeah, the locker room. Anyway, like I said, we were in a really good mood and were high-fiving and chest-bumping to have high school behind us. You know, guy stuff. Just talking about our plans for SSU while we changed our clothes. I'd been waiting for an opportunity like this for over a year, so I thought it was now or never. With the next chest bump, I lost all brain cells and grabbed him behind the neck, brought our faces together, and kissed him, right on the mouth. Tongue and everything."

"Get. Out," Garner said, unable to think of another suitable response.

"Oh yeah."

"And...?"

Hank looked up and rolled his eyes. "I'm still here, so that's proof he didn't kill me."

"Obviously," Garner said. "Stop stalling, Prince."

Hank's lips curved up into a smile. "He wrapped his arms around me, and I swear in the beginning he was actually kissing me back. He opened his mouth and everything, but then he suddenly put his hands on my chest and gently pushed me away."

"Did he say anything?"

"I'm paraphrasing here, but it went something like he'd suspected I was gay for a while and he was okay with it. And although he loved me and was very flattered, he was totally committed to Caroline. He also said we didn't need to ever speak of the incident again and that he hoped this wouldn't affect our friendship. And that was the end of it."

Garner whistled. "What a classy guy, even as a teenager. He could have blabbered that all over school and it could have been a nightmare for you."

"Don't I know it, and to my knowledge, he's never told another soul. And neither have I, until now."

Garner was genuinely touched. "I appreciate you sharing that with me." He hesitated for a moment before he decided to take this a little further. "If I ask you a question, will you promise to be honest with me?"

Hank hesitated and then nodded. "I'll do my best."

"Are you still in love with him?"

Hank hesitated again. "Good question. The most honest answer I can give you is probably yes. I don't think a person can ever get over Thompson Gray."

Garner must have had a knowing expression on his face, because Hank felt the need to clarify. "And... before you jump to any conclusions, let me explain."

Garner leaned back in his chair.

Hank's expression suddenly turned somber. "You haven't met the Thompson I used to know. At SSU he was the guy that everyone wanted to be with. Wherever Thompson went, there was always a herd of people who followed. He was funny and charming, but never at anyone else's expense. He always fought for the underdog, and no one was ever bullied when you were with Thompson Gray. He was very protective of all of us, especially Caroline, and was just the overall nicest guy you'd ever want to meet."

Hank looked up and his eyes appeared to be watering a little. "So am I still in love with him? The answer is yes and no. I don't think I'll ever be over the old Thompson, but sadly, that guy doesn't exist anymore."

Hank wiped his damp eyes with his sleeve. "Damn onions," he mumbled, clearing his throat. "So to finish the rest of the story, he and Caroline eventually married, bought the marina, and seemed really, really happy until...." Hank's voice cracked again. "Well, until she died."

Hank paused and looked right past Garner, seemingly staring into space. "He took her death very hard. And for the first year, we all tried to help him. And even when everyone else had given up on him, I continued to try and reach him, but in the end, he just didn't want to be helped. I would bet my life that there's something more to this story, but I've never been able to get Thompson to completely open up to me."

"What do you mean?" Gartner asked.

"I believed and still believe to this day that Thompson and Caroline were best friends and loved each other very much, but I don't think they were ever really *in* love."

"What makes you think that?" Garner asked, slipping off his stool and walking around to join Hank.

Hank continued, "On the rare occasion when he and I got to go out alone, after a few beers, he would sometimes open up to me a little. Cherishing those rare moments, I would just let him talk. He was normally so guarded when it came to Caroline, but once or twice in a very general way, he asked me questions like if I thought there was difference between loving someone and being in love with them. Of course my answer was yes. I loved a couple of my buddies, but I was so damn in love with Thompson it hurt, so I knew there was a difference."

Hank paused, then spoke again. "On one occasion he went as far as to ask what it was like to be with a guy."

"And...?"

"At the time I could never have imagined being with anyone else but him, so I hadn't known the answer."

Garner touched Hank's arm. "What did you tell him?"

"Just that."

"What was his reaction?"

"The most tender moment I ever shared with him." Hank hesitated, as if he was reliving the moment.

"It's okay if you don't want to share that," Garner said. "I totally understand."

"No. I've come this far, I might as well finish."

Garner squeezed Hank's forearm again and Hank laid his hand on top of Garner's. "He grabbed me behind the neck, and I thought he was going to kiss me. My heart was beating ninety miles a minute in anticipation, but he brought our foreheads together, held them there, and closed his eyes. All he said was 'I'm sorry, Hank!'"

Apparently coming back to reality, Hank cleared his throat again. "Yeah, well. I carried a torch for that man for years, but in the true Thompson fashion, when he made a commitment, he kept it. And I believe he must have made some sort of promise to Caroline, and well, if I'm right, nothing could have made him break his promise. That's just the way he is... or was."

Garner rubbed the back of his neck. *Man, that's so sad; admirable, but so damn sad.*

"And the worst part is that when she died, he shut us all out, especially me. After trying to save him for so long, we eventually gave up. We all realized in our own time—me much later, sadly—that it was impossible to save someone who doesn't want to be saved."

"I'm really sorry," Garner whispered. "But why do you think he took it so hard? I mean… people lose loved ones all the time, and most eventually recover."

"Look. This is all speculation, but I think he believes that he failed her in some way. And knowing Thompson, I don't think he can ever get over that."

"That's crazy," Garner said.

"I know it is, but try and tell Thompson that."

Silence loomed between them, and Garner suddenly wanted to change the subject and get Hank out of the interrogation room. "So what smells so good?"

Hank looked up with a slight smile. "Very subtle. Time to change the subject, huh?"

"No, I just wanted to give you a break is all."

Hank placed both hands on the counter. "Okay, I'm officially out of the hot seat, but you're not so lucky, mister. Before we start talking about food, you have a little *splaining* to do yourself."

"Me?" Garner asked. "About what?"

"For starters, you seemed pretty damn distracted and bothered by the fact that I'd seen you this morning and you hadn't known about it," Hank said, looking up through his eyelashes. "Is there something you want to tell me?"

Garner quickly contemplated whether to tell Hank about his semistalker, but in the end, he saw no reason not to. "If you must know," Garner said in a forced, overly dramatic tone, "I had a little stalking incident a while back in New York City, and although I thought I was over it, it is pretty obvious by my reaction the experience has stayed with me."

Hank moved to the stove, never taking his eyes off Garner. "You think I'm a stalker?"

"Of course not," Garner quickly said. "Are you?"

"No!" Hank said, sounding offended.

Garner walked around the counter and poured them another glass of wine. "Down boy, I'm just teasing you. I think it just brought back a few still-raw memories is all."

"Was it serious?" Hank said over his shoulder.

Garner again took his seat. "Not really, but it could have been. He was a patient and he was going through something called 'transference.' I kept seeing him everywhere. It continued for a few weeks, so I went to the police. They eventually put a tail on both of us and brought the guy in for questioning. I referred him to another doctor and took out a restraining order against him. I guess his new doctor eventually convinced him that I wasn't worth a jail sentence."

Hank walked over and placed a gentle kiss on Garner's cheek. "If it makes you feel any better, I'd go to jail for you."

"That's so sweet," Garner mocked.

"So, you're a doctor, huh?"

"Retired," Garner corrected.

"What's 'transference'?" Hank asked with the tilt of his head.

"It's when the patient thinks he or she has fallen in love with their doctor."

"Oh," Hank said. "I'm sorry you had to go through that. I'm sure something like that makes you feel very violated."

"It was creepy." Garner held up both hands, wanting to change the subject. "So what's next on the interrogation list?"

Hank gave him a questioning look.

"Earlier you said, 'For starters,'" Garner reminded him. "What else do you want to know?"

"Oh yeah, that's right. Thanks for reminding me."

Garner nodded. "My pleasure."

"What in the hell was going on between you and Thompson when I was leaving for that call this afternoon? I saw you hit him. Then he hugged you. Then you slipped out of his arms and jumped back like Bruce Lee. Then suddenly his arm was around your neck and you guys were walking up the dock killing yourself laughing. I mean, if I didn't know better, I think I might be a bit jealous."

Garner threw his head back and roared with laughter. "Really?" he choked out as soon as he could talk. "Jealous? Of Thompson and me?"

Garner noticed Hank was smiling but didn't seem to be laughing as hard as he was, so he thought he'd better tone it down. "Okay. Okay, sorry. Here's the truth, the whole truth, and nothing but the truth."

Garner told Hank about being pissed off at Thompson because he let him think he'd outed Hank. Then he explained the grief Thompson had given him about the rainbow sticker on his boat. And how one thing led to another and they were sort of at a showdown, and Garner pulled out a few self-defense moves because he wasn't going to allow Thompson to think he had the upper hand.

"Wow, that sparring sounds a lot like the old Thompson." Hank hesitated. "The Thompson before, you know, Caroline died."

"Really?" Garner asked, surprised.

Hank gave his shoulder a quick squeeze. "Yeah. You might just be what he needs to come out of his shell a little."

Garner's ears perked up for this one. "How so?"

"I don't know. Maybe it's good for someone who didn't know Caroline and what he went through to give him a little grief now and then. The rest of us used to; I mean, we all had that type of relationship. It was fun and harmless, but when Caroline died, he changed so much. We all felt so damn bad for the guy. I guess we started treating him *and* each other differently. Maybe a little more of the old norm might just do him some good."

Garner liked the idea of harmlessly sparring with Thompson. It was fun, and he had enjoyed the back-and-forth. He breathed on his fingernails and rubbed them on his shirt. "If grief is what he needs, lord knows he's come to the right place. I'll show him no mercy."

Hank chuckled. "I have no doubt." He folded the dishtowel and placed it on the counter. "I do believe dinner is ready."

CHAPTER SEVEN

THOMPSON CLICKED the "send" button, replying to the last unanswered email in his inbox, rubbed his eyes, and yawned. He glanced up at the clock hanging above the window. *11:35.* He looked back down at his desk and was amazed to see the surface, scarred from years of use, clearly visible.

Over the last few hours, he'd sorted and organized every bit of paperwork and then attacked it all with a renewed energy. He'd prioritized, written checks, and filed all the outstanding invoices, matched six months of time cards for spring and summer help with payroll reports generated by his payroll company, completed an inventory of the ship's store, and even put together an order for the first thing in the morning. Lastly, he'd returned every unanswered email in his inbox.

He rubbed the back of his neck, stood, and felt a stretch coming on. He lifted his arms way over his head and spread them wide and yawned again. He was tired but he was actually relaxed. He looked back down at his desk and had to admit he liked the neatness he saw there. And he also had to admit having all that paperwork behind him was a weight lifted off his shoulders. He made a silent vow to not let it get out of hand again but then questioned what had inspired the sudden surge of energy and interest.

He slid his hands in his jean pockets and looked at the large window. He'd resisted the urge several times during the evening to go over and take a peek to see if Garner was back, but this time he allowed himself to follow through. He first scanned the marina, and all appeared to be as it should. Then he honed in on Garner's sailboat. The same soft light that was emanating from the portholes when he'd left for his date with Hank was still glowing. He sighed and looked up at the clock again. *11:42. Go home, Thompson. If and when Garner gets home is no concern of yours.*

He walked back to his desk, opened the drawer, and retrieved his car keys. Attached to the ring was a note of some sort. He unfolded the piece of paper and began to read.

> *Dear Thompson,*
>
> *I really appreciate the use of your truck. My stomach and I thank you from the bottom of our hearts. Well, I guess technically, my stomach doesn't have a heart, but you get the idea. I filled her up with gas and she's all set to go. See you tomorrow.*
>
> *Thanks again,*
>
> *G*

Thompson read the note a second time and then smiled. He rubbed his thumb over the words, hesitating over the "G," and then folded the note back up and stuck it in his top pocket. He was locking the office door when a flash of light illuminated his entire body, then disappeared. He looked over his shoulder to see Hank's white pickup come to a stop in the parking lot. "Shit," he mumbled under his breath. "They're back."

As he turned the deadbolt, two doors slammed shut and he heard the sounds of soft laughter getting louder with each passing second. Not wanting to interrupt Garner and Hank's date, he turned in the opposite direction and was about to round the corner when he heard his name and stopped.

"Hey, Tommy boy," Hank called out. "What's doing? Isn't it pretty late, even for you?"

Thompson turned around and did his best to smile. "Hey, guys. Yeah, I had a shitload of paperwork to do, and with all the distractions during the day, I can never seem to make any headway." He raised both hands. "So here I am."

Garner raised a finger and flashed a broad smile. "You know I can help with that, right? Or at the very least, I can hold the phone, radio, and customers at bay to give you some quiet time."

Thompson put his hands together. "Thanks, man. But as of tonight, I'm all caught up." He recognized a tone of pride in his voice he hadn't heard in a long time.

"Well, if you ever get behind again, just let me know and I'll hold back the tides for as long as you need me to."

Genuinely touched by the gesture, Thompson smiled and nodded. "Will do. Now you boys go on along and enjoy the rest of your evening. I'll see you in the morning."

Thompson turned, but before he could take a step, Garner spoke with a detectible hint of nervousness in his voice. "Wait! Why don't you come down to the boat and have a nightcap with us?"

Shocked and a little flattered by the invitation, Thompson considered it until he glanced at Hank. He saw what he thought was a slight look of disappointment on Hank's face, which oddly enough saddened him, so he quickly decided against it. "I appreciate it, but it's late and you guys don't need a third wheel tagging along on your date."

"Are you sure?" Garner asked, sounding a little thwarted.

Thompson dipped his head. "I'm sure, but thanks for asking. You guys have a great night."

He turned on his heel and made a beeline for his truck.

He heard Garner yell, "Drive safely," so he looked over his shoulder and nodded.

Thompson slipped into the driver's seat, and from behind the steering wheel, he watched Garner and Hank make their way down to Garner's boat. When they disappeared below deck, he slid the key into the ignition and started the engine.

He lived only a few blocks from the marina, but he found himself passing up his driveway and turning into the next block. His mind started to wander as his truck cruised along on autopilot. Garner and Hank was where it stopped.

It had only been two days, but he really liked Garner and thought he was going to enjoy working with him. For some stupid reason, it almost felt like he was again sharing responsibilities with another adult who really cared about the business. Most of the teenagers that had worked for him over the years were just that: teenagers. He had nothing in common with them, and they were just there to do the least they could and still collect a paycheck. And there was certainly no intelligent conversation to be had. *Yeah, I think hiring him was a good move.*

Then he thought about Hank. Was he okay with them dating? Hank was a hell of a good guy and deserved someone nice to spend some time with. In an unconscious move, he reached up and brushed his fingertips over his lips, remembering that day in the locker room when Hank had kissed him. He remembered being caught off guard at first and then feeling like Hank had reached down deep into his soul and flipped a switch that would change everything forever. He'd always know he loved Hank, but the intensity of the moment had swept him away. Before he knew it, he was starting to kiss Hank back. But then reality reared its ugly head and he realized the consequences of what was actually happening. He'd made a promise to Caroline and was committed to her. He could never allow himself to get involved with anyone else.

He dropped his hand back down and rested it on the steering wheel. *Caroline!* She was never very far from his thoughts. No one had ever understood his commitment to her or the fact that he'd been her only lifeline. How could they? He couldn't tell anyone. And he couldn't even do anything about it.

"I hope that fucking bastard is rotting in hell," Thompson hissed under his breath, and then he sighed. "Why can't I get this shit out of my head?" *Cause you let her down, you asshole. She died on your watch. You promised to protect her, and you broke your promise.*

CHAPTER EIGHT

GARNER WOKE for the fifth day in a row to strumming guitars, and he had to admit he was starting to get used to the annoying ringtone. He rolled to his back, pulled the covers over his head, and thought about the last five days. Time had flown by with his daily marina responsibilities and being entertained by Hank in the evenings.

His thoughts shifted to Hank. He really liked the man and enjoyed spending time with him, but something was keeping him from taking it to the next level. It was right on the cusp of his consciousness, but he just couldn't put a finger on it yet. The night before, he'd stayed at Hank's, and although it was nice to sleep with someone and be held, he hadn't even considered taking it any further.

It was probably a good thing that Hank would be away at a boat show in Charleston for a few days. It would give them a little breathing room and him some time to think. Hank had begged Garner to go with him, but Garner had used the marina as an excuse. It wasn't an excuse really, it was his job, and although he knew Thompson would have given him the time off, he thought they needed this time apart. It's not that he wasn't enjoying spending time with Hank; he was. And he felt like Hank was really getting into their time together as well, but Garner knew deep down he had no intentions of staying around after his boat was fixed, and leading Hank on just didn't seem right. *Damn, I knew I should have jumped his bones the first night. Now I like him too much to lead him on. Shit! And besides, even if I stayed, with my track record of failed relationships, I just couldn't do that to Hank. He's way too nice a guy.*

Then his mind shifted to Thompson and he saw those sparkling emerald-and-citrine eyes. Gorgeous, funny, sensitive, forlorn, damaged Thompson. He wanted to do more than just help him out at the marina, and in some odd way, he felt like he was, but for the life of him he couldn't figure out how or why. He knew from his years of practicing that Hank had been right when he said a little normalcy might be good for Thompson. To be treated like the man he was before Caroline died was what Thompson needed. And that had been right up Garner's alley. He'd been teasing him and giving him shit all day long, and it appeared to be helping in some messed-up way. Little by little in the last few days, Thompson had slowly started dishing it out just like he was getting it, and he seemed to be actually enjoying it.

The smell of freshly brewed coffee wafted across his cabin and filled his nostrils. "God bless Juan Valdez," he said as he climbed out of bed. He threw on some sweats, slipped into his Crocs, and stomped into the galley. Instinctively he looked through the galley porthole to see if Thompson was on his usual perch. Each morning since he'd arrived, Thompson had stood in the same place on the dock with a cup of coffee and watched the sunrise over Savannah. After the first morning when he'd caught him teary eyed, he'd made a point to give him his privacy and allow him to deal with whatever demons he was fighting. But this morning all he saw through the porthole was a white smoky haze. *No visible sunrise for him today.*

He grabbed a jacket, climbed the companionway stairs, and gazed out over the bow of the boat. Visibility was no more than twenty feet, and the fog was billowing like strands of satin cloth in a light breeze. The air felt heavy and damp and the scene was downright eerie. He caught movement to the right, and lo and behold, Thompson was standing in his usual spot. Not wanting to disturb him, Garner attempted to back down the companionway door unnoticed. He froze when he heard Thompson's voice. "Not much of a sunrise today," he said, scrutinizing the misty haze.

"I'm sorry," Garner said. "I didn't mean to intrude."

"You're not intruding," Thompson said, still staring into the rolling fog.

A silence as heavy as the fog loomed between them, and Garner didn't know how to proceed. Luckily Thompson turned and walked over with a slight smile on his handsome face and shoved an empty mug in his direction. "Have any more of that coffee?"

The tense moment naturally waned and Garner accepted the cup. "Sure thing. Get up here."

Garner turned and headed down below but knew Thompson had followed when he felt the boat dip slightly from Thompson's weight. Garner filled Thompson's cup with steaming coffee and observed him quietly taking a seat at the banquette. "Black, right?" Garner asked over his shoulder.

"Good memory," Thompson said, accepting the cup.

Garner slid in the other side of the half-round banquette and waited. Thompson was resting his elbows on the table, hands wrapped tightly around the warm cup. Through his eyelashes, Thompson's eyes appeared dull and lifeless as they studied the dark liquid. When he finally looked up, his expression was full of apprehension, but there was a new openness Garner had not seen before. *Now's your chance. It's now or never, Garner.*

Garner set his cup down in front of him, linked his fingers, and rested his hands on the table. "I'm sorry, man, but I've gotta ask."

Thompson's expression looked as though he knew what was coming, and for a second Garner thought he might bolt, but to his credit he stiffened and appeared to brace himself for the question.

Garner paused momentarily, then spoke. "For the last five days you've stood in the same spot and waited for the sunrise. What's up with the ritual?"

Thompson winced a little at the question but didn't break eye contact. He opened his mouth to speak, then hesitated. Garner witnessed Thompson's eyes turn to a much deeper green and appear to cloud over. His expression turned to one of obvious pain and sadness.

Garner immediately regretted the question. "I'm sorry. I shouldn't have pried. It's really none of my busine—"

"Caroline and I... we used to do it together every morning." Thompson's voice was shaky and laced with anxiety, but he continued. "It was her favorite time of day."

A light switch went off in Garner's head. "So you continue the ritual," he said, realizing for the first time the weight Thompson was carrying on his shoulders.

Thompson nodded but didn't explain any further.

Garner sighed. "Man, that's got to be hard for you. Day after day."

Thompson seemed to be having some sort of internal struggle and was visibly contemplating his answer. "Yes and no," he finally said. "On one hand getting up and walking out here alone every morning is the hardest thing I think I'll ever have to do. On the other hand, and I know this is probably really hard to understand, I crave it desperately. It's the only time I still feel connected to her."

Garner thought about Thompson's response and could clearly see the internal struggle. He was literally stuck between then and now. "Can I be honest?" he asked.

Thompson nodded slightly.

"Are the few minutes of peace you get from that connection worth all the anxiety it brings before and the heartache it brings afterward?"

A single tear slid down Thompson's cheek, and Garner fought the urge to wipe it away with his thumb. "It's all I have left" was all Thompson said.

Garner lost the fight and reached over and gently wiped away Thompson's tears. Thompson stiffened a bit, but didn't pull away. When he was done, he laid his hand on Thompson's forearm. "Have you ever asked yourself what Caroline would have wanted for you? Or better yet, what you would have wanted for her if the situation were reversed?"

Garner waited silently.

The forefinger of Thompson's right hand was trembling as he nervously traced the outlines of the compass rose etched into the teak tabletop under layers and layers of polyurethane. "She needed me and I...." His voice cracked and trailed off.

"Look, man," Garner responded. "As hard as this is to hear, she died, you didn't. So I ask you again. What would she have wanted for you?"

"I guess she would have wanted me to be happy and go on with my life."

"You guess?" Garner asked.

"Our relationship was complicated," Thompson mumbled.

Complicated! What an odd word to describe what he'd been led to believe was an otherwise great relationship.

"Look, Thompson, we don't know each other very well, but I promise you that the details of your relationship won't change the outcome of my question. Did she love you?"

"Yeah... of course she loved me."

"Then I have no doubt she would have wanted you to go on with your life."

Another single tear slid down Thompson's cheek, and he wiped it away this time. "Like I said, it was complicated."

"Okayyyy," Garner said. "You've referred to your relationship with Caroline as 'complicated' twice now. If you ever want to elaborate, I'm a good listener, but until then I have no idea how to respond to that."

An uncomfortable silence fell between them again as Thompson appeared to be fighting this internal battle to continue their conversation or not. Suddenly the VHF radio at Thompson's hip sprang to life with a fishing boat requesting a fuel stop.

"Shit! I'm sorry," Thompson said, answering the call. When he was finished giving the approaching boat instructions, he slid out from behind the banquette, offering Garner a weak smile. "Duty calls."

Garner stood as well. "Give me a few minutes to brush my teeth and I'll be right there."

"Don't rush. I can handle this one on my own."

Thompson was halfway up the companionway when Garner spoke. "Hey! I was planning on cooking dinner on board tonight. You wanna join me?"

"I don't want to be a third wheel. Thanks, though, I really appreciate the offer."

"You won't be a third wheel. Hank's leaving this morning for a boat show. It'll just be the two of us."

Thompson was silent for a moment and then smiled. "Okay. I'd like that," he said. "Thanks."

GARNER WAS standing in the galley enjoying a glass of chardonnay, chopping cilantro, and happily humming along to Ella Fitzgerald's "I

Won't Dance" when his phone rang. He leaned over and glanced at the caller ID and saw it was Hank.

He wiped his hands and answered the call. "Hey, Hank."

"Hey, yourself. How's it going at the big Thundercloud? You and Thompson holding everything together?"

Garner laughed. "Yeah. You know us, an odd but efficient team. How's the boat show going?"

"Real good," Hank explained. "Today was setup, and we open for business tomorrow."

"Oh right. You told me that. I'm sorry, I should have remembered."

"Shame on you for not hanging on my every word. No! Look out! Shit! Garner, hold on for a second."

Garner heard some rustling, then Hank yelling at someone.

"Sorry," Hank said when he came back on the line. "I'd better run. A forklift almost hit one of my boats."

"Oh no!" Garner said. "Go take care of business. We can talk later."

"I just wanted to say hi. I'll try and call tonight. Wish you were here."

"Thanks, and look out for forklifts."

"Tell me about it."

Garner heard more yelling. "Okay! Okay! I'm coming! Sorry, Garner, I need to run. I'll try to call later. Have a good night."

"You too."

Garner chuckled, put his phone down, and stirred the black beans simmering on the stove before he went back to chopping. He added the cilantro to the mixture of fresh mango, red onions, green chilies, and lime juice, covered the bowl, and stuck it in the refrigerator. Before he closed the fridge door, he eyed the two beautiful sushi-grade tuna steaks he'd picked up with the use of Hank's truck at lunch and felt like he'd done all he could until it was time to get the grill going.

He leaned against the counter, crossed his legs at the ankles, and took a sip of his wine. The entire day had gone by in a blur, probably the busiest it'd been since he'd started. He and Thompson had barely even had a second to catch their breath between boats coming and going, but somehow they'd managed to close the office exactly at six. With a quick high five, Thompson had run home to shower and Garner'd headed down to the boat to start prepping for dinner.

Garner downed the last of his wine and glanced at his watch. *Time for a quick shower and a shave.* As he made his way to his stateroom, Ella was crooning "A Foggy Day," which reminded him of earlier that morning and his conversation with Thompson. While Garner shaved, he went over their exchange of words in his head. He'd felt certain Thompson was on the verge of telling him more about his relationship with Caroline before that call had come in and interrupted them. He hoped they would get the opportunity to talk about it again, but he didn't want Thompson to think he was prying.

He wiped the remaining shaving cream off his now-smooth face and stared at his reflection in the mirror. His face was a nice bronze color, but his eyes were a pale white where his sunglasses protected the skin beneath. *I think I need to go without sunglasses for a while. I look like a damn raccoon.*

He reached into the shower, turned on the water, and stepped out of his shorts and underwear. While he waited for the water to heat up, he realized that, for some peculiar reason, he felt like he now had a stake in this saga and really wanted to help Thompson if he could. But how? He didn't want to push or pry, but unless Thompson opened up to him, there was no way he could help. Instinctively, he felt as though Thompson was right on the verge of turning some kind of corner, but he wasn't there yet.

He stepped into the shower and allowed the hot water to beat down on his shoulders and back, and the warmth of the rising steam to embrace his entire body. The more he thought about Thompson, the more he believed he had to tread lightly.

Slowly, Garner. Just go slowly. If Thompson wants to talk about Caroline, let him broach the subject. That's the only way.

CHAPTER NINE

THOMPSON SAT at a red light and turned up the volume on the radio as the local county station played Luke Bryan's "Drunk On You." He tapped his fingers on the steering wheel, keeping up with the beat, feeling more lighthearted than he could remember in a very long time.

He'd made a beeline for home right after they'd closed the office, showered, and actually spent more than two minutes combing his hair and deciding on what to wear. The khaki pants and blue-and-white striped button-down he'd chosen had been hanging in his closet for so long they were still in the dry cleaner's plastic bag with a receipt stapled to the hanger dating back to before Caroline's death. Memories had tried to creep back into his mind, but he held them at bay. Tonight was about him having a nice dinner with a friend, his friend. Someone who didn't know Caroline or know him and Caroline together. Someone who didn't pity him because of what he'd lost. Someone who wasn't afraid to say the wrong thing or mention Caroline's name in conversation. *Yeah. For the first time in a very long time, this is about me.* He felt odd wearing something other than the blue jeans and Thundercloud Marina T-shirt or golf shirt that had become his everyday attire, but it felt good to break the norm for a change.

While still waiting for the traffic light to change to green, he caught his reflection in the rearview mirror. The crew neck of the yellow T-shirt he chosen to wear under his button-down was barely visible, but the bright color made the gold flecks in his eyes stand out. He leaned in a little and realized his sun-beaten face had taken on a totally different countenance. A more rugged, slightly older version of himself stared back at him from the tiny mirror. Age lines were now visible at his eyes. *When did that happen?* Those lines hadn't been there the last time he looked. But when had that been? He couldn't remember the last time he'd really paid any attention to his appearance. He leaned back in his seat and brushed a strand of his blond hair to the side. Now able to see most of his face, he decided he liked the older version of himself. Despite everything he'd been through, he thought he'd held up okay, a little older, a little weather-beaten, but okay.

The sound of a horn blowing startled him, and he realized the red light had turned to green while he'd been giving himself the once-over. He smiled, waved an apology to the car behind him, and hit the accelerator.

His next stop was the liquor store. He knew nothing about wine, so as soon as the automatic doors opened in front of him, he scanned the store for someone to help him make a selection. Instead he found the elderly owner behind the register and headed over. "Hey, Mr. Bigby."

"Thompson! Good to see you out and about, son," the older man said. "What can I do for you?"

Thompson held his breath. *Out and about? Really?* Shaking it off, he rubbed the back of his neck. "Uh, I need a really nice bottle of wine," he informed the man.

"I can handle that. You have any idea what you'd like?" Mr. Bigby asked.

"Oh hell, I don't know anything about wine. Can you just pick something for me?"

"Okayyyy," the owner drawled in his heavy Georgia accent. "Red or white?"

"What goes with tuna?"

"Both, actually," the older man said. "If you like white, I'd go with an oaked chardonnay. If you want red, I suggest a syrah or a pinot noir."

"Let's go with the pinot noir."

"The next question is how much do you want to spend?"

"Oh, I don't know. Something middle of the road, I guess."

Mr. Bigby walked over to a display and selected a bottle of Sea Smoke 2008, handing it to Thompson. "This will impress anyone, son. Big date, I hope?" he said with a hint of excitement in his voice.

"No, sir," Thompson replied, fighting the urge to scream and deck the old guy. "Just dinner with a friend."

"Oh, that's nice," the old man said, smiling weakly.

Before the man could say another word, Thompson turned and headed for the register. He looked over his shoulder. "Thanks for your help." He paid the clerk and hightailed it out of there.

Once again behind the wheel of his truck, he fought the frustration eating away at him. He knew the old man meant well. Everyone meant well, but the road to hell was paved with good intentions, and if he didn't do something very soon, he was going to send everyone on a one-way trip.

He threw the bottle of wine on the seat and clenched his fists in frustration. He smashed both fist against the steering wheel and cursed under his breath. "Will they ever get over the *poor Thompson* bit? It's fucking getting so old." Mentally exhausted, he rested his forehead on the steering wheel. In his fit of anger, a thought suddenly descended upon him. *You think maybe your actions have something to do with the way folks treat you?*

Thompson sat up again and stared blankly ahead. *Maybe it's time to stop blaming everyone else and finally take a good hard look in the mirror.* He rubbed his temples as he considered this new revelation. *Could that really be the case?* He slid the key into the ignition and started the engine, still contemplating the answer.

He had a five-minute drive to get himself under control before he reached the marina, and although he had a lot to think about, he decided for tonight, he was going to do his best to relax and have a good time.

Walking down the dock, wine bottle in hand, Thompson was well on his way to regaining some sense of control. Right before he tapped on the hull of Garner's boat, he glanced at his watch and saw he was right on time. "Anybody home?"

Garner stuck his head up through the companionway. "No one but li'l ole me."

"Li'l ole me?" Thompson questioned.

"Isn't that what you all say in the South?"

"Y'all," Thompson replied.

Garner tilted his head to one side and threw him a questioning look.

"What *y'all* say in the South."

"Oh, y'all," he drawled. "Well then, get y'all's ass up here."

Thompson toed out of his boat shoes and climbed on board, smiling and shaking his head. "I guess you have to be a southerner to get it."

"Yeah. Yeah. Yeah," Garner said, stepping down the companionway with Thompson in tow.

When they reached the galley, Thompson slapped Garner on the back. "Long time, no see."

Garner smirked. "Tell me about it. What is it now, about an hour and fifteen minutes?"

"About," Thompson replied.

"Good. That means you're right on time, then," Garner said. "And I like a man that's on time."

For some reason that statement made Thompson happy and he puffed up his chest with pride. "Glad I could be of service." He sniffed the air. "I smell beans."

"Nice nose."

"Thank you," Thompson responded. "I've been told that before."

Garner turned from the sink. "I meant the fact that your nose recognized the smell of the beans, you asshole."

"I knew what you meant," Thompson said, shoving the brown paper bag in Garner's direction. "I brought some wine."

Garner pulled the bottle out of the bag, inspected the label, and whistled. "Very nice, but you know I don't put out on the first date. Right?"

Thompson smirked and reached for the bottle. "Then give it back."

Garner moved the bottle just out of his reach. "Oh no you don't. Besides, I didn't know you were such a wine connoisseur."

Thompson leaned on the counter. "There's a lot about me you don't know," he said playfully. "But sorry to disappoint you. The guy at the store picked it out for me."

"I figured as much," Garner teased, searching through a drawer.

"What? I think that's stereotyping. A southern boy from the backwoods of Georgia can't be a wine connoisseur?"

"I'm sure some can," Garner snickered. "Just not you."

This back-and-forth banter had become part of their daily routine, and Thompson was really enjoying it. He decided to have a little fun with Garner and threw a wounded expression in his direction, then looked at his feet. "You're probably right."

"Oh, come on," Garner said.

Thompson looked up and flashed a big smile. "Gotcha."

Garner returned to searching in the drawer. "Fuck you, asshole."

"What does a guy have to do to get a drink around here?" Thompson asked.

"Get it your—fuck!" Garner hissed, sticking his left hand in his mouth.

Thompson crossed the small galley in one step. "Let me see."

When Garner surrendered his hand, Thompson saw blood was squirting from the base of his index finger.

It only took a second for Thompson to realize he'd probably sliced through an artery or something. "Let's go," he said, wrapping Garner's hand in a dishtowel, his instinct to protect flaring up and taking over. "Keep pressure on it."

"Wait a minute. Go where?"

"You need stiches," Thompson said, looking down at Garner's bare feet. "Where are your shoes?"

"Come on, it's not that bad. Just give it a few minutes to stop bleeding."

"It looks like you cut a major vessel, Garner. You're gonna need stiches. Now where are your shoes?"

"In my cabin, but…."

"But nothing. Hold it up and keep applying pressure to it. I'll be right back."

Thompson hurried to Garner's cabin, scanned the room, and found his boat shoes on the floor beside his bed. When he bent down, he saw Garner's wallet on the bedside table and snatched it up as well.

Back in the galley, he led Garner to the couch, slipped his shoes on, and tied the laces. "Okay, let's go."

Garner released his pressure hold just long enough to slap the empty pocket at his butt with his right hand. "Wait! I need my wallet."

"I got it," Thompson said, leading Garner to the companionway steps.

"Wait!" Garner whined.

"What now?"

"The stove?"

"Shit," Thompson said under his breath as he ran back and turned off the burner under the pot. "Anything else?"

"Not that I can think of," Garner said with a half smile.

"Good. Now up," Thompson said, pointing to the steps.

TWO AND a half hours later, Thompson and Garner walked down the dock with Thompson's arms locked securely under Garner's elbow, keeping his hand elevated. The emergency room doctor had confirmed Thompson's fears that he'd sliced into the radial artery that supplied the main blood flow to the index finger. He'd received five stiches in all, two inside and three outside. But the doctor said there would be no lasting effects, and he'd be good as new in a few weeks.

Just before they'd left the hospital, the nurse had tried to give Garner a couple of pain pills and an envelope containing a few more for later, but he'd refused them, arguing why take the pills if he wasn't sure he would need them. Thompson had forced the envelope in Garner's pocket, just in case.

"Boy, am I hungry," Garner whined. "Can you grill tuna?"

"I'll do my best," Thompson said with a grin.

When they reached the cockpit, Garner pointed to the lazaret. "The propane tank is in there."

Thompson opened the storage compartment and turned the tank's valve to the on position. He heard a slight hiss as the propane filled the hose and he closed the lid. Within minutes he had the grill going and starting to heat up.

"Tuna's in the fridge along with the mango topping," Garner explained. "The brown rice is in the microwave and all you need to do is put it on for ninety seconds, and of course you know where the beans are."

"I've got this," Thompson assured him. "Why don't you lie back and keep that hand above your shoulder. I'll be right back."

Down below, Thompson put the heat back under the beans, gave them a stir, and rummaged through the refrigerator for the tuna steaks and mango. He opened the drawer looking for grilling tools and found the bloodstained knife still lying where they'd left it. He put the knife in the sink and grabbed the tongs.

When he was again topside, Garner was right where he'd left him. Thompson put the tuna on the grill and took a seat next to him. "What can I get you?"

Garner smiled weakly. "A glass of that wine you brought might be nice."

"Do you think it's a good idea to drink? What if you need to take one of those pain pills?"

"I'll be fine, Mom," Garner said. "I have a high tolerance for pain and pills."

"Okayyyyy! You're the doctor," Thompson said.

Obviously surprised, Garner sat up. "What did you say?"

"Dr. Garner P. Holt. I saw it on your credit card when I paid the hospital bill. Why didn't you tell me you're a doctor?"

"Well, for starters," Garner explained, "I'm retired. Secondly, it never came up. And lastly, I hate people who throw the title around."

Thompson considered his answer.

Before he could respond, Garner asked, "Is it a problem?"

"Of course not. I was just surprised."

Garner sat up and gave him a strange look. "What? Do I look too stupid to be a doctor?"

"Well, actually, now that you mention it…," Thompson said.

"Asshole."

Thompson howled. "Of course it's not that, you idiot. I guess *surprised* is not really the right word." He cocked his head and considered carefully, not wanting to offend. "More caught off guard. Yeah, that's better."

Garner seemed to be okay with that answer and lay back against the seat cushion.

The aroma of grilling fish started to swirl around the cockpit. "How do you like your tuna?" Thompson asked.

"Rare," Garner responded.

Thompson stood and turned to the companionway. "Then I'd better get the rice on and make sure the beans aren't burning."

Garner raised his good hand. "And don't forget my wine."

Thompson smiled. "You're awful bossy when you're hurt."

"You know what they say about doctors?" Garner quipped.

"What's that?"

"We make the worst patients."

Thompson chuckled and climbed down the steps. Thirty seconds later he heard movement from above and he stuck his head out to see Garner standing at the grill, his bandaged hand in the air and the other flipping the tuna. "What are you doing?"

"If I waited for you to get back up here to flip these steaks, we'd have charred tuna."

"Okay fine. But after you flip, you get back to your seat."

"Yes, sir," Garner said with a grilling tongs salute.

GARNER WATCHED Thompson scoop a spoonful of mango salsa onto the last bite of tuna, shove it in his mouth, and apparently savor the fresh piece of fish. Thompson swallowed and downed the last of his wine and dropped his eyes to Garner's empty plate. Garner followed Thompson's stare and smiled shyly as he realized his plate was clean enough to put away without washing.

Thompson broke the silence. "By the condition of your plate, I guess I did okay with the fish?"

Garner shrugged. "Yeah, it was okay."

"Really, man? Just okay?"

"Fine, you're damned good at the grill. Is that what you wanted to hear?"

"Yep, that's it. Thanks," Thompson replied, looking down at his empty plate. He seemed to drift off to another place and Garner just allowed it to play out.

Eventually he spoke. "I used to be great at grilling, but I don't do it much anymore."

"One could never tell by this meal," Garner said, trying to sound as sincere as he could without sucking up. "The tuna was great. Really."

"Thanks," Thompson replied with a slight blush.

In an obvious attempt to change the topic, Thompson referred to Garner's bandage. "How's the hand?"

Garner looked down at the skin-colored bandage. "It's good. The nerve block is starting to wear off and it's a little sore, but other than that, I'm okay."

"Is it time for one of those happy pills?" Thompson asked, eyeing the little envelope sitting on the cockpit table.

Garner shook his head. "Nah. Not much pain right now." He hesitated, then added, "Seriously, though, I do want to thank you for coming to my rescue tonight."

Thompson smiled and nodded. "I was happy to do it. And don't take this the wrong way, but it's the most needed I've felt in a very long time."

Garner felt a flash of sadness for the man. He saluted with his bandaged hand and retorted, "Glad I could be of assistance."

"Very funny," Thompson said with a smirk as he wrapped both his arms around his body and rubbed his biceps. "Is it starting to get cold or is it just me?"

"I'm a little chilly too," Garner realized. "Why don't we head down below?"

"Sounds good. That way I can get the galley back in order before I go."

"No way," Garner argued as he stood, mindful of his sore hand. "You have to promise to leave everything right where it is and I'll take care of it tomorrow."

"Oh come on," Thompson grumbled. "One pot, a couple of plates, and some utensils. I think I can handle that."

Garner huffed but took a seat as Thompson went about cleaning the galley.

With the galley spotless, Thompson joined Garner in the saloon and the two men sat comfortably across from one another, legs stretched out and crossed at the ankles. Garner had his hand resting on the back of the couch, and Thompson was staring down at his wine as he twirled the glass in gentle circles.

"Want to share?" Garner asked.

Thompson looked up. "What?"

"You looked like you were pretty deep in thought. Do you want to share?"

"Oh. I was just thinking about what happened at the liquor store when I bought this bottle of wine tonight."

Garner's curiosity was now piqued. "Okay, I'll bite."

Thompson hesitated and then spoke. "It was nothing really. At least nothing out of the norm."

"It obviously bothered you, or you wouldn't have mentioned it," Garner pointed out.

"Yeah well, it's the same old thing," Thompson added. "You would think I'd be used to it by now."

Garner lifted his wineglass to his nose. He inhaled a few times and the smoky and earthy scents filled his nostrils. He looked up through his eyelashes. "So are you going to tell me or not?"

Thompson twirled his wineglass again, cleared his throat, and began to speak.

Garner listened patiently as Thompson struggled to verbalize what had happened to him in the liquor store with old man Bigby and how he felt about it.

When Thompson was through with the story, Garner remained silent.

"So?" Thompson asked. "Don't you have any words of wisdom for me?"

"What would you like me to say?" Garner asked.

"Oh I don't know. Maybe start with 'everything will work itself out' or 'it's all gonna be okay, Thompson' or maybe even 'Thompson, you'll see, it'll get easier with time.'"

Garner's wheels were turning as he silently crafted what he should say next. He wanted to gain Thompson's trust, and he instinctively knew the response right now was going to be a critical turning point in how they proceeded.

He went with a simple "Nope."

"Nope? That's it?" Thompson asked, leaning forward.

"Look. It's been, what, three or four years since Caroline died?"

"Four years and five days to be exact," Thompson recounted.

"So obviously everything didn't work itself out, right? It's not all going to be okay, and if time healed all wounds you'd be well on your way to coming to terms with it all. So no, I don't have any words of encouragement for you."

Thompson looked stunned. His mouth was hanging open and his eyes were as big as saucers.

"What?" Garner asked. "Did you expect me to lie to you?"

Thompson was obviously trying to compose himself. He leaned back on the couch and sighed. "Yeah, I guess I expected the same shit from you that I've been getting from everyone else."

"Listen, man," Garner said. "I've never been one to blow smoke up anyone's ass. It's painfully obvious that, for whatever reason, you are nowhere near being over Caroline's death. So what good would it do for me to lie to you?"

Thompson's face slowly morphed into a skeptical grin. "Well whaddya know," he drawled.

Garner relaxed and smiled back, knowing immediately that he'd taken the right path.

"You're the first person who's had the guts to be honest with me and not treat me like a victim," Thompson admitted.

"I'm really sorry about what you've gone through and the way you feel you've been treated. But all that aside, where do we go from here? I mean, now that you know I won't lie to you and I'll tell it the way I see it, can we be open and honest with one another? Will you talk to me about how you feel and allow me to try and help if I can?"

Thompson stared at his wine and didn't respond, so Garner kept going.

"Okay. Let me ask you a question. Why do you think everyone walks on eggshells around you?

"Hell if I know," Thompson muttered, shaking his head.

"Oh come on, Thompson. You're a very smart man and I think you know exactly what the answer is. Think about it. In the little time I've known you, even I know firsthand that saying the wrong thing can send you off into a dark place. Look what happened when I mentioned that shit about your face lighting up when you smile. How was I supposed to know that Caroline used to say the same thing?"

"You couldn't," Thompson agreed.

"Right, but it still affected you. Didn't it?"

Thompson looked up and met Garner's gaze. "So you think people walk on eggshells around me because they're afraid they'll say or do the wrong thing and hurt my feelings?"

"Bingo."

Thompson looked like he was considering Garner's explanation.

Garner continued. "And while we're at it, let's cover the victim issue. The same question applies. Have you been acting like a victim since Caroline died?"

In a split second Thompson's face took on a sinister expression. He looked like he was going to leap off the couch and punch something or someone. He appeared to be doing his best to hold his anger at bay. "I don't act like a fucking victim!" he hissed through closed teeth.

"Are you angry right now?" Garner asked.

"Fuck yeah I'm angry."

Garner nodded. "Then why don't you be angry? Yell at me. Call me an asshole. Tell me to shut up and go fuck myself. Say something."

"You want anger! Yeah I'm fucking pissed off," Thompson yelled as he jumped to his feet, his face getting redder by the second and looking like he wanted to pull his hair out of his head. "For the last four years, I've been going through the motions of living. I'm holding on to something that no longer exists, but I don't know how to get past it and move on."

Thompson looked around and started to pace. "God, I want to punch something right now."

He stopped in front of Garner and glared at him. "Look at me. Am I a fucking time bomb? Hell yeah! But. I. Do. Not. Act. Like. A. Victim!"

Garner remained calm as he sipped his wine and watched Thompson's reaction. He started pacing back and forth again, rubbing the back of his neck with one hand and squeezing his wineglass so tightly with the other, Garner thought it might explode between his fingers.

"I hesitate to ask in fear of getting a fist to the jaw, but do you want my opinion on this as well?"

Thompson paced some more, took some deep breaths, and eventually plopped down next to Garner on the couch. He sighed, ran his fingers through his hair and looked at Garner. "Fuck! What have I got to lose, Dr. Phil? Give it to me fucking straight."

Garner did his best not to grin at that comment. Thompson knew he was a doctor now, but he had no idea how close to the truth the Dr. Phil comment really was. "Okay. So maybe you don't act like a victim, but that doesn't mean that most people still don't see you as a victim."

Thompson opened his mouth to speak, but Garner held up his hand. "Let me finish before you jump down my throat. Okay?"

Thompson closed his mouth, but he didn't look happy about it.

Garner dipped his head. "Thank you. So as I was saying, I believe people still see you as a victim, but not a victim of your own choosing like you may think. I believe they see you as more a victim of circumstance. Does that make any sense?"

Thompson didn't answer.

"Look. Let me ask you a question. Did you do anything to cause Caroline's death?"

Garner waited patiently. By slipping this question in nonchalantly, it was a way to determine if Thompson blamed himself for Caroline's death. When no answer came, he had his answer.

Garner put that tidbit aside for later and continued. "But she still died and left you alone. So in all fairness, you are a victim, a victim of a tragedy that was out of your control. And by living the way you have for the last four years, you've just reinforced everyone's sympathy."

Thompson leaned his head on the back of the couch and closed his eyes. He was taking deep breaths, slowly inhaling and exhaling, and his hands were fidgeting with the empty wineglass. "I didn't protect her. I let her down."

"She died of a brain aneurism, Thompson—a condition that most times attacks with no warning. So tell me how you let her down?"

"She died on my watch!" Thompson choked out. "I made a promise to protect her. Hell, I'd been protecting her since she was thirteen years old, and I let her die."

Tears were now flowing freely down Thompson's cheeks, and all the pieces of the puzzle were finally starting to come together for Garner.

"You think you let her down because you couldn't save her? Is that what you've been carrying around with you for the last four years?"

Garner rested his bandaged hand on Thompson's leg. Thompson jumped at the simple gesture and then seemed to relax. He eventually nodded once but didn't say anything.

"Thompson," Garner whispered, "tell me what you could have done that would've prevented her death?"

Thompson's hands began to tremble and all the color drained from his face. He started rocking his body forward and back and appeared to be having trouble breathing. Garner had seen this before. Thompson was having a panic attack and all he could do was be there with him and ride it out. Thompson started mumbling incoherently as he rocked, and the only words Garner could make out were, "You don't understand."

Garner waited for the frantic behavior to wane before he finally spoke. "You're right," he said in a calm voice. "I don't understand, but I want to, and the only way I will is if you'll try to explain it to me. I want to help you get through this."

THOMPSON FELT like someone had reached in and was squeezing and twisting his heart, trying to rip it right out of his chest. His brain felt like it was in being crushed in a vise, and he was on the verge of hyperventilating. He'd never told another human being what he knew he was about to tell Garner, but he also realized that he could no longer hold it in, much in the same way Caroline had finally told him about the abuse. But why now? What had changed and why this stranger of all people?

Thompson felt Garner's hand resting on his leg and his soft voice gently encouraging him to speak. "Talk to me, Thompson. Please let me help you if I can."

Thompson kept his eyes closed tightly. One hand was clenching his stupid wineglass and the other was clawing the leather covering on the couch. He took a deep breath and attempted to speak, but no words found their way out of his mouth. He swallowed the huge lump in his throat and tried again. From somewhere deep down, he found the courage, but when he spoke, his voice didn't sound like his own. His words were raspy and broken and barely audible. "From the age of thirteen—" He hesitated again and swallowed hard. "—Caroline was being sexually abused by her alcoholic stepfather."

Thompson couldn't bear to open his eyes for fear of what he might see on Garner's face. He had no idea what Garner was expecting, but he felt certain it wasn't this.

But when Garner spoke, it wasn't surprise in voice, but compassion. "Oh, Thompson, I'm so sorry," he whispered. "That must have been horrible for her."

Thompson was still having difficulty speaking, so he just nodded.

"But you know her abuse wasn't your fault, right?"

Thompson concentrated and somehow found more words. "Yeah. I know it wasn't my fault, but I was the only one she'd told. I was fourteen."

"And did it stop when you went to the authorities?"

"We didn't."

"What?"

"Her stepfather had convinced her that if she told anyone, he would kill her, her mother… and me."

Thompson took a few deep breaths and continued. "She'd been petrified that he'd follow through with his promise and so she'd kept the secret from everyone—well, everyone but me. And… she made me promise to do the same."

Garner shook his head in apparent disbelief. "You were just a kid. Why did she pick you to tell?"

Thompson sighed. The words were coming a little easier as the heavy weight he'd been carrying around for so long got a little lighter. "I don't think she planned it that way, but I guess the burden and shame had become just too much for her to carry alone. She broke down one morning while we were out fishing. She just wouldn't stop crying, and I had no idea why. I kept begging her to stop and to tell me what was wrong, and she just cried harder. Finally I wore her down and she told me everything."

"Thompson, I… I'm sorry. That must have been an awfully big burden for you to bear. I mean… you were just fourteen years old."

"It changed my life forever," Thompson whispered. "But that didn't matter. All that mattered was keeping her safe. I was glad she'd told me and that I was able to do what little I could to help protect her, but keeping that fucking secret was the hardest thing I've ever had to do."

Garner blinked a few times and Thompson knew he was holding back tears. "I can't imagine that type of pressure on anyone, let alone a teenager."

"Each time he abused her, I could tell by the look on her face. I'd hold her in my arms when she eventually broke down, and I'd whisper those same fucking words of encouragement that people gave me after she died. *It would all be okay.* And I made a vow to her and to myself that I would do everything I could to protect her for the rest of our lives."

"You were just a kid, Thompson. You should have been out playing baseball with your friends and having a normal childhood, not fighting this battle alone and making a lifelong commitment to protect someone."

Thompson chuckled sarcastically. "Yeah, well. That didn't happen."

"Obviously," Garner said. "How did you do it?"

"Do what?" Thompson asked.

"Protect her."

"It was tough. I'd have to come up with excuse after excuse as to why she had to spend the night at our house. One late homework assignment after another, tutoring, anything I could think of. Anything to keep her out of her own house and away from that fucking bastard. On the nights when I couldn't be with her, I didn't sleep a wink knowing what was probably happening to her. I lived in constant fear. I mean… each time I let her down, she paid the price for my failure. Not me. I blame myself for every opportunity he had to abuse her."

"Again, Thompson, you were just a kid," Garner pointed out. "I can understand your feeling that way then, but as an adult, can't you see that you did all you could and none of this was your fault?"

"Logically, yes," Thompson acknowledged. "But emotionally I'm still that fourteen-year-old kid who *couldn't* protect her, and then I grew into an adult who *didn't* protect her."

"Thompson, stop. Man, you saved her life. She survived it *because* of you."

Thompson slammed his fist down on the leather couch. "But she didn't survive. She's dead."

"Through no fault of yours," Garner maintained.

"I wish I could believe that."

"So do I, Thompson, so do I."

The two men sat in silence for several more minutes.

Thompson heard Garner's voice crack as he spoke. "How long did this go on?"

"High school. Well into our sophomore year. I'd been trying to convince her that we needed to tell someone, but she was so scared he would retaliate. So on my sixteenth birthday, I finally took matters into my own hands and went to see the old bastard. By that time I was physically strong enough to stand up to him, and I told him that if he ever laid another hand on her, I would go to the police and expose him for the no-good son of a bitch that he was. And if that didn't make him stop, I'd kill him. And remembering how I felt at that moment, I believe I would have done it. But either way, the abuse stopped there."

"Where is he now?"

"The ironic thing is that I had just convinced Caroline to finally go to the police when the son of a bitch died of a massive heart attack. How fucking sick is that? But I have to tell you, it's a good thing the bastard was already dead or I'd be in prison today."

"What do you mean?"

"I remember the frame of mind I was in when Caroline died; I know I would have gone looking for him and… God only knows what I would have done to him."

Garner was apparently in shock with that admission, because silence loomed between them until Thompson spoke again. "You know the hardest fucking part about this whole thing? She survived his abuse, not totally unaffected, but she survived and was enjoying life with me. Every day was like a new beginning for her and the simplest of things made her so happy."

"Like watching the sunrise?" Garner whispered.

"Exactly," Thompson answered with an exhausted sigh. "Now do you get why I need to walk out onto that dock every morning and greet each new day? For her?"

When Garner didn't answer, Thompson found the courage to open his eyes. When he lifted his head, he saw Garner's tear-stained face staring back at him. They gazed into each other's eyes, neither saying a word, but complete understanding and compassion flowing between them.

Thompson leaned forward to get up. But before he could stand, Garner's arms were wrapped tightly around him. He had no energy to resist and eventually relaxed into the embrace. The human contact felt warm and encompassing. He hadn't had any real physical contact in such a long time and the arms surrounding him were Garner's. The warm gesture meant more than anyone could have imagined.

When Garner finally released him, Thompson accidentally bumped Garner's hand with his elbow. "Ouch. Shit." He hissed as he jumped off the couch.

"Oh God," Thompson said. "I'm so sorry."

Garner held his bandaged hand with his good hand. "Stop it. It wasn't your fault." Garner sat back down. "I think I'd better take one of those pain pills now. The damn thing is starting to throb."

Thompson got Garner a glass of water and handed him one of the pills from the little envelope. Garner popped the pill and downed the entire glass of water before handing the empty glass back to Thompson. "Thanks."

While Thompson was in the galley, he refilled his wineglass. He looked at Garner and held the bottle up. "More?"

"I'd better not since I took that pill. But please don't let me stop you."

Thompson came back and took his seat next to Garner. He again stared down at his glass, swirling the wine in gentle circles and thinking about what had just transpired between the two of them.

"Do you feel any better, getting that off your chest?" Garner finally asked.

Thompson thought for a few seconds and then realized that he did feel better. "Yeah, I believe I do."

"Good. Opening up almost always helps me as well. But there are a few things I really want to talk about a little more. Things that might help all of this make a little more sense and help you get past it."

Thompson was skeptical that he would ever get past this mess, but if there was a chance, he'd give it a shot. "Okay," he whispered.

"First off," Garner started. "Tell me what else you think you could have done to protect Caroline when you first found out about the abuse. And don't just speculate; I want real tangible things a fourteen-year-old could have done."

Thompson thought way back to that time and what resources he had at his disposal. No matter how hard he tried, he could only come up with one thing. "I could have told someone," he said.

Garner nodded. "Okay, maybe right now that seems like an option. But remember, you were fourteen years old and you promised Caroline. I don't know you that well, but from what I know, I don't see you as someone who easily breaks a promise. And besides, you both believed his threats. He was fearful of being discovered and may have said or done anything to keep his dirty little secret. Trust me, at fourteen, you didn't have the mental ability to decide whether he was bluffing or not. So, you take that one possibility away and what do you have left?"

"I guess nothing," Thompson said.

"You guess nothing?" Garner mocked. "Repeat after me, Thompson. There was nothing more I could have done to help her."

Thompson hesitantly repeated the sentence.

"Again," Garner instructed.

"There was nothing more I could have done to help her," Thompson said a little more forcefully.

"Next," Garner said, "after the abuse stopped, what did you do?"

"We finished high school and went away to college," Thompson explained.

"And after that?"

"We got married and bought the marina."

"Precisely," Garner said. "You married her, Thompson. You never turned away from her, you never left her side, and you continued to protect her just as you'd promised."

"But she died anyway," Thompson whispered.

"Yes, Thompson, people die. But instead of blaming yourself for her death, you should be proud of yourself for giving her the life that you did."

"I wish I could see it that way," Thompson said.

"You will," Garner said firmly. "If it kills me, you will."

In the silence that followed, Thompson concentrated on the tranquil sound of the water as it lapped against the boat's hull. The rhythmic lap-lap-lapping noise was a welcome distraction as he carried on a mental debate about what he should do next. Should he share the rest of his and Caroline's story? Or should he just let it go? On one hand, it wouldn't be fair to Garner not to be completely honest with him. Garner had already proven to be a compassionate and unbiased listener, and he'd made really good points. On the other hand, fessing up would change nothing in the end and only create more of a discussion that Thompson wasn't sure he wanted to get into. Before he made a conscious decision one way or the other, the words just flowed out of his mouth. "I loved her very much, but I was never in love with her."

With that admission, Thompson's stress levels were suddenly building again, and he looked Garner directly in the eye, trying to find any signs of disgust or pity. To his surprise all he found was more compassion, which seemed to take some of the edge off.

"I'm not surprised," Garner confessed in a hushed tone.

"What"—the hairs stood up on the back of Thompson's neck, and he sat up straight and squared his shoulders—"do you mean you're not surprised?"

"I'm just not," he repeated, obviously realizing that Thompson was not happy with his answer. "But look, man, if you want me to be honest with you, you can't get defensive every time I say something you don't like. You obviously want to talk about this or you wouldn't have brought it up, so it's up to you if you want to continue. As I said, I won't blow smoke up your ass. It's your call."

Thompson leaned back again and tried to relax. He knew Garner was right, but man, all this was really starting to get to him. "You're right, I'm sorry," he finally offered. "So why weren't you surprised?"

"For starters, with everything you've told me about how you and Caroline ended up together, you never once mentioned being in love with her. Or for that matter, the word love at all. But"—Garner held up a finger—"with that said, I know you couldn't have done all you did for her and sacrificed a majority of your life if you didn't care for her and even love her on some level."

Thompson realized that Garner was again spot-on with his assessment of his and Caroline's relationship. He nodded in agreement. "I guess what you're saying makes sense to me now. But for the record,

I did love her." He took a deep breath and continued. "Before the abuse started, she was a carefree kid and all of us, including Hank, had a lot of fun together. When the abuse finally stopped, it took her a while to get over all the crap, but once we married and bought the marina, I guess she felt secure again. Little by little the kid in her started coming back to life and she blossomed. We had a good life here, but even if I had wanted to end our marriage, I could never have taken that security away from her. She would have probably imploded."

Garner looked like he wanted to ask a question, but appeared to be mulling it over.

"Go ahead," Thompson said. "You can ask me anything. I mean, what do I have left to hide?"

Garner offered Thompson a weak smile. "How was your sex life?"

Thompson looked down at his feet. "Nonexistent. We tried a few times in the beginning, but Caroline just… she couldn't go through with it."

Garner nodded like he understood why. "And how did you feel about that?" he asked.

"I understood, I guess," Thompson said. "She went through a lot with her stepdad. I can only imagine how I would have felt if it had been me that was being abused."

"Did she ever get any kind of professional help?"

"You mean like therapy or anything?"

"Yeah."

"No. I tried to get her to talk to someone once. We made the appointment and drove all the way to the doctor's office. But in the end, she couldn't go through with it."

The two men sat in silence once again. Thompson almost jumped through the roof when Garner's cell phone went off right behind his head.

"That must be Hank," Garner said. "He said he would call back later tonight."

Thompson reached over his shoulder, retrieved the phone from the ledge, and passed it to Garner.

"It's Hank," Garner said after glancing at the caller ID and silencing the ring. "I'll call him back in the morning."

"No," Thompson argued. "It's okay. Go ahead and take it."

"You sure? I'll make it quick."

Thompson shrugged. "Take all the time you need."

"Hey, Hank," Garner said into the phone. "No. Not at all, I'm still up. Had a little excitement tonight, though."

Thompson listened patiently as Garner explained the evening's events to Hank and answered question after question.

When the call finally ended, Garner smiled. "Sorry about that. He was a little concerned."

Thompson felt a slight pang of jealousy. "Hank's a great guy." He looked at Garner with a raised eyebrow. "I just wish he could find a nice guy and settle down."

Garner held up his good hand. "Hold on there, cowboy," he said. "Hank *is* a really nice guy, but you know I'm just passing through, right?"

Thompson linked his fingers together, turned his palms outward, and stretched his arms. "Yeah, but you two *have* been spending an awful lot of time together. I thought you might consider staying on for a while."

Garner shook his head. "I don't think that's going to happen," he admitted rather reluctantly.

"Why not?"

"For starters, I suck at relationships big time. Secondly, I made a promise to myself to do some traveling, and I want to see that through. And thirdly and most importantly, I'm certain Hank's in love with someone else."

Thompson brushed over all the other reasons and focused on the last one. "Hank's in love with someone else? I didn't even know he was seeing anyone. Except you," he added.

"He's not. Exactly," Garner said, apparently choosing his words very carefully. To Thompson it looked like Garner was having some type of internal debate. "I think it's someone from his past" was all he said.

Thompson smiled, thinking back to that one kiss he and Hank had shared. "You know, Hank and I used to be best friends before... well, just before. He actually kissed me once in the locker room when we were in high school."

Garner again looked like he was deciding whether he should say something or not. He hesitated, then finally spoke. "Yeah. He told me over dinner one night."

Surprised, Thompson laughed out loud. "That shithead."

Garner laughed too. "Is that a problem?"

"Hell no," Thompson said. "After everything I told you tonight, you think I care if you know I once kissed another guy back in high school?"

"Good point," Garner agreed. "Hank said that you guys were pretty close back then."

"Yeah, we were. In fact, I think he had a little crush on me."

"How did you feel about that?" Garner asked.

Thompson thought back to that time. "Sad for both of us, I guess. But mostly for him," he added. "I'd already made a commitment to Caroline and I didn't have anything to offer him."

A weird sort of smile that Thompson couldn't quite identify crept across Garner's face. Then he dropped the bombshell. "Thompson Gray, are you a big ole homo?"

Oh fuck no! Thompson thought as he felt the blush consume his face from the bottom of his chin to the top of his forehead. *How in the fuck do I answer this?* Finally he decided on the truth. "Hell, Garner," he said. "To be truthful, I don't know what I am. It didn't really matter what I was or wasn't. From the minute Caroline told me about the abuse, my life was pretty much mapped out. I never really had a chance to figure out any of that shit."

"So tell me this," Garner asked. "Did you like the kiss with Hank way back when?"

Thompson smiled and brushed his fingers across his lips. "God yeah. It was my first real kiss. I mean... I was taken by surprise at first, but then it just felt, umm... it felt right. Until... well, until reality crept back in and I remembered Caroline. I knew Hank had been feeling neglected and he had every right to, but I couldn't tell him what was going on and it wouldn't have changed anything anyway. So I just pushed him away and said we never had to speak of it again. The look in his eyes broke my heart."

"But what about now?" Garner asked. "How do you feel about Hank now?"

"Hank? Man, I don't know how I feel about anything. After all I've been through, I'm no closer to knowing who I am now than when I was back in high school. Garner, you've got to remember. Right after my thirteenth birthday, my life was no longer my own. For better or for worse, I made a commitment to Caroline and I never allowed myself to think of any possibilities beyond that."

Garner leaned forward. "Look," he said, laying his hand on Thompson's leg. "I know you've been through a lot of shit in your life, but hopefully after tonight things will start to change for you. You got a lot of shit off your chest and got another person's perspective. Maybe it's time for a new beginning."

A light bulb suddenly went off in Thompson's head. "Holy shit! Are you saying what I think you're saying? Hank and me?"

Garner smiled coyly and didn't say a word.

"Now you just hold on there," Thompson protested. "I'm not sure what you have in mind, but I'm just now trying to work through the guilt I have about Caroline's death. And now you want me to get involved with Hank?"

"Thompson, what would say if I told you I know for a fact that Hank is in love with you? That's he's always been in love with you?"

"What? Am I the one you think Hank's still in love with?" Thompson replied. "Garner, that's ridiculous. It was nothing more than a high school crush, and I'm sure he's long over it."

Garner sat up straight and slid to the edge of the couch. "But what if he's not? You said yourself that Hank was the only one that hadn't given up on you in the years after Caroline died."

"But—" Thompson barked.

Garner cut him off. "But nothing. I'd bet my life that Hank is just as in love with you now as he was in high school. It was never just a crush. In fact, he said as much to me that night over dinner."

Thompson was in shock. *Hank in love with me? Hank and me?* Things were swirling around in his brain, and he was about to short circuit. "Stop it, Garner! No. This is all too crazy."

Garner started to speak, then a yawn consumed him. "Sorry, I think my pain pill is kicking in."

"My point exactly!" Thompson said. "Now I know where all of this is coming from. You're high on pain pills and you're not thinking clearly."

"Oh, that's nonsense and you know it. Relax," Garner pleaded. "For Pete's sake, I took one pill. I'm not high. This is all very real."

Thompson plopped back on the couch and closed his eyes. "And very weird if you ask me. I mean, I couldn't even think of Hank in that way after that day in the locker room. I just never allowed the possibility."

Garner plopped back next to him and both men sat side by side with their heads back and their eyes closed. "Just think about it, Thompson. It all makes perfect sense."

"Nothing makes sense right now," Thompson whispered.

Thompson's mind was reeling. For however long, he lay there in silence mulling over everything Garner had said to him. Most of it regarding Caroline made perfect sense, but the shit about him and Hank. That was just plain crazy. Or was it? He was mentally and physically exhausted and needed sleep. He was about to excuse himself and say goodnight when he heard Garner's light, whimpering snore fill the saloon.

He laid his hand on Garner's shoulder and shook him gently. "Garner, you need to get to bed."

Garner didn't move, so he shook him a little harder. "Garner!" he said, raising his voice a bit. Still nothing.

Finally, Thompson used both hands and, careful to not hit Garner's bandaged hand, shook him harder and said his name once more.

Garner finally opened his eyes. "What?"

"We need to go to bed, man."

"Together? I told you I don't put out on the first date," Garner slurred.

"No, not together," Thompson chuckled. "Come on, let me help you."

Garner looked like he wanted to stand but couldn't quite make it. Thompson pulled him up by his arms, mindful of his injured hand, and got him to his feet. Thompson lifted Garner's good arm over his shoulder and held on to it and then slid his other arm around Garner's waist. Once Garner was fairly stable, Thompson led him to his stateroom.

Thompson released Garner from around the waist long enough to pull the covers of his bed back, then gently laid him down and pulled the covers back up to his torso. He arranged Garner's bandaged hand across his chest and then went back into the galley, retrieved the little envelope of pain pills, and grabbed a bottle of water out of the fridge. He stooped down next to the bed and placed both items on Garner's bedside table. Garner was sleeping very soundly and he took the opportunity to really look at him. In his slumber, his otherwise strong jawline and sharp features seemed relaxed and stress free. He looked as handsome as Thompson had ever seen him. Without thinking, he gently pressed his lips to Garner's and whispered a heartfelt "thank you."

He got to his feet, turned out the lights, and went back to his office, where he collapsed on his couch. Unable to process another thought, he called it a night.

CHAPTER TEN

GARNER WOKE slowly, slipping in and out of a restless slumber. When he finally opened his eyes, he looked around his stateroom, trying to focus. His mind was clouded with sleep, but there was something else. He almost felt like he'd been drugged. He glanced at the clock and it read six thirty-two. He brought his hands up to rub his eyes and felt a sharp pain and a throbbing sensation. He looked down at his bandaged finger and little bits of the night started to come back to him. *Cooking dinner, injury, hospital, stiches, therapitizing Thompson.*

In the soft glow of the digital clock, he saw the envelope of pain pills and the bottle of water on his bedside table. *Thompson: what a caretaker that one is.* He felt his cheekbones rise as a smile consumed his face.

Attempting to readjust himself on the bed, his smile quickly faded when a sharp pain shot up his arm. He looked seriously at the little white envelope but quickly decided against taking another pain pill, knowing he'd have to be at work pretty soon. He gingerly climbed out of bed and made his way to the head. He held his injured hand up while he fumbled to get the zipper of his jeans open with the other. After a few failed attempts, he finally triumphed, peed, and, instead of going through that again, kicked the jeans off and left them on the floor. He rummaged through the storage cabinet, took two Advil, and climbed back into his bed. He rested his hand on a pillow and waited for the Advil to take effect.

Now wide-awake, he found portions of the evening quickly started to flood his memory in the form of little flashbacks. He slowly started to process everything. The therapist part of his brain was going a mile a minute, but there was one thing he knew for certain. *Thompson and Hank belong together. Thompson was handed a pile of shit as a kid, and he lived in it for a very long time. He deserves a chance to be happy. And Hank? He's carried a torch for Thompson all these years. The man did everything he could to help Thompson get over Caroline's death, and he deserves to be happy as well. It's all very simple from where I stand, but now I just need to convince them that they belong together. How in the hell am I going to do that?*

A hesitant tapping on the hull of his boat interrupted Garner's thoughts. He clumsily slipped on a pair of gym shorts and found Bubba standing on the dock, shifting from foot to foot. "Hope it's not too early, son. I was kinda hopin' to start tearin' that old engine up and gettin' her out of there."

Garner waved his bandaged hand. "Nope. Have at her," he said, backing back down the companionway. "I've got to get ready for work soon."

Bubba's eyes widened at the obvious injury. "What happened to your hand, son?"

Garner looked at his bandaged finger and frowned. "I guess I need to organize my knife drawer a little better before I go rummaging through it again."

Bubba gave him a knowing glace. "How bad is it?"

"Not too," Garner responded. "Just a few stiches. Be good as new in a few weeks."

"Glad to hear it," Bubba shared. "Mind if I get started?"

"Help yourself. Coffee?"

"Had three cups already. And since I quit smokin', any more than that will send me into hyperdrive."

Garner grinned hesitantly. "How's the not-smoking thing going?"

Bubba puffed out his chest. "I think I've kicked the damn beast," he said proudly. "Each day is gettin' a little easier."

Garner gave him a pat on the back with his good hand. "Good for you. I know how tough that can be."

Bubba smiled proudly and lifted the companionway stairs to the engine room. "How's it goin' round here?" he asked.

Garner looked over his shoulder while he poured his coffee. "I'd say pretty good." Bringing his coffee over, he took a seat and watched as Bubba started closing the through-hull holes and disconnecting hoses. "How long have you worked here?"

Bubba looked up, obviously doing the math. "Damn, well over twenty years now."

Garner's mind started wandering again. "That means you must have known Thompson when he hung around here as a kid."

"Sure enough," Bubba confirmed. "Hank and Caroline too."

"How well do you know him?" Garner asked.

Bubba stopped and looked up. "Pretty well, I think."

The two men held each other's gaze, Bubba apparently deciding if he should say any more.

"He seems to have been through a lot," Garner said inquisitively. Bubba nodded once and turned his attention back to what he was doing.

"Pretty horrible thing about Caroline, huh?" Garner added.

Bubba glanced up with a surprised look on his face. "Thompson told you about that?"

"Yeah," Garner said. "We've talked a good bit since I've been here."

Bubba patted his top pocket, apparently reaching for his cigarettes, and cursed under his breath. "I think that's good, son. The boy needs someone to talk to."

"Still reaching for them, huh?" Garner pointed out.

The old man grinned weakly. "That's a habit I don't think I'll ever kick." Bubba cocked his head to the side. "Look, son, I stick to my own business around here, ya know. Don't get me wrong, I try to do what I can, but I ain't got nothin' that can help that boy."

"I hear ya," Garner replied. "From what he's told me and what Hank's told me, I think Thompson's been through an awful lot."

Bubba nodded. "That he has. But I must say, I've seen a change in him in the last week or so. Can't quite put my finger on it, but he seems a bit happier, a little more at ease."

A long silence followed before Bubba spoke again. "If you don't mind me sayin', I think it might be good for him to have a little company. Someone who doesn't remind him of the past."

Garner looked down into his empty coffee cup. "Yeah, Hank says the same thing."

"Those two were thick as thieves growing up; then something changed between them. Don't know what it was, but that didn't stop Hank from trying to help him after she died. He was the last man standing until Thompson eventually ran him off too."

Garner stood. "You can't help someone who isn't ready to be helped."

"I reckon not," Bubba agreed.

"Well, it was good talking to you, but duty calls," Garner teased. "Got to change for work."

Bubba took off his ball cap and rubbed his head. "Good talkin' to you, son. I'll get as much done as I can so we'll be ready when the new engine gets here."

"Thanks, Bubba."

A BIT later Garner squinted against the bright sunshine as he walked up the dock. He lifted his left arm and glanced at his watch. *Seven fifteen.* "Thompson's always up for sunrise. Maybe I just missed him," he murmured to himself.

Looking at his bandaged finger, he realized the earlier throbbing was now just a dull ache, thanks to the Advil. *At least I can manage the pain without taking those damn drugs.*

Garner turned the knob on the office door, but it was still locked. He fished the keys out of his pocket and unlocked the deadbolt, then pushed the door open with his foot. As usual, he headed to the desk to check phone messages. Out of the corner of his eye he saw Thompson lying face down on the couch, face turned in the opposite direction and one arm puddled onto the floor. "What the fuck?" He froze as a quick chill ran up his spine and his heart started to race. He rubbed his face and felt a cold sweat forming on his forehead. Without thinking, he yelled, "Thompson!"

Before he could make it to the couch, Thompson was up on his feet, looking dazed and in shock. "What? What?"

Garner dropped onto the sofa holding his stomach. "Oh thank God," he hissed. "I thought…."

Thompson stood there like a deer in headlights. He rubbed his eyes and looked around. "What time is it?"

"It's after seven."

"After seven?" Thompson turned and looked out the window. "What in the hell?" He sat down on the couch and cradled his head in his hands. "This is the first time I've slept past sunrise since Caroline died," he muttered.

In a flash, Garner was in therapist mode. "You were up really late helping me, remember?"

Thompson simply shook his head still cradled in his hands. "No. No. You don't get it," he said. "You just don't understand."

Garner spoke softly. "Then explain it to me. Tell me what you're feeling."

Thompson slid his hands down and covered his face. He rubbed his eyes and jaw, then let his hands slide down and massage his neck. He leaned over, linking his fingers and resting his forearms on his knees, staring blankly into the floor. When Thompson finally looked up at him, the anger and self-loathing Garner expected to see wasn't there. In their place he saw looks that could only be described as relief and astonishment. There was even a hint of a slight smile.

Garner closed his eyes and sighed. He knew Thompson had made some sort of personal breakthrough, and he wanted to allow him a little time to process it.

After a couple minutes, Garner could no longer hold back and broke the silence. "You want to talk about it?"

Thompson stood and rested his hands on his hips, a hint of a smile still gracing his lips. His socked feet slid silently on the polished concrete floor as he paced back and forth, seemingly lost in thought. When he finally stopped pacing, he looked at Garner with an expression of disbelief. "I haven't slept past sunrise since Caroline died.

Not for lack of trying but because I never could. My internal alarm clock always woke me up, no matter what time I went to sleep."

Thompson paused and paced some more.

The pieces of the puzzle were finally starting to make sense for Garner, but he let Thompson continue working through his new discovery. "Go on," Garner urged.

"This probably won't make sense to you. Hell, I'm not sure it even makes sense to me yet, but here goes. Rain or shine, winter or summer, exhausted or not, I always woke just before sunrise. In the days after her death, I convinced myself that it was Caroline's gentle way of making sure I continued our tradition."

Thompson ran his fingers through his long blond locks. "On days when I didn't feel her with me, I figured it was me waking myself because I *needed* to do this. You know, for me." Then he chuckled. "And maybe it was both of those reasons. In the beginning, it was a way for me to hold on to her, but then it just became something I had to do."

Garner nodded and opened his mouth to concur, but closed it when Thompson continued talking. "Man, after my brain dump last night, I was mentally exhausted. When I got to the office, I just kicked off my shoes and collapsed on the couch. And who knows, if you hadn't come in, I might still be sleeping."

Garner smiled, realizing that Thompson was coming to all the right conclusions on his own. "Maybe you just needed that brain dump," he agreed. "You've kept these feelings to yourself for so long, never listening to anyone else's opinion, you eventually convinced yourself that there was no other way to live. You know, Thompson, survivor's guilt can be a bitch. You're alive, man. You need to give yourself permission to live and be happy. I didn't know Caroline, but I'm sure she would want that for you."

Thompson turned away, dropped his head, and again covered his face with his hands. Garner watched silently as Thompson's shoulders started to shake, his emotions obviously getting the best of him.

Garner leapt to his feet and crossed the room. Thompson turned and wrapped his arms around Garner tightly, resting his head on Garner's shoulder. The sounds that finally escaped Thompson's lips were sounds of laughter. To Garner's surprise, Thompson wasn't crying after all: he was laughing. Garner took a step back in disbelief. A smile formed on his lips from the sheer joy of seeing the sparkle in Thompson's beautiful green eyes. "Are you okay, man?"

Thompson nodded. He wiped at the tears of laughter with the sleeve of his shirt. "All these years I've hated myself for being the one left behind to sort through all of these unresolved issues. Why did I hate myself for something I couldn't control?"

Garner held on tightly to Thompson's shoulders and looked him straight in the eyes. "Precisely. Caroline's death was not your fault. Her abuse was not your fault. In fact, her stepfather abused both of you in a sense. He took away her innocence physically and emotionally, but he also took away your innocence too."

Thompson was listening intently, and Garner finally thought he might be getting through, so he continued. "That man is dead now, Thompson, and if there is a God, he's getting everything he deserves. He destroyed both of your childhoods; don't give his memory the power to destroy your adult life as well."

Thompson's smile faded and all the blood drained out of his face. "But Caroline paid a far bigger price than I did."

"But again, Thompson, not by any fault of yours," Garner insisted. "You took care of her and protected her as best as you could. You were a kid. Give yourself a break."

Thompson remained silent for a long time, and then the sobs slowly started. He appeared to be having trouble standing, so Garner led him to the couch and urged him to sit. As the intensity of the sobs increased, Garner realized that Thompson was crying from the deepest depths of his soul, releasing the years of pain and agony he'd kept hidden within his core. As Garner gently stroked Thompson's back, he imagined how he would feel after holding in all of these emotions year after year.

Thompson's sobs eventually turned into a quiet, almost peaceful sort of weeping, something Garner had seen over and over again in his practice. This was usually the turning point for his patients, and he suspected that Thompson too would soon be on his way to living and hopefully loving again.

When the weeping ultimately subsided, Thompson looked like he'd been through the wringer. His eyes were red and his face was swollen, but his color had returned and he looked at peace. "Go home and get some rest," Garner urged. "I can handle things here."

Thompson opened his mouth like he was going to protest, and Garner held up his hand. "I insist. You've come to a major realization here today, and you need some time to process it all completely."

Thompson frowned. "You're really starting to sound like a shrink."

"And your point is?" Garner asked.

Thompson's expression quickly changed to one of recognition. "Dr. Garner P. Holt. You *are* a shrink."

"I used to be. And… we shrinks prefer the term psychiatrist or therapist."

"Holy shit," Thompson said, wiping his tear-stained face.

Garner put his hands on his hips. "Is this going to be a problem?"

"Hell if I know!" Thompson snapped as he started pacing again.

Garner stuck his hand out and stopped Thompson from pacing. "Look, man. You've made a big breakthrough here today, but this is not over. This is going to take some time to work through, and I want to be here to help, if you'll let me."

"As a friend or as a shrink?"

"Can't I be both?"

"Look, you helped me see I still have a life to live. That's something no one has been able to do and I'll always be grateful to you for that, but…."

Garner interrupted. "But what? You don't need a shrink?"

Thompson inhaled deeply and sighed, rubbing the back of his neck. "I don't know what I need."

"Yeah. Well, I do, and a shrink is exactly what you need," Garner barked. "Let me ask you this. During all of our conversations, have you ever felt like I've been counseling or analyzing you?"

Thompson didn't answer right away, and Garner felt himself starting to get even more pissed. "Well?"

"No," Thompson whispered almost inaudibly.

"I didn't hear that?"

"No!" Thompson bellowed.

"Then please let me go on working here, being your friend, and trying to help you work through all of this."

Thompson went over to the couch and sat down again. He put his shoes on and exhaled. He looked up at his friend with a defeated look. "You win."

Garner sat down next to him and put his hand on Thompson's knee. "It's not about winning or losing, but thank you."

Thompson sighed and rested his hand on top of Garner's. "But none of that psychobabble, okay?"

Garner laughed. "Psychobabble? Please, I don't use psychobabble. Now get out of here."

Thompson looked hesitant but stood. "If you don't mind, I will go home and get a little rest, shower. I promise I'll be back by lunch time."

Garner nodded. "Take your time. I'll handle everything around here."

Garner stood, and Thompson threw his arms around him and held on tight. "Thank you."

"You're welcome. Now go get some rest."

THINGS HAD gone relatively smoothly so far, and Garner was walking back up to the office after helping a captain shove off. When he reached the top of the dock, he was surprised to find Hank standing there with his arms folded across his chest. "Hey there," he said with curiosity. "I thought you weren't back until tomorrow night?"

Hank lifted Garner's bandaged hand and gave it a once-over. "I was worried about you. I thought you'd be taking it easy today."

"Too much to do. Did you drive all the way back from Charleston just to check on me?"

"I called your cell phone this morning and I didn't get an answer, so I got worried."

Garner slapped his pocket and realized that he'd left his phone on the boat. "Oh, man, I'm so sorry. I must have left my phone on the boat this morning."

"It's okay. The attendees were in various seminars this morning, so I had a couple of hours to kill. Thought I'd drive back and make sure you were okay."

"That's really nice, and I appreciate it, Hank, but I'm fine. Really," Garner reiterated. "As I told you last night, it was just a few stiches, and Thompson was there to help."

Hank visibly stiffened. "Speaking of, where is Florence Nightingale?" he said, looking around.

Garner couldn't help but smile at that comment. "Oh, I sent him home to get some rest," he explained. "He should be back in an hour or so."

"You sent *him* home to get some rest?" Hank snapped. "You're the one with the injury; you should be the one taking it easy."

Garner paused, thinking about how he was going to handle the situation. It wasn't his place to explain Thompson's breakthrough to Hank. But it appeared that Hank was none too happy that he was working in Thompson's place. For some reason that level of anger from someone he'd known for a little over a week pissed Garner off. *Damn, this is why I'm not good with relationships.*

"Look, Hank," Garner said, recognizing the matter-of-fact tone in his voice. He stopped midsentence and took a deep breath. Trying to ignore the hairs standing up on the back of his neck, he spoke calmly. "He took care of me, took me to the hospital, cooked dinner for me, and after the painkiller took effect, he put me to bed. And… just for the record, the little sleep he got was on the couch in his office. I sent him home to take a nap and shower. He'll be back soon. Again, I appreciate your concern, but everything is fine."

Hank's expression turned from one of concern to obvious hurt. "He put you to bed?" He flashed a disingenuous smile and held up both hands. "I'm sorry, none of my business. My bad. I can see that you and Thompson have things under control and you're obviously okay, so I'll be on my way and let you get back to work." He turned and started walking away.

"Fuck," Garner hissed, looking down at his feet. Garner took a mental step back and realized Hank was just projecting. His anger at Thompson had nothing really to do with Garner or the current situation; it was all related to their history. Garner was just the outlet. "Hank! Wait a second."

Hank stopped but didn't turn around.

"I'm sorry. I didn't mean that the way it sounded."

"No problem, I heard you loud and clear," Hank said. "I need to get back to Charleston. I'll see you when I get back." Hank started walking again and this time he didn't stop when Garner called his name.

"Shit," Garner said under his breath. He kicked the side of the building in frustration and cringed when the pain from his foot reached his brain. "Way to go, Doc. For a psychiatrist, you sure suck at communicating."

THOMPSON OPENED his eyes and squinted against the bright sunshine streaming in through the skylight above his bed. "This is a new experience," he said to himself. As hard as he tried, he couldn't remember the last time he'd been in bed when it was light outside. He was always up long before sunrise, let alone—he glanced at the alarm on the bedside table—eleven fifteen in the morning.

He rolled onto his back, tightened his hold on the pillow in his arms, and stared up at the bright noonday sun. As he lay there feeling better than he had in years, his first conscious thoughts were of Garner Holt and how this stranger had triggered something in him, making him want to leave the very dark place that had become his existence. This savior had helped him realize that he was still alive and had single-handedly put him on the path to reclaiming his life. As he studied the particles of dust dancing through the sun's rays, he wondered how someone he'd known for just over a week could make such a huge difference in his life.

He broke into a contented yawn that was instinctively followed by a long, gratifying stretch. He hopped out of bed feeling revitalized, as though he'd been sleeping for a week. He showered, dressed, and was out of the house in just under twenty minutes.

Thompson pulled into the marina parking lot right after noon with a large brown paper bag filled with various sandwiches and chips from the local deli. It was normally pretty slow midday, so he fully expected to find Garner in the office with his hand propped up, taking it easy. But when he found the office empty, he dropped the lunch bag on the desk and nervously walked over to the window. He scanned the marina and relaxed when he saw Garner fueling a fishing boat with his back to the office.

Thompson walked down the dock with a bounce in his step and a natural smile he couldn't contain. When he reached the other man, Garner was leaning on the pump, still holding on to the nozzle.

"Hey, dock boy," Thompson teased, reaching for the fuel nozzle. "Let me give you a hand with that."

"Dock boy?" Garner asked, matching Thompson's smile.

"You heard me," Thompson said, rather pleased with himself. "Oh, and I brought lunch."

"Lunch, huh?" Garner said. "Then I guess I'll overlook the 'dock boy' comment and let you live."

Thompson put the nozzle back into the pump. "Okay, killer, calm down. I was just teasing. Hey, how's the finger?"

Garner looked down at his bandage. "Not too bad, actually. The Advil seems to be doing the trick."

"Glad to hear it." Thompson leaned around to the front of the fuel pump and turned to the boat captain. "That'll be eight sixty-seven and fifty-two cents."

He took the credit card from the captain and walked over to the hut. "Why don't you head up and start on lunch, and I'll finish up here and join you in a minute."

"Are you sure? I can certainly finish up."

"I know you can," Thompson said, swiping the credit card through the terminal. "You've covered for me all morning. Go take it easy for a while. I'll be up in a minute."

"If you insist," Garner said through a smile. "I'll see you in a few, then."

When Thompson finally walked through the office door, Garner had turned his desk into a spread of deli sandwiches, chips, and soft drinks. "How many people did you expect to feed today?" Garner asked.

"Just us," Thompson said hesitantly. "I really didn't know what you liked, so I bought a little of everything."

"So I see," Garner concurred, looking over the spread. "It all looks great. Thank you."

Thompson sat down and picked up half of what looked like a turkey club and held it in his hands. "Are you kidding?" he said. "This is just the beginning of me trying to pay you back for everything you've done for me."

"Whoa, man," Garner said, holding a roast beef sandwich inches from his lips. "All I did was lend an ear and make you see what you already knew. You don't owe me anything."

"We'll just have to agree to disagree on that one," Thompson said, taking his first bite. He held his hand in front of his mouth and added, "But for now I'll just say thank you."

Garner smiled. "And I'll just say you're welcome. Did you get any rest?"

Thompson nodded. "Yeah, I did, and thank you for that too."

Garner raised his bandaged finger. "Nothing to thank me for; you took really good care of me last night, so now we're even."

Before Thompson could protest, Garner added, "Oh, and I had a visitor this morning." But he didn't elaborate.

Thompson's curiosity was now piqued. "And…?"

"It was Hank," Garner explained.

"Hank? I thought he was in Charleston."

"He said he called my cell this morning, which I mistakenly left on the boat, and when I didn't answer he got worried and wanted to check on me."

"He drove all the way from Charleston?"

"Yep, and right now I'm pretty sure he's second-guessing that decision."

"Garner? What happened?"

Thompson listened intently as Garner filled him in on his and Hank's conversation. "I just didn't feel comfortable telling Hank why you'd gone home," Garner explained. "It wasn't really my place to discuss your personal life with him."

Thompson sighed. "I'm sorry I put you in that position. And believe me, I appreciate your discretion, but now he's pissed at you and thinks I'm an ass for making you work with a hurt finger just so I could home to get some sleep."

"I get that. And I'll apologize to him for the way I handled the situation when he gets back, but I think he should know you a little better and trust that you had a good reason to not be here. My God, you practically live here."

Thompson dropped his head, feeling a little ashamed. "In all fairness, he hasn't seen the old Thompson in a very long time. I'm sure he thinks he doesn't know me at all anymore, and he's probably right. Hell, I look in the mirror and most times I don't recognize the person I see."

"Come on," Garner said, laying a hand on Thompson's forearm. "You've got to start giving yourself a break; it's been a tough few years. But with that said, I think you're going to start seeing things little differently now."

Thompson opened his mouth to agree, but before he could speak, the VHF radio came to life with a boater requesting a fuel stop. "I'll take it," Garner said, taking the radio off his belt and answering the call.

"Oh no you don't," Thompson barked. "You sit right back down and take it easy for a while. Tell him I'll meet him at the dock."

"You're very bossy," Garner whined, backing up and plopping down on his chair and answering the call. When he was through, he clipped the radio back on his belt and looked at Thompson, whose hand was already on the doorknob. "How long are you going to baby me like this?"

"Not sure, but I'll let you know," he replied, closing the office door behind him.

"THANKS FOR the business," Thompson yelled as he pushed the boat away from the dock. He looked up at the office and went back into the fuel hut. He dug his cell out of his pocket and pressed the speed dial button for Hank.

While Thompson waited for Hank to answer the call, he wondered how much he should tell him about what had transpired since he left. Hank had been his best friend and, if he were being truthful with himself, might have been a lot more if Caroline's abuse hadn't put an end to life as he'd known it. He decided that Hank deserved to know. But did he *want* to know? That was the question. Hank had washed his hands of Thompson just like the others, with good reason, of course, and they'd been distant at best since then.

Thompson knew that if he had any hopes of forging another friendship with Hank, he'd need to be honest with him.

The ringing stopped and Thompson heard distant voices mixed with all sorts of loud noises. "Hank Charming. Hello! Can you hear me?"

"Prince. It's Thompson." Thompson regretted using Hank's nickname the minute the word left his lips, but it was too late to take it back.

"Who?"

"Thompson."

"Wait! Did you say Thompson? It's very loud in the convention center." Hank's words weren't able to hide the surprise in his voice at who was calling him.

"Yes, Hank, it's Thompson."

"Is Garner all right?"

"Yeah. He's good. In fact, that's why I'm calling."

There was silence on the other end of the phone. Thompson cleared his throat and started talking. "Hank, I wanted to explain why I left Garner to run the marina this morning."

"What? Say it again. I can't hear you."

Thompson repeated his reason for the call, a little louder this time.

"Hang on, Thompson, let me get somewhere where I can hear you."

Thompson waited patiently as little by little the background noises quieted.

"Can you hear me now?" Hank asked.

"Yeah. Can you hear me?"

"Much better now. Sorry about that."

Thompson repeated for the third time why he'd called.

"Thompson, neither of you owes me any explanation."

"But we… I do."

There was silence on the other end of the line.

"Look, you know I was with Garner last night when he cut his finger. He asked me to join him for dinner and I'm glad I was there or he would have never gone to the hospital. But after we got back, we did a lot of talking. Hank, he really helped me. I don't know how or why, but he made me realize that I still had a life to live. Did you know he was a psychiatrist?"

He didn't give Hank a chance to answer before he continued. "Anyway, we talked most of the night, and then I slept on the couch in the office. This morning he woke me after seven. Seven o'clock, Hank! Every day since Caroline died, I have been up long before sunrise. I'm sure you remember the ritual. Then we talked more, and I was just exhausted, mentally and physically. He insisted I go home and get a couple of hours sleep, and you're right, I shouldn't have, but I was just so damned worn out I made a bad judgment call. I'm sorry I left him here alone."

Thompson took a deep breath. He knew he was rambling, but suddenly he had so much to say.

"Hank?"

"I'm listening."

"Garner's a psychiatrist and he helped me see a lot of stuff and I'm so sorry, Prince," he said with a crack in his voice, realizing suddenly that he was now apologizing for a lot more than leaving Garner to fend for himself.

"For what?"

"For a lot of things," he whispered. "Which I hope we can talk about later, but right now for coming between you and Garner. Garner should have explained more things to you, but he didn't want to betray my confidence."

"Thompson," Hank said in a somber voice, "you didn't come between Garner and me. There was nothing to come between. He's a nice guy, but he's only passing through, and just like you did so many years ago, he made it painfully obvious that my concern for him was neither needed nor wanted."

Thompson felt like he'd been sucker punched. Of course he knew Hank was right, but that didn't make it hurt any less. He could hear the pain in Hank's voice and it broke his heart.

"I'm sure he didn't mean it like that, Hank. Please talk to him. He meant well; I think he was just trying to protect me."

Hank laughed sarcastically. "Protect *you* from *me*? Really? Look, Thompson, I appreciate the call, but I've gotta go. I'll see you when I get back."

"Prince, wait."

Thompson had so many things to say, but they were all running together in his head. And he really didn't want to do this over the phone.

Hank interrupted his jumbled thoughts. "I'm listening," he snapped.

Anxiety and fear won over and Thompson lost his nerve. "Never mind. We'll talk when you get home. Take care, Hank."

Thompson disconnected the call without another word and dropped his head, suddenly overtaken with an array of daunting emotions. A mixture of guilt, shame, and defeat consumed him, almost sending him to his knees. He braced himself on the dock railing while he slipped the phone back into his pocket. Instinctively, he brought both hands to his now-churning stomach in an attempt to steady it. "I'm so sorry, Hank," he whispered.

He felt his skin go damp and he realized he was close to losing his lunch. The magnitude of the pain he'd caused others while wallowing in his own sorrow was now such a stark reality. He tried to calm his stomach and the dread he was feeling by looking out over the waterway, but the encompassing wretchedness didn't seem to ebb.

His realization of how he'd treated the people who cared the most hit him hard. He had so much he needed to make up for, but he didn't really know where or how to begin.

Somehow Thompson made it up the dock, but by the time he reached the office door, his skin was clammy and his hands were trembling uncontrollably. Thompson realized he had only one option. He had to impose on Garner one last time. He needed to know how to start to make it right with Hank and anyone else he'd hurt. He owed everyone, but especially Hank. He knew simply apologizing would never be enough to ease his remorse, but short of that he didn't know what else he could do.

He grabbed the doorknob to try and stop his hand from shaking, but it did no good. Thompson's feet were frozen in place and his legs were wobbly, almost to the point of collapse. The guilt flowed into him like the mighty storm surge from a category five hurricane, and he willed himself to step away from the door. He turned around and looked out over the waterway again. He felt the tears welling up in his eyes as he heard Hank's words over and over in his head: "... and just like you did so many years ago; you made it painfully obvious that my concern for you was neither needed nor wanted."

The pain in Hank's voice as much as the words he used stuck in Thompson's brain. He remembered the last time he'd heard a similar tone and the scene unfolded in his head.

Hank was pleading with him to not give up on life, his words laced with pain and distress. At the time Thompson hadn't detected any of that. All he wanted was to be left alone. Finally, Hank dropped to his knees and began to plead, "Thompson, please. Somewhere deep down you know how I feel about you. And if you let me, I know I can help you. Please don't give up on yourself. On me. On life. I love you. I've always loved you."

Thompson shook his head in an attempt to release the painful memory, but it was as vivid as if it had happened just an hour ago. "Hank said he loved me." *Why didn't I remember that?* He searched the far reaches of his mind to see if he'd missed anything else, but all he remembered was staring off into the distance, listening, but not hearing. *His* words came flooding back to him this time. "I don't want to be helped by you or anyone else. Can't you see that?" he'd said. "Fuck!" he said now, hanging his head. *And I wonder why people treat me like I'm pathetic?*

Thompson's knees were about to buckle, but just before he let himself go, he felt strong arms around him. He jumped at the mere touch and craned his head to see Garner standing behind him supporting his weight. "I got you, big guy. It's okay."

Thompson tried to speak, but his voice cracked and his chin started to quiver. He closed his mouth, took a deep breath, and tried again. "I...." He swallowed the lump in his throat. "I... was awful to everyone after Caroline died, but especially to Hank. I really hurt him. I need to make it right."

"Come on, let's get you back into the office."

Garner helped him inside, and they sat side by side on the couch. A heavy silence loomed between them, each waiting for the other to speak.

Thompson wanted to start, but the lump in his throat was so massive he couldn't form an audible word. He sighed with relief when Garner finally spoke. "Was Hank the one you were talking to on the phone at the fuel dock?"

Still struggling to find the words, Thompson closed his eyes and nodded. It took every ounce of strength he could muster to utter the next sentence. "I wanted to fix this for the two of you."

"Fuck," Garner cursed under his breath. "I figured as much." Garner rested a hand on Thompson's leg. "This is all my fault, man; I should have never told you what happened between Hank and me."

Thompson attempted to speak again, but Garner held up a hand. "Thompson, all this is coming on way too quickly. You barely had time to process your breakthrough from last night, and now you're dealing with a different kind of guilt, but guilt just as powerful. But you need to know one very important thing," Garner whispered as he turned to Thompson and looked at him with conviction. "There is no *two of us*. Hank is a great guy, but we have no future. We hung out a little and enjoyed each other's company. That's it. And as I told you last night, I believe Hank is still very much in love with you."

Thompson again tried to swallow the lump still very present in his throat. He chuckled nervously. "After the conversation he and I just had, I think you're way off base with that assumption."

Thompson finally regained control of his voice and started relaying the conversation from start to finish, barely stopping to breathe. When he finished Garner leaned back and rested his head on the back of the couch.

"Well?" Thompson said.

After a few minutes, Garner lifted his head and looked at Thompson. "I'm trying to sort through all of this, but based on everything you just told me, I'm more convinced than ever that he's still in love with you."

Thompson stood. "I know you're the expert, but how can you come to that conclusion from the conversation I just relayed to you?"

"It's basic textbook," Garner said. "His choice of words indicates that he's still hurting, and he's still hurting because he's still in love with you. It's that simple."

Thompson thought about the answer, and he had to admit it made a great deal of sense, but he still had trouble believing it.

"And look," Garner added. "I didn't make it any better for either of you by reacting the way I did when he came looking for me. I told you I suck at relationships or anything that even resembles a relationship."

Before Thompson could say anything else, the VHF radio came to life again, announcing an arrival. "Damn," Garner hissed, looking at his watch. "Looks like our time is up."

Thompson was still pretty shaken, but he was grateful for the interruption. He quickly retrieved the radio and handled the call. Identifying the slip number from the reservation chart above his desk, he gave the captain the preassigned docking instructions and was about to stand when Garner laid a hand on his knee. "You realize we're not finished here."

"I know," Thompson said. "Can we talk more over dinner?"

"Sure."

Thompson smiled. "Thank you."

"Don't thank me yet," Garner teased. "You're buying."

"Oh really?" Thompson said with a smirk. "It would be my pleasure." Right before he got up, he laid his hand on top of Garner's and squeezed.

Garner winked and returned the gesture. "Let's go make some money."

IT WAS nearly seven o'clock when Thompson and Garner finally finished up for the night. All the check-ins were docked and secure, the end-of-day paperwork was done, and Thompson was standing in the window looking out over the marina, waiting for Garner, who had gone down to his boat to take a quick shower before dinner.

Although mentally and physically exhausted, Thompson felt exhilarated. He had a new hope and energy about him. *How could my life have gone from spiraling out of control and desperate to...?* He stopped short before he continued his thought process. *Do I dare to think... hopeful? Am I actually hopeful of the future? A little over a week ago I could barely function. Barely even breathe. Then Garner Holt comes into my life and...! How could a stranger get into my head so quickly and make me see what so many had tried and failed to do? Why now? Hell, why was Garner able to get through when Hank hadn't?*

Hank. The more he thought about his friend, the more he wondered if Garner could actually be right. *Could Hank still be in love with me?* Beyond those few stolen moments in the locker room when he'd lost himself in Hank's kiss, the possibility of life with Hank was just never an option he was willing or able to explore, for obvious reasons. "Hell, I don't even know if I'm into Hank that way."

He sat down and rested his head on the back of the couch and closed his eyes. In seconds he was transported back in time to his high school locker room with Hank. He pictured the two of them alone, half-naked, face to face, and eyes locked on one another. He instinctively brushed his fingers over his lips, remembering his and Hank's first and only kiss. It felt like it had happened so many lifetimes ago, but yet he remembered it now like it was just yesterday.

In his mind he felt Hank's grip firmly planted behind his neck. When their lips met, he was instantly lost in the moment. No Caroline. No commitment. No abuse. Nothing but him and Hank frozen in time. He imagined Hank's lips pressed tightly against his and the roughness of Hank's day-old beard against his face, then the warmth of Hank's tongue desperately combing every inch of his mouth. The sheer masculinity behind the sloppy wet kiss was raw and exhilarating but tender and passionate at the same time. Hank was taking complete control of him physically and emotionally and he quickly came to the realization that he was gladly giving in to him.

Then in one second it all came to a crashing halt. *Caroline!* He abruptly remembered coming back to his senses when he'd thought of Caroline. And that was the end of that.

Again in his office, he opened his eyes and lifted his head. He was drenched in sweat, and his hand was resting on his aching erection. "Holy shit!" he whispered. "I guess that answers my question about being into Hank."

In frustration he allowed his head to fall back against the couch again. He stared up at the ceiling and willed his racing heart to slow down. As his erection slowly faded and his pulse returned to normal, his breathing followed and within minutes he was again in control.

His mind was reeling from every realization he'd come to in the last thirty-six hours, but one thing was certain: he had to see Hank. But he needed a game plan. He just couldn't show up on Hank's doorstep and beg forgiveness. Or could he? He had so many things he needed to say, but where to start? *The truth.* Hank had a right to know what had transpired so many years ago and why he had promised to take care of Caroline. And maybe, just maybe, Hank might understand.

He'd barely just decided that he was going to wait on Hank's doorstep and make him listen, make him understand what had transpired all those years ago, when the office door swung open and Garner was standing there staring at him. Thompson looked up and froze. His heart rate doubled again immediately. Garner looked like a sports model. His wet brown hair, now almost blond from spending so much time on the docks, was slicked back behind his ears, accentuating his strong jawline and rich brown eyes. Thompson shook his head and whispered, "What the fuck's the matter with me?" *Did I flip a switch or something and now I'm going to start checking out every guy I see?*

Garner smiled. "Now that's a loaded question," he teased. "Where do I start?"

"Ah… never mind, you weren't supposed to hear that," Thompson mumbled. "I was just thinking out loud and… fuck you for that comment," he added.

Garner chuckled. "What? No foreplay?"

Thompson rolled his eyes and looked down at Garner's hand. He had a bright new bandage around his finger. In a feeble attempt to change the subject, Thompson asked, "How's the finger?"

"It's better than I expected." Garner lifted his hand up and looked at his skillful work. "I removed the bandage, showered with a Ziploc bag on my hand, added a little antibiotic ointment, and put this on," he said, pointing his finger at Thompson. "To be honest, the cut looks

pretty good and doesn't hurt much either."

Thompson stood. "Good to hear."

The two men stood in an awkward silence for a few moments before Thompson spoke. "I'm starved. You ready to go?"

"Yep. Anything wrong? Something you want to tell me?"

"Why?" Thompson snapped.

"'Cause you're acting stranger than normal," Garner said with a smirk.

"Fuck you again."

"Really? More obscenities," Garner teased.

Thompson ignored that comment and grabbed his keys from his desk. "Come on. I'll fill you in over dinner."

CHAPTER ELEVEN

ON THE way back to Savannah, Hank clutched the steering wheel tightly in an attempt to stop his hands from trembling. He tried to control his anger and frustration and focus on maneuvering the two-lane road between Charleston and Savannah, but he wasn't having much luck. Highway 17 was well known for speed traps and overzealous traffic cops, and the last thing he needed was an accident or a speeding ticket while pulling a boat and trailer. No matter how hard he tried to put the events of late out of his mind, his anger from the day before hadn't waned a bit. In fact it had intensified.

He'd tossed and turned the entire night, and even now, almost twenty-four hours since the infamous call from Thompson, anger and frustration still welled deep inside him. The only problem was that during the night, he'd realized this really had nothing to do with Garner; this was really between him and Thompson.

For years, Hank had tried to put aside his love for Thompson and simply be his friend. And for the most part, he'd succeeded. Although they were never going to be close again, Hank had tried to be civil, friendly even, when they interacted. But lately this thing with him and Garner, and then with Garner and Thompson, was dredging up all those old feelings he thought he'd dealt with and put behind him.

"And speaking of Garner and Thompson, what in the hell is going on with those two?" he murmured. "First Garner gets pissed off and blows me off after I drove two hours to check on him. When did caring about another human being become a bad thing?" And then the call from Thompson after having some sudden epiphany and wanting to make it all right. "Fuck his 'too little too late' weak apology. As a matter of fact, fuck 'em both. The last thing I need is to get mixed up in some stupid love triangle. Have at it, fellas, you're on your own. You deserve one another."

An hour later, Hank backed the twenty-five-foot Carolina Skiff into an empty spot in his dealership parking lot and disconnected the trailer. He quickly glanced at the office door, debating whether he should go in and check on things. "Fuck it," he said. "I was only away for a few days. If anything's wrong it can wait until tomorrow." He climbed back into his truck and headed for home.

During the five-minute ride home, Hank had all the windows down and was enjoying the cool fall air rushing through the cab. All he could think about was stripping off his clothes, taking a long hot shower, and crawling into his own bed. But when he pulled into his driveway, he quickly realized that none of that was going to happen anytime soon.

He dropped his head against the steering wheel and cursed under his breath. Thompson was sitting on his front porch swing, his face clearly illuminated by the bright porch light. "Man. I really don't want to deal with this crap right now," he murmured to himself.

He forced the truck into Park, and before he could get all the windows up and turn the engine off, Thompson was leaning in the truck window.

"Welcome home, Prince," he said in a shaky voice.

"I told you to stop calling me that," Hank snapped.

Thompson winced and stepped away from the window.

"Shit," Hank muttered, regretting the words as soon as they left his mouth. "It's late, Thompson, and I'm really tired. What are you doing here?"

"I know it's late and I'm sorry, but I… I had to talk to you."

"Can't it wait until tomorrow?"

"I'm afraid I've put this off way too long already."

Hank stared straight ahead, contemplating what good all this would do.

Eventually he sighed, put the windows up, and grabbed his duffel bag.

He watched Thompson take another step back when he opened the truck door and slid out. When Hank slammed the door shut and turned, he stepped right into Thompson's open arms. Before Hank had time to react, Thompson's hands were cupping his face, and Thompson's lips were pressed firmly against his. When Thompson's tongue sought entry, Hank was so caught off guard he opened; willingly or unwillingly, he wasn't sure.

Thompson's kiss was sweet and gentle, not like the first kiss they'd fumbled through way back when. Hank suddenly felt warm all over, and he allowed the sensation to flow all the way through him to the tips of his toes. He dropped his duffel bag to the ground and was about to wrap his arms around Thompson, when he abruptly came to his senses and realized what was happening. Instead he planted both hands on Thompson's chest and pushed as hard as he could. Thompson stumbled back and looked like he caught himself right before he tripped over his own two feet.

The two men stood in Hank's front yard staring at one another until Hank finally spoke. "What in the hell do you think you're doing?"

Thompson ran his fingers through his hair. "I… I don't know, Prince. I don't know anything anymore. I have no idea what just came over me. I'm sorry, but can we please just talk?"

"Is that your idea of talking?" Hank asked.

"No!" he explained. "That just… just sort of happened. I swear I didn't plan it."

"Oh great! Now I don't know whether to be relieved or offended," Hank said.

Thompson gave him this pitiful look, and Hank moaned in frustration. He threw his hands in the air in complete surrender. "You know I never could say no to you, Thompson."

"To be honest, Prince, I was sort of counting on that."

Hank chuckled sarcastically. "At least you're honest."

Hank picked up his duffel bag and walked right past Thompson and up the porch steps. He unlocked the front door and glanced over his shoulder at Thompson, who appeared to be frozen in place.

"If you're waiting for a formal invitation, you're not getting one," Hank grumbled, pushing the front door open and stepping inside, purposely not looking back again. He sensed more than heard Thompson on his heels as he walked through the house, turning on lamps as he went. When he got to the kitchen, he dropped his bag again and went directly to the fridge. He pulled out two beers and tossed one to Thompson, who was standing awkwardly in the doorway but caught the projectile beer bottle.

Hank leaned against the refrigerator and glared at Thompson, whose hands were trembling so badly he could barely open the bottle. For a split second, Hank's heart melted, and he felt some level of pity for his once-best friend, but he quickly remembered the last time he'd cared for this man and where that had gotten him. He pushed those thoughts out of his mind and took a long pull from his beer bottle. "Okay, talk."

Thompson opened his mouth like he was going to speak and then closed it again. His entire body was now shaking and all the blood had drained out of his face. Looking at him now, Hank realized just how pitiful Thompson had become. But at the same time, he also realized how angry he still was at this man for casting him aside and shutting him out the way he did. With all these emotions running through his head, he still had to fight the urge to run over and throw his arms around Thompson to try and comfort him. But luckily all the years of pent-up anger kept his feet firmly in place.

"You've got five seconds to start talking or I'm—"

"I'm fucking scared, all right," Thompson blurted out. "Can you give me just a little bit of a break?"

"Why should I give you a break, Thompson?" Hank snapped, quickly running out of patience. "And what in the fuck are you scared of?"

"Of you, okay! Of caring again! Of everything! The last fucking time I was this scared, I was running up the dock with Caroline's lifeless body in my arms."

In that instant Hank's blood pressure shot up, and the anger that he thought he'd long ago dealt with rose to the surface again with a vengeance.

Four years of pain, rejection, and loss finally sent him into well-deserved rage. He slammed his beer down on the counter, the bottle shattering and sending shards of glass in every direction. "Caroline! It always fucking comes down to Caroline, doesn't it, Thompson? Why don't you just get the fuck out? Just. Fucking. Go! That's what you always do anyway. Isn't that your MO, Tommy boy? You retreat to somewhere deep inside of yourself and lock everyone else out."

Thompson dodged the shards of glass and then froze. His eyes looked like they were going to pop out of his head, and he seemed to be in complete shock. Then his expression turned to one Hank could only identify as defeat. He slowly put his beer on the counter and turned to leave.

"No wait," Hank yelled. "On second thought, I think I've waited long enough for this conversation. Let's get it all out, right here, right now! I think you owe me that much."

Thompson stopped but didn't turn around. He said something that was barely audible and for some reason that made Hank even angrier.

"Come on, Thompson. Is it that tough to say out loud?"

"Yes," Thompson said, louder this time. "Yes, you've waited long enough."

"Now we're getting somewhere," Hank hissed. "So tell me. Why did you turn your back on me? What in the fuck kind of hold did she have on you? I know you weren't in love with her."

"She didn't have any hold on me," Thompson said in a monotone voice.

"That's interesting, because one day it was you and me, the next it was you, Caroline, and me, and then it was just you and Caroline. How could you just cast me aside?" Hank's voice cracked. "For her."

Thompson slowly turned around, tears streaming down his face. "She was being sexually abused by her stepfather."

Hank felt his heart drop to his stomach. His mind heard the words, but they didn't quite register. *Did he say sexually abused?* Of every excuse he was prepared to hear, sexual abuse was not one of them. He staggered back until his ass found a barstool and he sat.

"One morning after she'd been abused, she asked me to take her fishing. I guess she wanted some sense of normalcy, to try and forget. She wasn't herself and cried the entire time, and I noticed that both her wrists were bruised. After a couple of hours of begging her to tell me what was wrong, she finally broke down and confessed."

Thompson took a seat on the barstool next to Hank and continued. "By that time, it had been going on for several months, and he told her that if she ever told anyone, he would kill her and her mother. And later, after we started spending so much time together, he also added me to that list. She was terrified."

"Why didn't you tell me, or anyone for that matter?" Hank asked. "Someone could have helped."

Thompson shook his head. "She made me promise not to tell anyone. She was so scared that he would hurt her mother or me."

"Could she not see how unfair that was to you?" Hank asked.

Thompson rested his head in his hands. "I guess not. We were kids, Prince. Fair or not, it was what it was."

"But you were just a kid yourself," Hank admitted. "I can't imagine how you handled all of that."

"All I knew was that I had to do everything I could to protect her, so I started spending every moment I could with her. In my mind, I thought if I was with her, he couldn't get to her."

Hank was having a hard time comprehending everything he was hearing. So many questions were swirling around his head, he felt like he was going to explode. "But you married her?"

Thompson shook his head. "By the time we graduated high school, she was not the same girl we all grew up with. She was fragile, insecure, and frightened of her own shadow. I could have never turned my back on her."

"So you married her?"

"I had to," Thompson argued. "By this time I'd pretty much convinced myself she was my responsibility. I had to take care of her."

Hank looked down and slowly shook his head. So many things were not as they had appeared to be back then. How could he have not known?

Then a thought hit him. He looked up at Thompson and their eyes met. "After she died you went into such a tailspin, no one could reach you, not even me. Why?"

Thompson lowered his head, his voice shaky and barely audible. "I promised to protect her and I failed," he said. "She died on my watch."

"Fuck," Hank said under his breath. In that moment, he quickly realized the magnitude of guilt Thompson had been carrying around with him for the last four years. The anger flowed right out of him, and his heart suddenly melted. He stood and wrapped his arms around his old friend. He rested his forehead against Thompson's and whispered, "You didn't let her down, Tommy. It was a brain aneurism. It was not your fault."

Thompson reached up and gripped Hank's forearms, which were now wrapped securely around his shoulders. "I think I'm slowly starting to believe that now," he said. "Garner was the one who—" Thompson stopped without finishing.

"—finally got through to you?" Hank asked, finishing the sentence for him.

Thompson turned around to face him, his rich green eyes dark and cloudy. He rested both hands on Hank's shoulders. "Prince, I know you did everything you could to try and help me, but Garner… for some reason he was able to make me see things more clearly. Things that were right in front of me, things I couldn't see on my own."

Hank's jealousy tried to creep in, and his heart broke a little bit more. He cringed at Thompson's admission that Garner was the one who finally helped him see things, but he knew he had to put those feelings aside for now. "It's okay," he said, trying to reassure Thompson. "Maybe you just needed someone that wasn't so close to the situation. Someone with no emotional involvement and nothing to lose."

Thompson was silent, apparently trying to find some words to express how he was feeling. When he spoke, it sounded like his voice was very far away. "I don't know, Prince. You're probably right. I was in such a dark place and so completely lost."

Hank watched a single tear slip from Thompson's right eye, and unable to resist the urge, he reached up and wiped the tear away with his thumb. Hank was totally taken off guard when Thompson leaned into the touch and covered Hank's hand with his own.

When Thompson brought Hank's palm to his mouth, gently kissed it, and then clutched it against his chest, Hank's stomach began to flutter. He had dreamed of a moment like this, and now that it was finally happening, it was unexpected, yet comfortable. He could feel

Thompson's rapidly beating heart against his palm and it was so intimate, like their two bodies were one.

Hank closed his eyes and tried to sort through his own feelings.

"You know, Prince," Thompson said in a low, hesitant voice. "I won't ever say that I regret giving up my life for Caroline. If I had to go back, I know I would do the same thing all over again. But... by saving her, I lost you, and that I'll regret until the day I die."

Hank had waited so many years to hear Thompson say those words. He grabbed him behind the neck with his free hand and brought their foreheads together again. Hank was now trembling and his legs were beginning to feel unsteady. Hearing those words made his heart soar, but deep down somewhere he was also feeling a great deal of apprehension. Was this real? What did it all mean?

Hank felt Thompson's hands gripping his shoulders, gently pushing him back. When they were far enough away from one another for their eyes to meet, Thompson stopped. "I'm so deeply sorry for abandoning you. I may be way out of line and I probably have no right to ask this of you, but can you ever forgive me?"

Hank felt the tears welling up behind his eyes threatening to break free at any moment. He thought he'd long ago moved on and all this was water under the bridge, but now he knew exactly how badly he had needed to hear these words. He tried to speak, but his voice cracked. All he could manage was a nod.

A wave came across Thompson and his dark and cloudy green eyes were now shining like emeralds, with the familiar flecks of citrine and gold Hank remembered from when they were kids.

Thompson's lips formed a playful smile. "Prince, do you remember that kiss we shared in the locker room on our last day of school?"

"I remember" was all Hank managed to choke out.

Thompson's face now broke into a broad smile. "It was my first kiss, and I was completely lost in it. Lost in you."

"Me too," Hank said, fondly remembering the scene in his head like it was yesterday.

Thompson stood and put his hands on Hank's biceps. "Prince, make me feel that way again."

Hank looked up into Thompson's sparkling eyes, unsure of what he'd just heard. "Wait. What? Say that again," he asked hesitantly.

"Kiss me again, Prince" was all Thompson said. "Please."

Hank couldn't believe his ears. He simply stared up into those gorgeous eyes trying to decide if he'd heard what he just heard or if he was going mad.

Thompson took both of Hank's hands and clutched them to his chest. "Please, Prince. I want to feel that way again."

"Fuck it," Hank murmured. He stood and cupped Thompson's head with his hands and pulled him closer. When their lips met, Hank felt lightning bolts running through his body. The inexperience and awkwardness that had been there with their first kiss was long gone. Hank had kissed a few men in his day and if Thompson asked to be kissed, by God he wasn't going to hold any punches.

When Hank's tongue pressed against Thompson's closed lips, Thompson freely opened to him. Hank explored Thompson's mouth just the way he'd done so many years ago, but with a renewed intensity. As their tongues flirted and danced, Hank thought that Thompson tasted every bit as magnificent as he did way back then. Hank melted into the feeling of Thompson's hands sliding urgently across his chest, over his pectorals, down to his waist, over his shoulders, and up and down his back.

Hank desperately needed to feel Thompson's warm skin against his hands, so he released his head long enough to grab Thompson's T-shirt and yank it out of his blue jeans. He raised it enough to get his hands under and explored every inch of the man's naturally muscular chest. Needing more, Hank lifted the shirt farther, and Thompson instinctively raised his arms as the thin cotton slipped over his head, grunting in apparent disapproval when their lips came apart long enough to get the shirt over his head.

Thompson did the same with Hank's shirt, and now they were both naked from the waist up, caressing smooth, hot skin.

Hank could feel Thompson's erection against his own as they explored every inch of each other's bodies, their movements getting more frantic by the second.

Hank broke the kiss once more and took Thompson by the hand and led him across the room to the couch. He shoved Thompson back onto the couch and then toed off his own shoes. He grabbed each of Thompson's feet one at a time and removed his boat shoes, never once breaking eye contact.

Hank then lowered himself on top of Thompson, straddling him at the waist. He placed his hands on each side of Thompson's head and hovered over him until their lips finally met again. They made out like teenagers, Thompson's hands anxiously moving over Hank's tanned chest.

Hank felt long sweeps of Thompson's hands up and down his back, his fingernails gently scratching as he moved in slow deliberate movements.

Hank quickly tossed the pillow cushions over the back of the couch and slid to Thompson's side. He bent his leg at the knee and draped it across Thompson's groin, resting it on his solid erection. Hank broke their kiss just long enough to look at Thompson more closely. The lines around his eyes that had developed and seemed to harden over the years were suddenly relaxed and smooth. The sparkle in Thompson's beautiful green eyes was back, and his entire face lit up when he smiled at Hank. Hank gently ran his fingers through Thompson's hair over and over while Thompson simply stared at him with a look of sheer contentment. Hank hadn't seen that look since they were kids, and his heart filled with joy that he could finally be the one who put it there.

Hank gently kissed Thompson again and felt Thompson's erection jump against his leg. He smiled and reveled in the fact that he was able to get that simple reaction out of Thompson.

"Penny for your thoughts," Thompson whispered.

Hank rolled his eyes and his smile broadened. "I was just thinking about how relaxed and happy you look right now, like the old Thompson. I haven't seen that look in so many years."

"That's because I am happy and relaxed," Thompson shared. "For the first time in a very long time," he added.

"I'm glad," Hank said. "But look, do you mind if this stops here?"

Thompson gave him a disappointed look.

"Please don't get me wrong," Hank tried to explain. "This is incredible, but I think we both need a little time to reflect on what has just happened and where it might go from here."

Thompson tilted his head to one side and waited.

"I don't want a one-night stand," Hank confessed. "If you're just experimenting, I'm not your guy."

Thompson lifted up and rested on his elbows. "Hell no. I'm not experimenting, and I don't want a one-night stand either," he said. "I imagine I've been waiting for you since high school, but Caroline, she needed...."

Before Thompson could finish the sentence, Hank rested his fingertip on his lips to quiet him. "Shhhh. I just think we need a little time to process all this. At least I know I do."

Thompson lay back down and closed his eyes. "I can wait," he said. "I've waited this long, I can certainly wait until you're ready."

"What do you mean waited this long?" Hank asked.

A deep red quickly flooded Thompson's face, and he turned away.

"Please don't turn away," Hank pleaded. "Talk to me."

Thompson turned back and looked Hank directly in the eyes. "I'm a virgin, Prince."

"What?" The shock on Hank's face must have been obvious because Thompson turned his head away again. "I mean... I thought... you and Caroline?"

Thompson explained that after Caroline's abuse they had tried to make love a couple of times, but she just couldn't follow through, so they had accepted it and gone on with their lives.

Thompson came back up and rested on his elbows again. "Don't you see, Prince? I never once thought about cheating on her or leaving her just because we weren't intimate. It's almost like somewhere deep, very deep down, I knew I belonged to you."

Hank's eyes welled with unshed tears, tears that had been building up since he'd lost his best friend so many years ago. He placed a gentle kiss on Thompson's lips and laid his head on Thompson's chest. Hank sighed when he felt Thompson's arms tighten around him, believing now that all this might actually be real.

THOMPSON OPENED his eyes and quickly closed them against the intrusion of morning. When he attempted to open them again, he squinted against the bright sunshine flooding the room. Hank was curled up to next to him in the same position in which they'd both fallen asleep. Hank's smooth, even breathing was comforting as he watched the particles of dust floating through the sunbeams from the skylight over the couch.

The night before, Thompson hadn't known what to expect when he'd camped out on Hank's front porch swing, finally ready to bare his soul. He'd almost lost his nerve more than once, but a quick call to Garner had given him the encouragement he needed to follow through with his plan. But this, he thought, looking down at Hank comfortably stretched out in his arms, was never in the realm of possibility as far as he had been concerned.

Once Hank had learned the truth, he'd been as understanding and supportive as he'd been when they were kids. But what surprised him the most was the intimacy they'd shared. It hadn't gone as far as Thompson would have liked, but it was incredible. Hank had taken control and Thompson had gotten lost in him, just he had so long ago. So lost that Hank could have done anything to him, and he would have begged for more. He hadn't wanted it to stop for fear that it may never happen again.

Lying quietly in the early morning hours with Hank tucked tightly under his arm, Thompson had nothing else to do but really think about that feeling of abandon he was experiencing.

Of course Hank was right to stop it where he had, but damn it felt good. I was always the strong one with Caroline, the one in control. Maybe that's why it feels so good to just let go with Hank and let him take the lead. I've been to hell and back over the last four years and damn it, I want to be happy. If Hank will have me, I want to see this through.

Thompson realized he was unconsciously stroking Hank's hair over and over, and he abruptly stopped, not wanting to wake him.

"Please don't stop," a sleepy voice mumbled.

Thompson smiled and started stroking again. "I'm sorry, did I wake you?" he whispered. "I didn't realize I was even doing it until it was too late."

Hank stretched his legs and arms out and appeared to be stifling a yawn. "You didn't wake me," he said. "I've been lying here for a while just listening to your heartbeat."

Thompson smiled again and kissed the top of Hank's head. "Good morning, Prince."

"Morning," Hank said as he looked up and matched Thompson's smile. "Sleep okay?"

Thompson thought for a moment. "The best night's sleep I've had in forever," he replied, knowing it was absolutely true.

"Me too," Hank added as he snuggled back down into Thompson's arms.

They both lay there quietly for the next few minutes, obviously content to be in each other's arms. Then Thompson heard an alarm coming from another area of the house. "Sounds like it's time for someone to get up."

Hank made a swatting motion like he was trying to turn off the alarm from the couch. "Damn alarm," he said. "It goes off automatically at the same time every morning."

As the shrill beeping bellowed through the quiet house, Hank sighed and started to stir. "Give me a second while I get my sledgehammer."

"Now, now, Prince. Don't go murdering your alarm clock. I don't know what the sentence is for that is, but you're way too pretty to go to jail. And besides," he added, "I'm hoping to get you back in my life; I don't want to lose you to some Bubba in prison before it ever happens."

Hank looked up at him and chuckled, his crystal-blue eyes full of amusement. "Well, Tommy boy, I see you still have that vivid imagination," he teased. "And just for the record, I'm not going anywhere."

Hank leaned up and gave Thompson a quick peck. "Let me turn off that wretched alarm and I'll make some coffee."

"Sounds good. Can I help?"

"Nope," Hank said, reaching down and grabbing last night's discarded T-shirt and putting it over his head. "Just relax and I'll be back in a few."

Hank got up and shuffled his stocking feet across the hardwood floors toward the other side of the house.

Thompson took this opportunity to enjoy a long morning stretch, and then he got up, doing the same with his T-shirt, and went in search of a bathroom. He thought he remembered seeing one off the foyer, so he went in that direction first. His memory served him well and just in the nick of time, too.

In the distance, he heard the shriek of what he assumed was the coffee grinder and followed the sound back to the kitchen. He walked up behind Hank and slid his arms around his waist, gently kissing Hank on the back of the neck. Hank lifted his shoulder and bent his head as he shivered.

"Note to self," Thompson whispered. "Hank is ticklish on the neck."

"Ha-ha," Hank responded as he poured water into the reservoir of the coffee pot and pressed the start button. "Just a couple more minutes."

He turned in Thompson's embrace and reached up on his toes and gave him a quick kiss.

"No fair," Thompson whined. "You brushed your teeth."

Hank chuckled. "My bathroom, top drawer on the right, you'll find a new toothbrush."

Thompson smiled. "That would be perfect if I knew where your bathroom was."

"Come on, man, it's off my bedroom," Hank teased.

"Oh yeah, that makes perfect sense. Now where's your bedroom?" Thompson asked.

"Down the hall, third door on the left," Hank replied with a hint of mischief.

"Hold that pose and I'll be right back."

"Hurry, the coffee will be ready momentarily."

Thompson saluted and turned on his heels. He found his way down the hall, peeking into each open door as he went. "Man," he said to himself. "This place looks like it's right out of a magazine. Nothing like my shabby two-bedroom bungalow."

Thompson found Hank's bedroom and was amazed how the massive floor-to-ceiling windows allowed the morning sunlight to completely flood the room. The king-size bed was all rumpled like it had been recently slept in, and not being able to control himself, Thompson lifted Hank's pillow, brought it to his face, and inhaled deeply. Hank's scent was strong, and Thompson reveled in it.

"Coffee's ready," he heard Hank yell from the kitchen.

"Be right there," he yelled back as he inhaled one last time, tossed Hank's pillow back on his bed, and found the bathroom.

Minutes later he was following the wonderful scent of freshly brewed coffee back to the kitchen. When he rounded the corner, he found Hank standing in the doorway with a steaming mug.

"Thanks," Thompson said, taking the hot mug from Hank. "This smells incredible."

Before he took his first sip, he leaned over and kissed Hank on the lips. Hesitant at first, but then he went all in and deepened the kiss. When he withdrew, Hank was smiling broadly, and his piercing blue eyes were sparkling like the bright blue sky.

"Thank you," Hank said. "That was nice."

"My pleasure."

They sat at the breakfast bar sipping their coffee, both of them seemingly deep in thought.

"You know?" Thompson said.

"I owe you…," Hank said at the exact same time.

They both looked at each other and laughed. "You go first," Thompson insisted.

"No you," Hank protested.

"Okay," Thompson said in obvious defeat. "I was just thinking. So much has happened in our lives, a lot of it out of our control and a good bit of it my inability to slay my own demons. But right here in this moment, I feel like we've never been apart. Prince, I know it's crazy, but what I'm trying to say is that we may have been apart physically, but I feel like we were never apart in mind and spirit."

Hank reached up and brushed the backs of his fingers down Thompson's cheek.

Thompson turned into the touch, reached up, and grabbed Hank's hand, kissing his palm, but not releasing it. "Your turn," he said.

"I was going to say I owe you an apology and wish I could go back and do things differently."

Thompson cocked his head to one side. "You owe me an apology? How so?"

"I shouldn't have given up on you all those years ago."

"Prince...."

Hank raised a finger. "Let me finish," he asked.

Thompson shut up and nodded.

"Thompson, I know you. I know you very well, and I should have known you would never have abandoned me without good reason. And I also know you've never ever felt sorry for yourself in all the years I've known you. So after Caroline died and you withdrew from everyone, including me, I should have known there was more to the story than grief alone."

"But you couldn't have known," Thompson countered.

"Yes!" Hank retorted. "But I *should* have known. And I should have followed my instincts and continued to try and reach you. You see, when Caroline died, I naively thought it might be a second chance for us. And on that day when I begged you to come back to me and you shut me out again, I was devastated. My pride kicked in and I vowed to never give you the power to hurt me again."

Thompson put his mug on the counter and stood. "I'm the one that's sorry, Prince, so sorry for hurting you. But if you'll let me, I'll spend the rest of my life making it up to you." Thompson dropped his head and brushed his lips gently across Hank's. "I love you, Prince. I think I always have."

Hank set his cup down and wrapped his arms around Thompson's neck. "I love you too."

Hank smiled seductively and took him by the hand. He led Thompson down the hall to the bedroom and the closer they got, the faster Thompson's heart raced. When they reached the bedroom and crossed the room to the bed, Hank once again covered Thompson's lips with his own. Hank turned him and guided him down to the edge of the bed and grabbed the hem of Thompson's T-shirt. Hank broke the kiss just long enough to get the shirt over Thompson's head before he continued his assault.

Every one of Thompson's nerve endings was on fire. His erection was now aching and begging to break free of his blue jeans, and his heart was racing in anticipation.

Thompson felt a gentle push and found himself lying on his back looking up at Hank. Hank pulled his own T-shirt up and over his head and tossed it aside, his broad, muscular chest now fully exposed. He unbuttoned his blue jeans and let them drop to the floor.

Never taking his eyes off Thompson, Hank stepped out of his jeans, removed his socks, and knelt down at Thompson's feet. Hank slowly unfastened Thompson's jeans, freeing his hardening length. Instinctively, Thompson lifted his torso off the bed while Hank slid his pants down and off and knelt between Thompson's legs.

When Hank gently rubbed Thompson's erection through his briefs, Thompson was surprised at how suddenly his arousal had built, a simple touch almost pushing him toward orgasm. He had to bite his bottom lip as he fought the instinctive urge to thrust his hips up. He took several deep breaths and willed himself to relax.

Hank slid his fingers through the opening of Thompson's boxers and took him in hand. No one, other than himself, had ever touched him in such an intimate way; the feeling was both foreign and exhilarating. When flesh met flesh, Thompson's heart literally skipped a beat and then sped to double time. Unable to resist the urge, he arched his back and pushed into Hank's grip.

When Hank started moving his hand up and down Thompson's length, an unfamiliar sound of pleasure escaped his lips. The feeling of Hank gripping him, applying just the right amount of pressure and moving so slowly and deliberately, was overwhelming his senses, almost taking his breath away. Hank slid his hand upward, stopping only to brush his thumb over the tip of Thompson's now-moist member, causing him to jerk uncontrollably. When Hank's hand moved back down, another moan escaped Thompson's lips. Hank's hand was now slick, and the feeling added yet another sensation to his overloaded brain cells. Thompson gazed into his lover's piercing blue eyes and then at his own dick as it glided through Hank's skillful hand. The sight was just too much, and he quickly put his hand on top of Hank's to stop him from moving in an attempt to ward off his pending orgasm. Hank gently nudged his hand away and whispered, "Come for me, Thompson."

Those four simple words of encouragement were all Thompson needed. As Hank's hand moved along his now almost painfully hard erection, he felt the orgasm building from the tips of his toes. The sensation worked its way up his legs at breakneck speed and headed right for his balls. When he opened his eyes and saw Hank's beautiful face gazing up at him, he lost it. He closed his eyes and threw his head back, clutching the bed linens in his fists while releasing a roar of ecstasy. He came like he'd never come before, the overwhelming pleasure indescribable.

The tension in Thompson's muscles began to relax, and he melted into the mattress, breathing harshly through parted lips that were curled into a smile as he savored the moment. When he opened his eyes again, panic caused his gut to roll when he found Hank gone. The unease quickly dissipated when Hank stepped out of the bathroom carrying a white cloth, a smile on his face. Hank slid Thompson's boxers down and off and then laid the cloth on top of Thompson's softening erection. It was warm and felt good as Hank slowly moved it around, thoroughly cleaning him. When Hank was through, he tossed the cloth aside and kissed Thompson's flat stomach. Hank's breath was warm and tickled the sensitive skin. Thompson couldn't stop the perpetual smile that had formed on his lips, and he opened his arms for Hank to join him.

"That one was just to take the edge off," Hank murmured as he laid his head on Thompson's chest. "The next round will go much more slowly, and I guarantee it will make your toes curl."

Thompson kissed the top of Hank's head. "The only thing I can ever imagine that will be better than what we just did is when I get to do it to you."

"Oh, man," Hank said with a chuckle. "It gets so much better, and I can't wait to show you everything you've been missing."

Thompson wrapped his arms around Hank and held him tight. "I promise I'll be an eager student." He rolled over on top of Hank and pressed their lips together.

The incredible pleasure Hank had just given him was still fresh in Thompson's mind, and without bothering to break their kiss, Thompson slid his hand under the waistband of Hank's briefs and gently wrapped his hand around Hank's manhood. They were about the same size, but the sensation of having another man in his hand was so absolutely unfamiliar to him, it was a major turn-on, and Thompson felt himself getting hard again.

Holding on to Hank firmly, Thompson could feel Hank's pulse vibrating against his palm as he started to move his hand slowly up and down Hank's entire length.

Thompson broke their kiss, leaned up on one elbow, and ran his hand lightly over Hank's chest, stopping at the nipple and pinching gently. Hank moaned with pleasure, encouraging Thompson to continue. He gave the other nipple the same treatment, rolling the taut nub between his fingers before moving his hand farther down Hank's body. When he got to Hank's tight stomach, he pushed Hank's underwear down and rolled over on top of him and straddled Hank at the knees.

He looked down at Hank, who was lying there seemingly so content and most definitely so beautiful. His Prince was smiling up at him so seductively it warmed Thompson's heart. Thompson intuitively knew what he wanted to do next, but his nerves were getting the best of him.

The idea of tasting Hank and sharing this intimacy with him had his mouth watering, but the overwhelming need to please Hank was the driving force. His gaze met Hank's, and Hank was looking at him with such emotion and encouragement, Thompson's apprehension quickly faded. He lowered himself down and hesitantly took Hank into his mouth. Hank hissed and Thompson immediately retreated. "Did I do something wrong," he whispered.

"No," Hank responded. "That felt incredible."

Thompson, very relieved, picked up where he'd left off. Hank's skin was silky smooth against his tongue, and the sensation of Hank in his mouth was strange at first but soon felt as natural as anything. He slipped down a little farther, and his gag reflex kicked in and he pulled up again.

"It's okay," Hank assured him. "Just take your time; it will get easier."

And of course Hank was right. Within minutes Thompson's mouth was sliding up and down Hank's length with Hank making the sexiest sounds Thompson had ever heard come out of another human being.

Hank hooked his arms under Thompson's armpits and urged him up until they were once again face-to-face. "That felt so good. And you're damn good at it."

Thompson couldn't help the pride he felt at finally doing something right for Hank. "Thanks, I really like it."

Thompson felt Hank's erection jerk while pressed tightly between their stomachs, which in turn forced a similar reaction out of him.

"This feels really good," Thompson whispered as he kissed Hank's neck and slowly started to rub his erection against Hank's.

Hank ran his fingers through Thompson's hair and down his back. "I've waited for this moment for most of my life," he replied.

In a very quick and impressive move, Thompson was now on his back and looking up at Hank. "Do you trust me?" Hank asked.

Thompson smiled. "With my life."

Hank placed a soft kiss against Thompson's lips. "Good. If I do anything that makes you uncomfortable or hurts, please tell me, okay?"

Thompson nodded. He was somewhat nervous, but he did trust Hank and that made all the difference.

"There's so much I want to show you," Hank said. "So much I want you to experience."

"I'm yours and I'm ready," Thompson whispered.

Hank reached into the bedside table and pulled out a small bottle of something and laid it on the bed next to them. "Lubrication," he said with a wink.

Thompson watched in awe as Hank moved down the bed and stopped when his head was even with Thompson's groin. Hank lightly brushed his hand over Thompson's erection, tickling and teasing. Thompson's erection jerked at the attention as Hank continued his assault. Thompson gasped when Hank took him into his mouth. Hank's tongue did wonderful things to him as his mouth slid up and down his length. Thompson had never had a blowjob and now he finally knew what he'd been missing. The sensation of the warm wetness was almost enough to push him over the edge again, but Hank seemed to sense that he was getting close and stopped.

Thompson heard the sound of the flip-top bottle being opened and felt a warm sensation on his erection. "Smells like strawberries," he said.

"Great nose," Hank teased. "It's edible and strawberry flavored."

Hank's hand was like silk sliding over his erection. He was almost lost in the feeling when he felt the same warm sensation at his opening. He instinctively tensed up at the odd feeling, but did his best to try and relax.

"That's it," Hank said. "Just relax. I won't hurt you. But remember, if you're the least bit uncomfortable, please tell me and I'll stop, okay?"

Thompson nodded and allowed Hank to spread his legs a little wider. He felt Hank's finger lightly massaging his opening, around and around as his other hand slid up and down his erection. Thompson began to tremble at the indescribable sensation. He was again fisting the linens as he arched his back, fighting the urge to thrust into Hank's hand.

Thompson felt another odd sensation as Hank's finger slipped inside him and slowly started moving in and out. He tried to determine if it was uncomfortable or not, but the blend of Hank's hand moving up and down and his finger moving in and out were the perfect combination. Just as Thompson was relaxing into Hank's actions, Hank did something inside of him and he saw stars. "Oh God," he moaned. "What the hell was that?"

"Feel good?" Hank asked.

"Hell yeah," Thompson said just as Hank moved his finger against the same spot again. This time he moaned with pleasure.

"It's called your prostate," Hank explained. "And it's a huge source of pleasure for men when stimulated correctly."

Thompson leaned up on his elbows and looked down at Hank. "Man, you've got to stop for a minute or I'm gonna lose it again."

Hank slowed but didn't stop completely.

"Come on, Hank," Thompson pleaded. "I want to taste you again, and I want you in my mouth when you come."

"You are a quick study," Hank teased as he flip-flopped positions, aligning his groin with Thompson's head. "This is called sixty-nine," he explained.

Thompson chuckled. "I'm not that naive. I have heard of sixty-nine, I just haven't done it."

Hank lay on his side and Thompson followed his lead. As Thompson took Hank into his mouth and slowly started to move, his gag reflex was almost nonexistent.

Hank took Thompson into his mouth as well, still gently moving his finger in and out of his opening, brushing against Thompson's prostate, driving him crazy with pleasure every time.

As Thompson's orgasm became imminent, he picked up his pace, frantically moving along Hank's length. Within minutes, Hank's moans led to frenzied thrusts, and Thompson felt a warm, slightly salty presence at the back of his throat. The idea that Hank had just come in his mouth along with the combination of what Hank was doing to him sent him over the edge as well. Both of them were now moving frantically, holding on to one another for dear life. Eventually their movements slowed and they both rolled over onto their backs in an attempt to catch their breath.

"Oh my God," Thompson groaned when he could finally speak. "That was incredible."

Hank spun around in the bed so their heads were together, and Thompson brought them close, wrapping both arms around Hank tightly.

"I hope your first time didn't disappoint," Hank murmured.

"Are you kidding? I couldn't have dreamed of anything better."

"And I still have a lot more to teach you," Hank said wryly.

"Like I said—"

"I know," Hank interrupted. "You're a quick study."

"You got it, Prince."

CHAPTER TWELVE

GARNER LEANED back against the diesel pump as he listened to the click-click-click of the numbers flipping while the amount of gallons climbed. He'd gotten very little sleep the night before and the entire morning he'd had this very uneasy feeling. Thompson hadn't shown up for work at his usual time and knowing what Thompson had been planning the night before put him very much on edge. He nervously glanced at his watch for the twentieth time in the last three hours. "Half past ten," he mumbled. He'd tried Thompson's cell phone numerous times, but it had gone straight to voice mail every time.

"Where in the hell could he be?" Garner paced back and forth on the dock while the pump clicked away, quietly cursing himself for getting so involved in Thompson's and Hank's lives. He didn't need this shit. He was supposed to be retired and following his dream, yet here he was waiting for a new engine and playing cupid with two guys he barely knew.

"Aw fuck," he said under his breath. *You're not really being fair. Neither of these guys asked for your help, although it was painfully obvious how much they needed it. You jumped in with both feet; no one to blame but yourself, Holt.*

Garner had just finished casting off the boat he'd been fueling and was making his way up the dock when he saw Thompson's truck pull into the parking lot. A feeling of relief washed over him that Thompson was at least alive. He picked up his pace, dying to know what had happened the night before.

When he reached the office, Thompson was standing in front of the large window, arms folded across his chest, gazing out over the marina.

"Thompson," Garner said softly, not knowing what to expect.

When Thompson turned around, Garner couldn't believe his eyes. Thompson looked ten years younger than he had the day before. He was flashing a broad smile and his emerald-and-citrine eyes were sparkling like Garner had never before seen before. Before Garner could say anything, Thompson bolted across the room, planted a huge kiss on Garner's lips, and picked him up and spun him around in circles.

Garner couldn't help but laugh, but he was starting to get dizzy, and now that he knew Thompson was all right, worry gave way to annoyance. "Put me down, you idiot," he yelled. "I'm pretty pissed at you."

Thompson stopped and put Garner down, tilting his head to one side, his smile never faltering.

"Pissed at me?" Thompson asked. "Whatever for?"

"Wait, let me get the list out," Garner said, making a motion to dig into his pocket. "Oh no, never mind, I forgot, I memorized it last night when I couldn't sleep while I was worrying about you."

Without giving Thompson an opportunity to speak, Garner babbled on. "Let me see. For starters, not calling me to let me know you were all right and for not answering your phone all morning."

Thompson's smile waned a little, but it didn't totally disappear. "I'm so sorry, Garner. You are absolutely right. But everything just happened so fast."

"No fucking excuse," Garner said. "It only takes a minute to dial a number." He paused and then added, "And now you've managed to make me fucking sound just like my mother. I hate you." Garner plopped down in the desk chair, exhausted and irate.

Thompson chuckled and stooped in front of his chair. "You're right, Gar. I wasn't thinking. I should have called you."

Garner felt some of the anger start to subside and the muscles in his face start to soften. "I guess you're forgiven. And for the record, I'm really glad you're okay."

Thompson stood and walked over to the window again. He spread his arms as wide as they could go. "I'm better than okay, Garner. For the first time in my adult life, I feel alive. Really alive."

Garner couldn't help but smile. "I guess I don't have to ask how everything went with Hank last night?"

Thompson turned and crossed the room again. "You don't but I'll tell you anyway," he said, sitting on the corner of his desk. "You were right, Hank does still have feelings for me, and we worked everything out."

"Yes!" Garner said. "I knew it. And…?"

Thompson's smile again broadened. "Let's just say I'm no longer a virgin."

"What?" Hank asked. "Man, you move quickly."

"Hell, I have a lot of years to make up for and I'm certainly not getting any younger," Thompson said wryly.

Garner fidgeted in his seat. "Look, I don't want the gory details, but you have to give me the *Reader's Digest* version since I'm sort of responsible."

Thompson chuckled. "That you are."

Thompson was just about finishing telling Garner about the events of the evening when the office door opened and Hank appeared.

Garner suddenly felt invisible. Hank crossed the room without even acknowledging him and took Thompson into his arms. He pressed him against the window, holding both hands over his head, and kissed him good.

It's a good thing that window has a one-way glass, or they'd be putting on one hell of a show.

As Garner closely watched them together, he felt a sense of pride. He realized that all the cursing he had done at himself this morning for getting involved in their lives was for naught. He'd do it again in a heartbeat if it meant these two guys would be happy.

Tired of waiting for the kiss to end, Garner cleared his throat. Thompson and Hank stopped and turned, Thompson blushing a bright red and Hank appearing to be in complete shock that they weren't alone.

Before anyone could speak, the VHF radio sounded, and Garner jumped out of his seat. "I'll get that."

"No!" Thompson protested. "Let me. You've been here all morning alone."

"No really," Garner said. "I insist."

Hank finally joined the conversation. "Let Thompson get it, Garner. It will give us a moment to talk."

Obviously outnumbered, Garner handed the radio to Thompson and sat back down.

"Be right back," Thompson said, pecking Hank on the cheek and bouncing out of the office.

There was an awkward silence before Garner spoke up. "I hear congratulations are in order."

Hank nodded. "Thanks to you."

"I'm really happy for you guys," Garner said as he nervously shuffled through some papers on the desk.

He hated the tension between them and needed to find some way to make it right. He needed to start by finding some way to apologize for being an ungrateful and insensitive ass the last time they were together. But before Garner could decide how to say what he needed to say, Hank crossed the room and rested a hand on his shoulder. "I owe you an apology. I have a tendency to be a little possessive, and I had no right to treat you like a child. Please forgive me."

Garner reached up and laid his hand on top of Hank's. "No," he argued. "I'm the one who owes you the apology. You were just being a good friend. You drove all the way back here to check on me, and I was an ass. I'm really sorry for the way I behaved."

"Fine," Hank said, stepping back and opening his arms. "We were both asses and now it's behind us." Garner smiled, stood up, and stepped into his embrace.

"Should I be concerned?" Thompson asked, standing in the open doorway with a smile as broad as his chest.

"Been there. Done that," Hank said wryly. "Not a thing to worry about."

"Hey! That's not fair," Garner yelled. "I know I suck at anything that even remotely resembles a relationship, but am I that bad?"

"Now, now, boys," Thompson said. "Can't we all get along?"

"I'll try if he'll try," Hank said.

"And I'll try if he'll try," Garner added.

Thompson opened his arms and both men stepped into them. "Then it's settled; we're all just one big happy family from now on."

IT WAS a Friday afternoon in December, and the snowbirds had long ago made their treks south, so the marina was very quiet. Garner had gone with Hank on a rescue, and Thompson was sitting at his desk mindlessly signing the checks for the past week. He'd kept his promise to stay on top of the paperwork and found it much easier to manage the marina when everything was in order.

The last four weeks had passed in the blink of an eye, and he was as happy as he'd ever been. He and Hank were solid as a rock, and Hank was even starting to hint that Thompson should move into his house but hadn't really come out and asked him yet. If and when he did, Thompson would say yes, of course. They were spending every night together anyway, so why not make it official?

For the first time in a long time he was looking forward to the future, and Garner had had so much to do with that. The sad part was that Garner's engine was due to arrive by the end of the week, and once Bubba installed it, Garner would surely be moving on.

The three of them had become quite good friends, and Thompson knew he was going to miss Garner terribly. Garner had not only become a cherished confidant, but he and Hank had become sounding boards regarding his marina business. Together they'd identified and put into motion several improvements that would make the marina a better one, including renovating the shower house and laundry rooms. Garner had even convinced Thompson that he should start delivering Krispy Kreme donuts along with the newspapers to the marina guests each morning. Thompson knew he and Hank were both going to take it hard when they had to cast Garner off on his journey.

Thompson was snapped out of his thoughts by the ringing of the telephone. He lifted the phone to his ear. "Good afternoon, Thundercloud Marina, this is Thompson."

"Is this Thompson… Gray?" the soft but raspy voice on the other end of the line asked.

"Speaking."

"Good afternoon. My name is Sherri Peters, and I'm the head nurse at Hospice Savannah."

"Yes, ma'am," Thompson said, immediately thinking of his parents. When they had planned their estate, they had both chosen Hospice Savannah as the place they wanted to end up if the situation ever presented itself. As it turned out, they both died there, his mother first of colon cancer and his father of a stroke less than a year later. They had received excellent care when they were there, and every year since they'd died, Thompson had made a donation in their names. So his first thought was that it must be time to write that check.

"Mr. Gray, do you know a Beatrice Reilly?"

Thompson sat up straight in his chair. *Caroline's mother!* Just the mention of that woman's name made his pulse race and his stomach turn.

"Are you still there, Mr. Gray?"

"Ah yes, ma'am," Thompson replied. "I know a Beatrice Reilly, but I haven't seen or spoken to her in many years."

"I understand you were married to her late daughter Caroline Reilly Gray."

Thompson lowered his head. Old memories were trying very hard to bore their way back into his very existence, but he knew he had to hold them at bay.

"Yes, I was."

"Well, sir. Mrs. Reilly's a patient here and very near the end of her life, and she's listed you as her next of kin."

"What? Why me?"

"You are her son-in-law and, according to her, her only living relative."

Thompson fell silent. The nurse cleared her throat, bringing Thompson back to the conversation. "Look, I'm very sorry to hear that she's dying, but like I said, we haven't spoken or seen one another in many years."

"That may very well be the case, Mr. Gray, but she's asking to see you."

"See me?"

"Yes, sir."

"Why?"

"She hasn't shared the why of it with me, Mr. Gray. But in my experience, when people are near the end they sometimes want to right a wrong or make amends in some way or, in many cases, just say goodbye."

"I really don't think that would be such a good idea," Thompson replied.

"I understand," the nurse said. "The decision is yours, but I told her I would make the call, and I did. Should you change your mind, she is in room two fifteen. Have a nice day, Mr. Gray."

"Thank you" was all Thompson said as he hung up the phone.

Thompson sat in silence for a few minutes, contemplating what he should do about Beatrice. Suddenly the office door swung open, and Hank and Garner came in with their usual boisterous banter.

Hank must have recognized the look of unrest on Thompson's face, because he was at his side in a flash. "Thompson. What's wrong?"

"I just hung up to the phone with Hospice Savannah."

"Why?" Hank asked, resting his hand on Thompson's shoulder.

"Apparently Beatrice Reilly is near death and is asking for me."

"Caroline's mother?" Hank asked.

"Yep," Thompson said, explaining to Hank and Garner what the nurse had told him.

Garner looked at Hank and then at Thompson. "What are you gonna do?"

"I told the nurse I didn't think it would be such a good idea."

Apparently Garner was slipping into psychiatrist mode. "And how does that make you feel?"

"I don't quite know yet, Dr. Phil," Thompson said with a slight smile. "But for starters, it's pissing me off."

"I hear you loud and clear," Garner said. "I'll just head back to my boat and let you two deal with this."

"No," Thompson said. "Stay, I didn't mean it like that."

Garner stood and made his way to the door. "Look, you guys are two grown men and you have each other now. You can work through this without my help."

Hank squeezed Thompson's shoulder. "He's right, Tommy boy. We can get through this."

Garner smiled, opening the door. "I'll catch up with you later."

Thompson looked up at Hank. "What do I do?"

Hank pulled Thompson up from his chair and wrapped his arms around him. "We'll figure this out together." He took him by the hand and led him to the couch and they sat side by side.

"So what are you most afraid of?" Hank asked.

Thompson thought for a moment but he knew the answer immediately. "Prince, for the first time in so long, I'm looking forward to the future. I'm so happy with you, but I'm terrified of going back to that dark place."

Hank took his hand. "I won't let that happen again. I promise you that."

"I just don't see what good could come from it," Thompson said.

"What about closure?" Hank asked. "Like the nurse said, maybe she just wants to thank you for taking such good care of Caroline."

"Maybe," Thompson agreed.

"Look, I can't tell you what to do, but think about this," Hank said. "What if you don't go and you regret it? You don't get a do-over with this one."

"Good point," Thompson said. "I don't like the idea of seeing her and dredging up the past, but I think I need to go."

Hank stood. "I think that's the right decision, and I'll drive you if you like."

Thompson stood as well. "Thank you, but I think I need to do this on my own."

Thompson thought he saw a flash of disappointment on Hank's face, but it was gone just as quick as it came. He thought about changing his mind and allowing Hank to go with him, but he knew deep down he needed to prove to himself he was strong enough to handle it alone.

THOMPSON WALKED into Hospice Savannah and immediately thought of his parents. It was the first time he'd been there since his father died, and the smells and sounds triggered quite a few old memories.

Because he and Caroline had spent so much time there when his parents were sick, he was pretty familiar with the layout. The two-story building was built in the shape of a cross with a one-story atrium in the center. He walked past the reception desk and the elevator bank on autopilot, heading to the same stairwell he traveled up and down every day when his parents were there.

When he reached the second floor, he followed the corridor signs indicating rooms 210 to 220. At the head of each wing was a nurse's station, and he stopped and asked for Nurse Peters. After a few minutes, a very attractive woman of average build with blue eyes and very chiseled features approached him.

"Thank you for coming, Mr. Gray."

"How did you know it was me?" Thompson asked.

"Because you look just like you do in your picture."

Thompson started to ask where she'd seen a picture of him, but he decided to let it slide for now. "If you don't mind my asking, what is she dying of?"

Nurse Peters hesitated. "With today's HIPAA laws, Mr. Gray, we have to be very careful about what medical information we divulge, but Mrs. Reilly signed a medical release, and since you're listed as her next of kin, I think we're covered."

Thompson waited.

Nurse Peters's expression turned to one that could only be described as sadness. "I'm very sorry to inform you that Mrs. Reilly is dying from complications from AIDS."

Thompson felt weak in the knees. "How can that be?"

"From what she told me, she contracted it from her late husband, who died before he even knew he was infected with HIV. Apparently he was quite promiscuous."

Promiscuous? That's one way of putting it. Thompson felt lightheaded and shaky. Now he wished he had allowed Hank to come with him, if only to catch him before he hit the floor. *You can do this, Thompson. Man up.*

He straightened his back, bit his lower lip, and steadied himself on the counter of the nurse's station. "Can I see her now?"

"Certainly, right this way. But I must warn you; if you've not seen her in years, she will not look like you remember her."

Thompson nodded as he followed the nurse to Beatrice's room.

When the nurse opened the door, Thompson was struck with a double blow. Beatrice looked like a frail old woman. *My God, she can't be any older than*—he did the math—*fifty-seven or fifty-eight, yet she looks like she is ninety.*

He silently studied her as she lay still in her hospital bed. She was so thin he could barely see an outline of her body under the blankets. If he hadn't seen her head and shoulders, he would have sworn the bed was empty.

Oxygen tubes were coming out of her nose, and an IV was at her bedside pumping God only knew what into her body. She was ghostly white, her hair sparse and very thin, and her eyes, although closed, were deep set in her head. She looked like a frail baby bird that had fallen out of its nest just after hatching.

But the second blow hit him the hardest. It was a picture of him and Caroline on their wedding day, placed on the table beside her hospital bed.

Tears suddenly stung the back of his eyes, but he wouldn't allow them to drop. He was going to listen to what the woman had to say and be out of here as soon as he could. He was so ready to forget and move on with his life.

He stepped into the room and up to Beatrice's bedside. She slowly opened her eyes and attempted to smile. "Thompson," she said in a strong Southern drawl. "I'd hoped you'd come."

"Hello, Beatrice," Thompson said with as much compassion as he could muster.

"Son, you haven't changed one iota," Beatrice said, now gasping for breath between words. "Just as handsome as ever."

Thompson forced a smile and said, "Thank you, ma'am."

Beatrice lifted one tiny arm out from under the covers and fidgeted with her oxygen tubes as she tried to speak. "I'm sure they told you my—" She coughed a couple of times, apparently attempting to clear her throat. "—life is nearing its end. But I couldn't move on to wherever I'm going without thanking you for taking care of my baby as you did."

Thompson stiffened. "She was my best friend and then my wife, Beatrice," he explained. "I would have moved heaven and earth to protect her."

A tear slipped out of Beatrice's eye, and she turned her head away.

Thompson's heart started to melt and he quickly realized that this woman hadn't asked for her plight in life. Maybe she was just a victim, like Caroline, and wasn't strong enough to get the help she needed to get out of the situation.

Thompson laid a hand on her forearm. "It's okay, Beatrice. I did what I did for Caroline because I loved her."

Beatrice looked back at him with lifeless eyes. "You did more than love her. Thompson, you saved her... from him."

Thompson froze. "What do you mean, I saved her?" he asked, horrified at what she was alluding to.

"I wish I would have been as strong as Caroline," Beatrice said, her thin lips curving into a slight smile. "I heard them through the walls; she kicked and fought him every time. Of course he always won, but he never came out of her room without battle scars."

Thompson's blood pressure and his anger were quickly rising. Was he hearing right? Was Beatrice saying she knew about the abuse and did nothing to stop it?

Thompson withdrew his hand to avoid snapping her birdlike forearm in two. "Are you telling me you knew?"

"I knew," she responded coldly.

"And you did nothing?"

"I was barely surviving myself." She gasped, fighting for oxygen. "What could I have done for Caroline?"

Thompson couldn't control his anger, and he was on the verge of losing it. "You could have told someone!" he yelled. "Like the police or child protective services. A minister maybe. Anyone who could have helped both of you."

"Then everyone would have known what was going on," Beatrice barked back with renewed strength. "We were raised not to air our dirty laundry," she drawled. "My God, people would have talked."

"Fuck people, Beatrice," he screamed at the top of his lungs. "You allowed your teenage daughter to be sexually abused by your husband to save face? You ruined her life. And mine as well."

"What about my life?" she snapped back. "It was ruined right along with yours and Caroline's."

"Damn you! That was your choice," Thompson snapped. "Caroline didn't get a choice and neither did I."

By this time Sherri Peters was standing in the doorway. "I'm sorry, Mr. Gray, I'm gonna have to ask you to leave. I've already called security."

"Gladly!" Thompson said as he turned back to Beatrice. "I hope you rot in hell for what you did to Caroline and me. As far as I'm concerned, you got exactly what you deserved. Damn you!"

He looked again at the picture of him and Caroline on the bedside table and snatched it up, waving it in her face. "You don't deserve this."

He headed for the door and then abruptly stopped when he heard his name. He cast a quick glance over his shoulder. "I have nothing more to say to you! Christ, woman, how could you have been so heartless? Damn you!" he said, slamming his fist right through the wall.

Thompson angrily made his way down the hall. *I can't breathe.* He felt like he was suffocating. *I need air now!*

He picked up his pace, and by the time he reached the stairwell, he was running at full speed. Taking the stairs two at a time, Thompson quickly reached the ground floor and pushed the door open without stopping. He bolted across the sun-filled atrium, dodging everything in his path and finally through the front doors, gasping for any bit of air he could get into his burning lungs. Angry, confused, and out of breath, he sat on a bench and dropped his head between his legs, trying not to hyperventilate.

Bits and pieces of his conversation with Beatrice started ringing in his ears, but he fought hard to block them out, focusing only on his next breath.

The burning in his lungs slowly started to subside as his breathing returned to normal, but the anger and disgust were still very much front and center. Images of Caroline's tear-stained face after each time she'd been abused flooded his memory. Tears threatened, welling in his eyes, but he blinked them away. "Not here," he mumbled and scanned the cold concrete parking lot. Pushing the horrible images and memories down, Thompson stood on shaky legs and made his way to his truck. He dug his keys out of his pocket and pressed the "unlock" button.

Once behind the wheel, he realized that the fingers on his right hand were bleeding, but he ignored them as he struggled to get the key into the ignition. He hissed at the stinging pain as he wiped his knuckles on his blue jeans. He took a deep breath, opening and closing his throbbing fist several times, and it still took a few attempts, but he finally got the engine started.

The next thing he knew, he was again fumbling with his keys, but this time he was at his own front door. The ride home was a blur of color and sound. Mechanical. But somehow he'd been able to maneuver his way through the streets without thinking, or perhaps refusing to think. He let himself in and nearly collapsed as he headed for the couch. He dropped down with a thud, his legs finally giving out on him.

Cradling his head in his hands, he shook it from side to side.

She knew. The bitch knew and she did nothing. What kind of parent would let their daughter go through all that just to save face and avoid a scandal?

Thompson squeezed his head between his hands until it hurt. A long, agonized sound escaped him as the weight of it all crushed down on him. "Gone," he screamed. "That bitch took half my life."

Rage surged through Thompson like wildfire. He screamed until his throat was raw, his cheeks damp from angry tears. So many wasted years. So many missed opportunities. How could Beatrice have done that to them?

Thompson's cell phone rang again, for at least the fifth time, and Hank's number once again flashed across the screen. This time he'd calmed down enough to answer it.

"Prince?"

"Thank God, Thompson, I've been worried sick."

"Prince, my entire life has been one big fucking cover-up."

"Where are you, Thompson?"

"Home."

"Stay on the line with me," Hank ordered. "I'm on my way."

"She knew, Prince," Thompson said. "She knew and she did nothing."

"About what?"

Thompson tried to answer but his throat constricted, and he could only sit and stare at the wall beyond.

"About what, Thompson?" Hank asked again. "The abuse? She knew about the abuse?"

"Yes," Thompson finally squeezed out and dropped the phone. He leaned back on the couch and looked up to the heavens.

I'm so sorry, Caroline. We were just kids, and we didn't know what else to do. But she was your mother and an adult. She could have done something. I'm so sorry.

Thompson closed his eyes with a heavy heart as the all too familiar darkness started to seep in all around him. He tried to fight it, but eventually gave in, accepting the darkness as part of him, something he would never shed. *How could I have been so stupid as to think I could have actually had a chance at a new life?*

Strangely enough, as he accepted his lot in life and continued to stare upward, there was no anger, no tears, but a sense of calm that descended over him.

AS SOON as the line went dead, Hank did the only other thing he could think of and hit the speed dial for Garner.

"Did you find him?" Garner asked, evidently checking the caller ID.

"Yes, and it's bad, Garner." Hank's voice cracked with the well of emotion. "Thompson said Caroline's mother knew about the abuse and did nothing. He thinks his life has been one big cover-up."

"Shit," Garner cursed. "This could be all it takes to send him right back into a death spiral."

"Please," Hank begged, unable to control his sobs. "Meet me at Thompson's house? I can't do this alone."

"I'm on my way. Hank?"

"Yeah."

"Pull yourself together before you get there. He needs us, and we need to be strong."

"I'll try. Please hurry!"

"I'll be there in under ten minutes."

"What do I say when I get there?"

"Just be with him and comfort him. I'll know more about what to do when I get there."

Hank grabbed his keys and slammed the front door behind him, not bothering to even lock it.

"I shouldn't have encouraged him to go," he muttered while getting in his truck. "Just for once, Hank, why didn't you just keep your big mouth shut?"

Earlier that evening, after four hours of not hearing from Thompson, Hank had tried Thompson's cell phone numerous times with no success. He'd hoped that maybe he was having a nice long visit with Beatrice and had turned his ringer off on his phone. But something hadn't felt right....

Hank had been about to dial Thompson for the umpteenth time when his cell phone rang first. "Oh thank God!" But he'd looked at the caller ID and had been disappointed to see Garner's name on the display.

"Garner."

"Hey, man. Just calling to see how the visit with Caroline's mother went."

"I don't know," Hank said. "He's not home yet."

"Oh," Garner replied with surprise in his voice. "Have you heard from him?"

"He's not answering his cell, and I'm really starting to get worried. I knew I should have gone with him."

"Come on, Hank," Garner assured him. "Thompson is stronger now. You're going to have to give him a little room to grow."

"I know. I know," Hank responded, "but he's just so vulnerable when it comes to Caroline and her family. Plus, something just feels off, call it a gut feeling, I don't know."

"Let's not overreact," Garner said. "Maybe he's getting the closure he needs and everything will be okay."

"I sure hope so," Hank said, feeling very apprehensive about the whole damn thing. "Let me go, Garner. I'm gonna try and call him again, and if he doesn't answer, I'm going to his house, and if he's not there, I'm going over to the hospice place."

"Okay, but keep me posted."

"Will do. Gotta go."

As Hank sped over to Thompson's house, his nerves were definitely on edge, and the fear of not knowing what to expect was eating him alive.

Whatever condition he's in, I've got to get through to him. I will not fail this time.

Hank pulled into Thompson's driveway, his heart hammering, and bolted up the front steps. The front door was wide open, keys still dangling from the lock. Hank found Thompson sitting on the couch, staring unblinkingly into space.

Hank crossed the room and sat down next to Thompson, who continued to look straight ahead. When he laid a hand on Thompson's leg, Thompson jumped as if he were startled.

He looked at Hank with a surprised expression. "Hank. When did you get here?"

"Just now," he whispered. "Thompson, are you okay?"

Thompson studied Hank for a moment, shrugged, and then shook his head. "I don't know."

"What do you mean, you don't know?"

"I think I may be losing my mind."

"You're not losing your mind. Talk to me," Hank pleaded.

Thompson shifted on the couch to face Hank, a confused expression on Thompson's handsome face. "One minute I was feeling like I was quickly slipping back into that very dark place and wasn't going to survive this, and then the next minute this calm came over me and I heard Caroline's voice…. She helped me."

Garner rushed through the front door, looking back and forth between Hank and Thompson and then joining them on the couch.

"Garner," Thompson said very calmly. "What are you doing here?"

"Oh, I don't know," Garner said. "I thought you might need a friend right about now."

"Thanks, but I think I'm okay."

"Good to hear," Garner said cautiously. "What were you just saying about Caroline?"

Thompson laid his hand on top of Hank's, which was still resting on his leg. "I think her spirit or whatever was here. I never saw her, but I just heard her in my head like she was right here."

Hank looked at Garner with a concerned look while Thompson continued his story.

"She told me how sorry she was that she wasn't able to deal with the abuse on her own and how unfair it was that she'd burdened me with it as well. She also said how happy and safe I made her feel and how sorry she was that I'd sacrificed my happiness for hers. But more importantly she said it was my turn to live. My time. She said that Hank and I are meant to be together and that I needed to put all the heartache, including her, in the past and leave it there."

"Well," Garner said. "That Caroline's one smart cookie. I couldn't have said it any better myself."

Thompson squeezed Hank's hand and smiled. He leaned over and placed a gentle kiss on his lips and rested his head against Hank's. "I think it's all finally over. I love you, Prince."

"I love you too."

IN THE predawn hours of the day that Garner was finally going to continue his journey, Thompson chuckled and tightened his hold when Hank shivered and snuggled up closer against his chest.

"What are you doing awake?" Hank said in a sleepy voice, looking over at the clock. "It's four thirty in the morning."

"Been up thinking for the last couple of hours."

"About Garner?"

Thompson kissed the top of Hank's head. "I just can't believe he's actually leaving us today."

"I know how you feel, but we knew he wouldn't stay."

"I know," Thompson agreed. "I just hoped, ya know, he'd change his mind."

Hank looked up and smiled. "Yeah, me too."

Hank brought his knee up and rested it on top of Thompson's groin. "Looks like something else is awake as well."

Thompson thrust up a couple of times and tightened his hold on Hank again. "Yep, that head's been doing a little thinking of his own as well."

"Oh I'm dying to hear this," Hank said wryly as he slid his leg up and down Thompson's length.

Thompson smiled. "All in good time."

Hank had proved to be a patient, sensitive, and very loving teacher over the last few weeks, and he'd opened Thompson's eyes up to so many wonderful things, things that just felt so damn good. And in return, Thompson had tried to be as open and adventurous as Hank was, and so far, he'd never been disappointed. Of all the things they had done, Thompson loved being inside Hank the most. He felt closest to him when they were joined as one, and Hank really seemed to be into it as well. But lately he'd been curious about what it would feel like to have Hank inside of him. He loved it when Hank did that thing with his finger. It always drove him mad, and he wanted to experience everything that Hank wanted to teach him. He really wanted to do it as much for Hank as he did for himself, but he just didn't know how to bring it up.

While Thompson had drifted off in thought, Hank had been softly caressing his erection, and he was now fully erect and ready to go. Hank climbed on top of him and Thompson could feel that Hank was just as hard.

Hank obviously had plans of his own and was attempting to slide down to give his lover's erection some attention when Thompson grabbed him under the arms and pulled him back up. "Not so fast," he said. "I like you on top of me."

"I like being on top of you, 'cause I get to do this," Hank said, quickly moving down just enough to force his erection between Thompson's legs. Thompson opened just a little and then closed his legs tightly against Hank's erection. Hank gently thrust in and out while rubbing Thompson's erection resting between their stomachs.

"I love the feeling of you thrusting like that," Thompson said. "What does it feel like when I'm inside of you?"

"Amazing," Hank whispered. "In the beginning as you work yourself inside me, it burns a little bit. Then when you enter me completely, it's a strange feeling of well… fullness. But as soon as I relax around you, the fullness turns pleasurable. And then when you begin to move inside me, my nerve endings ignite and my world comes unraveled."

"I want to feel that," Thompson whispered.

Hank's piercing blue eyes were now filled with a look of desire Thompson hadn't recognized before. "Are you sure?"

"I'm sure," Thompson said. "What do I do?"

Hank eased off him and reached into the bedside table for the lubricant. "Just relax and let me take care of everything. The preparation for your first time is the most important."

Hank slid down, taking the covers with him. Thompson watched as Hank urged him to open his legs and bend them at the knee.

Thompson jumped a little when he heard the flip-top of the lubricant and then the squish as Hank slicked up his fingers.

Thompson closed his eyes when he felt Hank's finger circling his opening and tried to relax. Hank slid one finger gently in and held it there for a few minutes. He took Thompson's erection in his other hand and slowly started to move. Thompson had done this much before and he loved it. When his body began to relax against the invasion, he started to move in time with Hank's rhythm as Hank started to move his finger gently in and out.

Thompson felt a slight burn as Hank slid a second finger inside him. But as with the first, after a few minutes, he started to relax around the finger and the burn diminished. With two fingers now inside him and Hank sliding up and down his length, he laid a hand on top of Hank's to slow his movements to control his pending orgasm.

The burn was a little greater with an added pinch when Hank slid a third finger in, but Hank held them in place without moving and allowed Thompson the time he needed to adjust to the increased stretch and burn.

Hank had been right. His nerve endings were starting to spark, and Thompson quickly realized how connected his body was. Every movement by Hank inspired another movement to counteract.

"I think you're ready," Hank whispered. "You okay?"

Trying to hide his nervousness, Thompson nodded and offered a weak smile. He laid his head back and closed his eyes. He wanted this, wanted to feel Hank deep inside him, but he was worried he wouldn't be able to handle Hank's full girth.

He heard the tearing of foil and lifted his head again to see Hank rolling a condom onto his erection. "It that necessary?" he asked. "I haven't used one with you."

"I think it is," Hank answered. "I've been with other people. You haven't. And although I'm negative and tested regularly, we can't take any chances. We'll get tested together soon, and if all goes well, we can do away with them."

Thompson laid his head back down and closed his eyes once more. He again heard the squish of the lubricant, Hank obviously getting himself ready.

Thompson felt a chill run up his spine when Hank lifted his legs and rested them on his shoulders. He took a long deep breath and tried to relax.

The next thing he felt was Hank at his opening, gently but firmly pushing against him. His heart rate sped up with anticipation, and he fought the urge to tighten against the intrusion. Hank pushed in farther, and Thompson hissed under his breath. As he'd suspected, three fingers were nothing compared to Hank's girth. The burn and stretch was way more intense, but he bit his bottom lip and pushed through the pain.

"You okay?" Hank asked.

Thompson didn't answer, but he nodded.

"Put your hands on the backs of my legs and help guide me," Hank murmured. "If it hurts, push against my legs and I'll stop."

Thompson placed his hands on the back of Hank's thighs as instructed and had to admit he felt a little more in control.

Hank must have sensed the initial burn was probably subsiding and he pushed in a little more.

Thompson hissed and pushed against Hank's legs when the pain became more intense.

"We don't have to do this," Hank said. "We can stop now."

"No," Thompson protested. "I want to. I just need you to take it slow."

Hank stilled and took Thompson in hand. "We can take it however you like." Hank started sliding his hand up and down Thompson's length with steady, even strokes.

The wonder of Hank inside him and stroking him at the same time was an indescribable combination, and within seconds, Thompson felt himself relaxing. With the pain now quickly lessening, Thompson felt so full. The feeling was strange but not uncomfortable.

With one more slight push, Hank was all the way in, and to Thompson's surprise, there was no pain with the last push, only more of the strange feeling of fullness, a sensation not altogether unpleasant.

As Hank slowly withdrew, the fullness turned to an empty feeling and Thompson suddenly wanted Hank back inside him. With his hands still on the backs of Hank's thighs, Thompson pulled Hank back inside in one continuous move.

It was during that move that Hank brushed against that magical spot that drove Thompson crazy. A loud moan escaped his lips and he threw his back, his eyes rolling into his head.

"Prince!" Thompson hissed.

Hank froze.

"Noooo!" Thompson begged. "Don't stop. Feels so good."

Hank started to move again, and Thompson had a hard time comprehending the sensations that were invading his body.

When one movement felt the slightest bit strange or uncomfortable, the countermovement sent him over the edge with pleasure. Thompson's head was now thrashing from side to side as Hank moved in and out of him with quicker, shorter strokes. Thompson felt like he might implode at any minute.

Thompson's orgasm was quickly building from somewhere deep inside him, and Hank was now suddenly trembling as well, the early sign of his impending orgasm. Thompson leaned up, rested on his elbows, and froze. When their eyes met, the world went away and it was just the two of them. Hank's movements quickly became sporadic and desperate. The sight of Hank coming inside him, mouth open and head thrown back, was the most beautiful thing Thompson had ever seen. Hank came with a loud roar, and Thompson took himself in hand and pumped frantically as Hank continued to move inside him. When he came his entire body erupted with pleasure as he yelled Hank's name. Hank collapsed on top of him.

"I love you, Thompson Gray," Hank whispered as he placed a gentle kiss on Thompson's lips.

"You've awakened me, and you'll always be my Prince Charming. I love you, Hank."

Hank slid off Thompson and rested at his side. Thompson snuggled up next to him and laid his head on Hank's chest.

As they lay there, sated, the sun started to peek above the horizon, and Thompson tightened his hold on Hank. The room slowly filled with a soft orange glow, and together, completely secure in each other's embrace, they watched the sunrise over Savannah.

EPILOGUE

"WHY DID you have to pick the coldest damn day since the summer to leave," Hank whined to Garner, clinging to Thompson for whatever warmth he could get.

"Quit your whining," Garner said wryly. "I need to get down south before winter really kicks in. And besides, I thought towboat captains were supposed to be tough."

Hank puffed out his chest. "I am tough, you shit, I'm just cold."

Thompson listened to the usual back-and-forth banter the two of them had fallen into, and it saddened him more than anything that he might never hear it again. Thompson hadn't said very much this morning because he didn't think he could speak without his voice cracking. But he sensed that Hank knew how difficult this was for him, so he'd taken up the slack and talked enough for both of them.

Thompson had known he was going to take Garner's departure pretty hard, but he had no idea it was going to be this hard. Garner had been the only one able to save him from himself. This man had also brought Hank back to him. Thompson would be indebted to him for the rest of his life.

"What do you think, Thompson?" Garner asked. "Thompson?"

"I'm sorry, what?"

"I was just asking Hank if he thought I could make it as far as Ossabaw Island today."

Thompson looked out over the horizon. "Probably," he said. "You have the tide in your favor for the next four hours. So yeah, I think you can make it."

Garner stood in the cockpit, listening to his new engine. "Listen to that," he said. "She's purring like a kitten."

The three of them stood there in silence, looking everywhere but at each other, not one of them willing to say goodbye first.

Garner finally broke the painful silence. "I guess it's that time," he said with a hint of sadness in his voice. Hank offered Garner a hand, and he climbed up onto the dock. Hank opened his arms and Garner stepped into them. They exchanged a few quiet words that Thompson couldn't hear, but he understood all too well that they were probably about him. Hank slapped Garner on the back, and the two of them stepped away. Hank was looking away and Thompson knew there were probably tears streaming down his face.

Garner turned to Thompson, and before he could say anything, Thompson barreled into his embrace and wrapped his arm around him as tightly as he could. He buried his head in Garner's neck and did the best he could to hold back the sobs.

"I love you, man," he whispered. "You gave me my life back, and I'll never forget you. Thank you."

Garner tightened his hold. "I love you too. And you better not forget me, you asshole."

Thompson laughed through his tears. "Fuck you! You're the asshole."

"Okay," Hank said. "So as soon as you get to Key West, you call us. I'm trying to convince Thompson that we can sneak away for a long weekend and come to see you."

"Will do," Garner said, hopping back onto his boat.

Hank untied the bowline and tossed it onto the boat. Thompson had the stern line in hand but couldn't bring himself to let it go. He had this odd feeling that once he did, Garner would be gone and he would never see him again.

"Ah, Thompson," Garner said wryly. "I can't leave until you let go of the line."

"Fuck you!" Thompson hollered over the sound of the engine, forcing himself to toss the line into the cockpit.

Hank slipped his arm around Thompson's waist, and Thompson draped his arm over Hank's shoulder. The two of them waved as the boat eased away from the dock. They watched in silence until Garner was no longer visible, the morning sun, now bright and warm on their faces, somehow lessening the chill Thompson knew they both felt.

Hank kissed Thompson's cheek, took him by both hands, and looked deeply into his eyes. "He's living his dream, Thompson. Just like I am."

Thompson wrapped his arms around Hank and held on tight. "I hope you know how much I love you."

"I think I have an idea," Hank said, taking his hand again. "Let's get inside, I'm cold."

Thompson took one last look out over the waterway. He kissed his finger and held it in the air. "Safe journeys, my friend. I hope you find whatever it is you are looking for."

SCOTTY CADE left Corporate America and twenty-five years of marketing and public relations behind to buy an inn & restaurant on the island of Martha's Vineyard with his partner of fourteen years.

He started writing stories as soon as he could read, but only recently for publication. When not at the inn, you can find him on the bow of his boat writing m/m romance novels with his Shetland sheepdog Mavis at his side. Being from the South and a lover of commitment and fidelity, most of his characters find their way to long, healthy relationships, however long it takes them to get there. He believes that, in the end, the boy should always get the boy.

Scotty and his partner are avid boaters and live aboard their boat, spending the summers on Martha's Vineyard and winters in Charleston, SC, and Savannah, GA.

Visit Scotty at http://www.scottycade.com and Scotty Cade on Facebook and Twitter. You can contact him at scotty@scottycade.com.

The Love Series from SCOTTY CADE

http://www.dreamspinnerpress.com

Also from SCOTTY CADE

http://www.dreamspinnerpress.com

Also from DREAMSPINNER PRESS

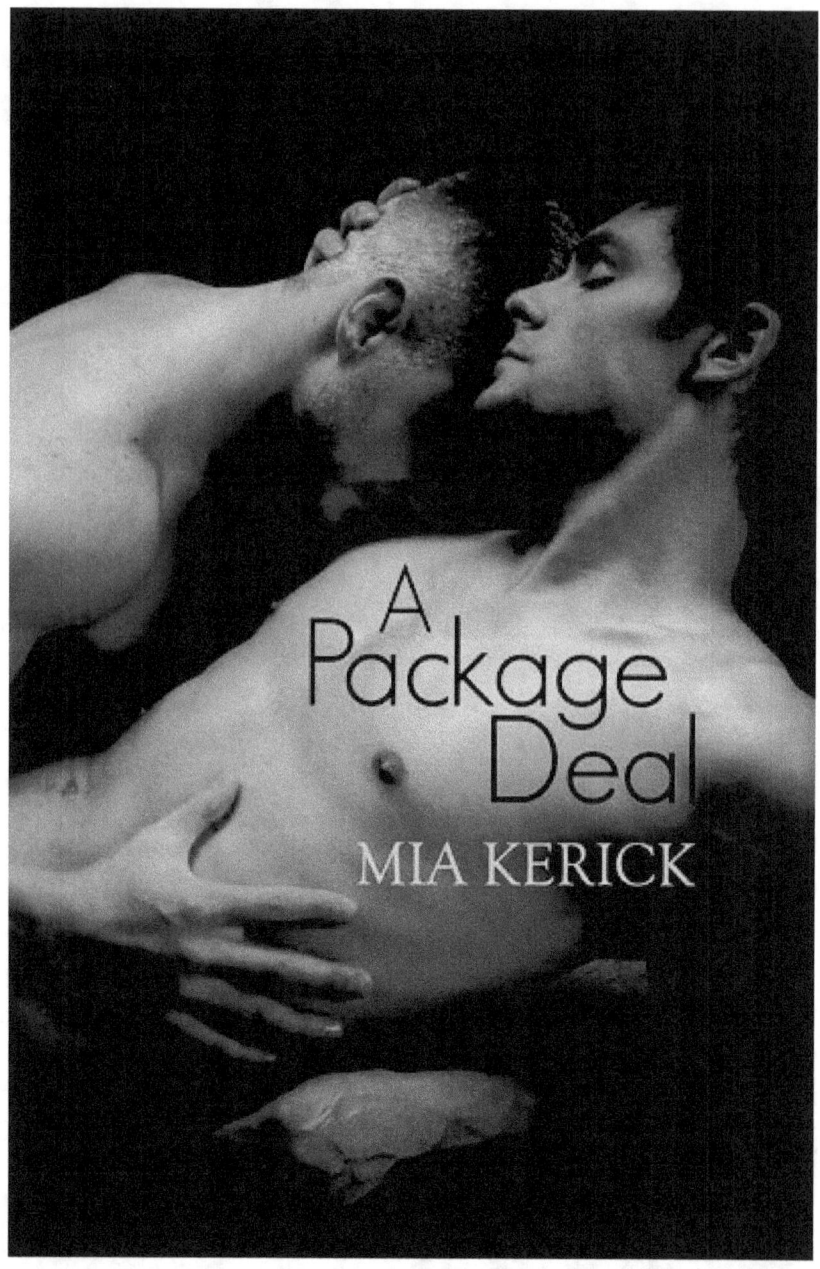

A
Package
Deal

MIA KERICK

http://www.dreamspinnerpress.com

Also from DREAMSPINNER PRESS

RICK R. REED

LEGALLY WED

http://www.dreamspinnerpress.com

For more of the
best M/M romance,
visit

Dreamspinner Press

www.dreamspinnerpress.com

www.ingramcontent.com/pod-product-compliance
Lightning Source LLC
Chambersburg PA
CBHW060052260626
47160CB00005B/1657